ELLE GRAY

BLAKE WILDER

THE
LOST
GIRLS

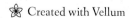 Created with Vellum

PROLOGUE

Stacy's breathing was ragged. The muscles in her legs burned as if they were actually on fire. She doubled over and clutched her midsection, the pain so intense she felt as though she was being split in two. Stacy's breath came out in thick plumes of steam as her heart thundered in her ears. Tears spilled from her eyes, and an icy fist of terror squeezed her so tightly, it drove the air from her lungs.

Stacy was exhausted. Spent. She just wanted to find some place to lie down and rest for awhile. But when the sound of a branch snapping echoed through the woods around her, Stacy knew she had to keep moving. They were coming. And if they caught her, they would kill her. Nobody left the compound. Nobody escaped. Once you'd pledged your life and your body to them, you belonged to them. They owned every square inch of you. They took what they wanted from you when they wanted it. They even took...

Stacy pushed those thoughts away. They wouldn't do her any good right now. Not when they were coming. Coming for her. She had to stay ahead of them. She had to keep running.

She couldn't let them catch her. If they did, there would be no forgiveness. There would be no mercy.

In the distance, Stacy saw the beams of light from their flashlights cutting through the darkness. They bounced crazily as the men holding them ran, sweeping the lights from side to side in search of their prey. Stacy had no idea where she was or how to find her way out of the woods, but she lowered her head and ran anyway. Legs pumping, arms churning, pain radiating through every square inch of her body, and her breath a series of ragged gasps, Stacy ran.

She heard them crashing through the brush behind her, the clamor of their voices driving her onward. Stacy was running as fast as she dared in a blind panic, tearing through the bushes, pushing branches out of her way, trying to keep from tripping over rocks or exposed roots. The last thing she needed was to trip over something and break her ankle.

"Over here. She's this way!" his voice echoed through the night.

A soft squeal of fear passed her lips as she powered on. They were closing the gap, and Stacy was starting to panic. She grit her teeth and pushed through a screen of bushes—and was suddenly weightless. Stacy found herself falling, having just run off the edge of a bluff. She hit the ground with an impact that jarred the bones in her body and drove the breath from her lungs. Almost from a distance, as if it was happening to someone else, she heard a loud cracking sound as she hit the pavement, then felt a lance of white-hot pain shoot straight up her leg.

Stacy gasped in agony. It took all her strength to barely struggle back to her feet. Her muscles were trembling and tears spilled down her face. She used a rock to prop herself up and finally stood to her full height, just as the splash of headlights rounding the bend blinded her.

She felt her eyes widen and a choked scream burst from her throat. It was drowned out by the sound of tires screeching. She dove toward the side of the road, but she wasn't quick enough. Something hard clipped her in the side, sending another sharp spike of pain through her body. The impact sent her spinning like a top, finally dropping her into the ditch that ran beside the road.

As Stacy lay there, a collection of bumps, bruises, broken bones, and sheer agony racking her entire body, she stared up at the darkened sky overhead. She marveled at the sight of the stars above. There were so many of them in the vast blackness above her that she suddenly felt absolutely insignificant. A small speck of nothing among the endless field of stars above. She enjoyed the way they twinkled. Stacy relished the soft caress of the cool breeze on her skin. Everything felt heightened, her senses sharper. The world around her suddenly seemed so vivid, and she didn't understand why.

Stacy heard the voices of the people in the car that had clipped her, but they sounded far away. Stacy thought they might as well be on another planet. Darkness crept in at the edges of her vision and kept eating away at her sight until there was nothing left but a pinhole of light in the dark.

But then that too was gone, and her entire world went black.

ONE

"WHAT I'M SAYING IS that we don't have enough information to move yet," Mo says, looking exasperated. "That's all I'm saying."

"I think we've got enough to bring her in and rattle her cage," Astra counters.

"You do that, you'll tip her off that we're looking at her," Mo fires back.

"Perhaps. And perhaps it also forces her to pull back. Saves some lives while we're building our case," Astra argues.

With my arms folded over my chest, I pace the front of the room, listening to the two of them go back and forth, absorbing their arguments as I try to come up with the best decision I can. But in a case like this, there is simply no good decision to make.

"What do you think, Blake?" Astra finally asks.

"Honestly, I think you both have compelling points," I tell her. "However we choose to proceed, we're going to need to be very careful."

"Way to straddle the fence, boss," Astra cracks.

I give her a small smile and shrug. "It's just the truth. Mo is right that we don't have enough to get a warrant yet, let alone make an arrest," I state. "But on the other side of that coin, if we put her on notice, as you said, maybe she's forced to pull back and stop killing."

"Not to be the harbinger of doom or anything—"

"Hey, we're all playing to our strengths right now, so you're good," Astra cuts Rick off, earning her a middle finger that makes us all laugh.

"Anyway, as I was saying before I was so rudely interrupted, there's another possibility I haven't heard floated yet," Rick goes on. "If you tip her off, she could also decide the walls are closing in and start killing everybody."

The room falls silent as we all weigh Rick's words. I mean, he's not wrong. It's something we hadn't considered, and it's a very strong possibility. We've seen people do that before. It's rare when you're talking about an Angel of Mercy, but it's not unheard of, either.

Astra stumbled onto this case when she was reviewing data on nursing homes and assisted living facilities. She found that a nursing home in Seattle called Tender Care had a higher-than-average number of patient deaths. While it was still within the tolerated range of deaths for a hospice care facility, it was much higher than the facility's numbers, historically speaking, which is what pinged Astra's radar.

The increased number of deaths was swept under the rug, of course—it's a facility for the elderly and hospice care, so nobody ever takes too close a look. And because it's a hospice care facility, it's going to have a higher mortality rate than a standard nursing home. But what Astra dug up was downright chilling. We ran a quiet behind-the-scenes investigation of the facility and quickly keyed in on a nurse who was hired about a month before the deaths began. After she was hired, deaths in the facility spiked. Again, it was still within the expected norms, but it was scraping the ceiling and seemed out of balance with the facility's historic trendline.

We did a deep dive on Nurse Misty Crane and found that she had left quite a trail of death behind her. Over the past ten years, she'd worked at three facilities before Tender Care—and those, too, had increased numbers of patient deaths exactly correlating with her employment history. Nothing so outrageous that it set off any official alarms, of course, but enough that internally, the facilities recognized they had a problem. In each case, it seemed that they'd narrowed their own suspect pool to a small handful of employees—Misty Crane among them in all cases.

From what we'd been able to dig up on our own, along with a few discreet conversations with former employees, we learned that rather than dig deeper, the administrators at the facilities had chosen to cover it all up. They'd apparently concluded it would be easier to hire new staff they could vet a little more thoroughly than have the public spectacle of an Angel of Mercy on their wards. Covering it up would avoid a PR nightmare in each case by keeping it all internal. So, the administrators of these care homes gave glowing letters of recommendation and tidy severance packages to that small group of people they'd identified as possible murderers and sent them all on their way.

"I'll tell you who I want to arrest and prosecute," I start, "It's these administrators who let Crane keep on killing knowing full well what kind of monster she is."

"I second that," Astra says. Mo nods with us in agreement. "They knowingly turned a murderer loose, letting her kill again. All so they could keep their six-figure bonuses. It's disgusting."

"It's beyond disgusting, and you can bet your butt that I'll be talking to one of the Assistant US Attorneys about it," I reply. "If there's a case to be made against these administrators, we'll make it."

Through the glass doors of the shop, I see Rosie—SAC Rosalinda Espinoza—standing in the corridor talking with a woman who has her back to me. I catch Rosie's eye and she gives me a look that tells me to wrap up what I'm doing because she needs to talk. I nod and turn back to my team.

"As for the here and now, I'm going to err on the side of caution and agree with Mo. Right now, all we have is circumstantial. It won't get us a warrant, let alone hold up in court," I say. "So, let's do a deeper dive on Nurse Crane, guys. I want you to go full Pac-Man and gobble up every bit of information you can find. I want to cast as wide a net as possible on her. If we need to match a shoe size to her, I want that information in hand. Got it?"

"You got it, boss," Mo says, clearly happy I'd come down on her side of the argument.

Astra looks at me, then cuts her eyes to the door to the shop and arches an eyebrow at me. She'd clearly seen the woman in the corridor with Rosie. Astra is subtle, slick, and doesn't miss a trick. I didn't even see her glance at the doors, so how she knew Rosie and a friend were out there, I have no clue. It's a pretty neat parlor trick, though, I'll give her that.

"Who's the suit?" she asks.

As if Astra's question summons her, the doors to the shop open with a pneumatic hiss. When I finally see who Rosie is walking in with, I groan. Astra cuts a glance at them, then back to me, and I see the question in her eyes. I give her a subtle shake and a look that says I'll fill her in later. She can obviously see I'm not thrilled with our visitor, so she gives me a wink and a smile to boost my spirits. If it were any other person with

Rosie, I might be able to crack a smile, but I can't seem to muster one right now. Rosie points to my office and I give her a nod and hold up a finger to tell her I'll be there in a minute—and then have to physically restrain myself from giving her visitor a different finger.

"Okay guys, let's get to work. We need hard evidence," I say. "We want to take this woman out of play permanently, so you know what to do."

"Good luck," Astra mutters.

"Thanks," I reply quietly. "I think I'm gonna need it."

TWO

Rosie and her guest stand as I step into the office and close the door behind me. She gives me a tight smile and a look that tells me to mind my P's and Q's. It's as though she can read my mind or something.

"SSA Blake Wilder, I'd like to introduce—"

"Representative Kathryn Hedlund," I say as I step behind my desk and drop down into my chair. "Yes, I know who you are. Please, have a seat."

Rosie gives me a frown, but she should know better than this. I don't play politics any more than she does, so for her to bring somebody like Hedlund, one of the slimiest operators around—not to mention somebody I absolutely despise—into my office, was her mistake. They both sit down and Hedlund looks at me with an amused smile playing across her lips.

"And I take it from the icy reception you are not a fan of my politics," Hedlund comments, her voice rich with her perfectly prim, suburban attitude. If she wasn't in Congress, you'd think she'd be on the board of some Home Owner's Association snooping in people's business.

I lean back in my chair and give Rosie a meaningful glance before turning my sights back onto Hedlund. She's taller than I thought, standing five-nine without heels. She's got a full head of silver hair and slight crinkles around the corners of her eyes. She's thin, but athletic looking—a runner or a swimmer, I'd guess. Her skin is smooth and youthful, the gray hair the only thing that betrays her age. But if she colored it, her age would be absolutely ambiguous. She looks as though she could be anywhere between thirty and fifty.

"I'm an FBI Agent and do my best to avoid politics at all costs," I say evenly. "Politics is a messy business, and I'd prefer to keep the knives out of my back, thanks very much."

Rosie shoots me a dark look as Hedlund laughs softly, a light of genuine amusement in her cornflower blue eyes. The Congresswoman is impressive as a person. At least on paper. She came up from nothing and earned her BA from Cornell at twenty-one, a Master's degree from Harvard at twenty-three, a law degree from Yale at twenty-five, and was arguing before the Supreme Court before the age of thirty. She's a woman who's driven and determined. But strangely enough, she's also a woman who seeks to deny other women the same advantages and successes she enjoyed. She's a classic example of one of those people who pulls the ladder up after her. How she manages to keep the cognitive dissonance from making her head explode is beyond me.

Hedlund advocates for a return to what she calls "simpler times" and "traditional values". You know, when women wore strings of pearls to vacuum the house, had dinner for their husbands on the table by five, and stayed home to raise the two-point-five children the perfect nuclear family would have. She's railed against basic equal rights policies like Title IX more times than I can count—and has even taken court cases designed to erode it, if not abolish it altogether. She's argued against having women in the military, on the job as police officers, and within the halls of the FBI and other agencies under the auspices of Homeland Security—unless they were to work there as secretaries, of course.

She's espoused these positions and advocated essentially purging women from the workplace while standing in the halls of Congress itself. The irony seems to be completely lost on her. So, no. I'm not a fan of her politics. Nor am I a fan of her as a person. That she uses her position to try and cut the legs out from under other women looking to climb the ladders beneath her is abhorrent to me., I find her particularly reprehensible as a person. And I'm utterly perplexed as to why Rosie would bring her into my office.

"I trust we're not pulling you away from anything too important," Hedlund says.

I shrug. "If you don't consider running down an Angel of Mercy important, then no, I suppose not."

"Blake," Rosie growls.

"What's an Angel of Mercy?" Hedlund asks.

"This is a nurse who is murdering the residents of a hospice care facility," I explain. "She believes she's putting them out of their misery, thus displaying mercy."

"Oh, dear," Hedlund says.

"Yeah. 'Oh, dear,'" I say. "But, as I can guess that you're not here to tell me how much you approve of the work we're doing in this unit, may I ask what it is you want?"

"Blake, let's take it down a couple of notches," Rosie warns.

Hedlund smiles. "No, it's all right, Rosie. I much prefer somebody who is unambiguous in her beliefs and opinions. More than that, I prefer somebody who isn't afraid to speak to her convictions," Hedlund says. "Honesty in all things is something I can respect—even if it is delivered very bluntly. I find it refreshing, though. As you can imagine, I don't get much of that on Capitol Hill."

"As we're in the mood for blunt honesty, may I ask how it is you can advocate for the positions you do, all while sitting in the halls of Congress?" I ask. "How can you justify cutting the legs out from under other women who simply want an opportunity to make something of themselves? Who want to build better lives?"

"Blake, we're not here to have a policy debate," Rosie warns. "We're here for something far more serious."

"Oh, I don't know. I consider empowering women to be very serious," I press. "Or, in this case, disempowering women."

"Not. Now," Rosie growls again, her voice hard.

I sit back in my chair and glower at the Congresswoman—and for the first time, see a tightness around her eyes. I didn't notice it before, but there's a hardness in her expression. She's troubled by something, and given that they're both sitting in my office, I assume it's something she wants my help with. Which is also ironic, given the fact that in her perfect world, I'd be home making a meatloaf and preparing to perform my wifely duties right now.

I glare hard at Rosie for a minute before turning to the other woman. "What can I do for you, Representative Hedlund?"

"Please, call me Kathryn."

"I'd rather not, since that implies a level of familiarity I don't aspire to. But thank you," I reply. "As I asked, however, what can I do for you, Congresswoman?"

Hedlund's expression darkens, and I can see I've managed to get under her skin. Apparently, that much blunt honesty isn't quite as refreshing. I'm sure there's going to be a price to be paid with Rosie later, but at the moment, I can't bring myself to care. I have no idea when or if I'll ever get the chance to speak to her again, so I figure I might as well get in a few solid jabs and body blows while I have the chance.

"All right, let me cut to the chase," Hedlund says. "My daughter, Selene, has gone missing and I would like for you and your team to find her."

"Isn't this a matter for local PD?" I ask.

She arches an eyebrow at me. "I think you and I both know that SPD is sometimes—problematic."

"I'm sure they'd pull out all the stops for a VIP like you."

"Let me put this simply, SSA Wilder," she says. "I don't trust SPD to get the job done. There are some within the power structure who are more interested in chasing headlines than criminals. I know you know to whom I refer."

Wow. Common ground. There actually is something Representative Hedlund and I can agree on. Knock me over with a feather. I'm still not convinced this is a case for my team, though. I glance at Rosie and arch an eyebrow, but she remains blank and expressionless. Though I'm sure she's upset with me for letting my temper get the better of me, I see something else in her eyes—she's not thrilled with this ask, either. Maybe that will somehow mitigate the lashing she's going to give me later.

"I understand that abduction cases are outside your usual bailiwick, but I've been told that your team is one of the best in the Bureau. I've heard that your team gets real results," she goes on. "And that's what I need right now, SSA Wilder—results. I need you to find my little girl."

I frown and look down at my hands. The idea that I have to pull my team off an important case—one where real lives are at stake—to go chasing some socialite who's likely drunk on a beach in Cancun, infuriates me. I look over at Rosie, hoping for a lifeline, but get nothing back from her. She stares back at me, her expression completely blank.

"Representative Hedlund, while I appreciate your confidence in my team's abilities, I think if you insist on Bureau involvement, missing persons would be better qualified," I tell her. "As you said, this isn't our usual bailiwick."

"I would feel more comfortable if your team handled this," she replies.

"SSA Wilder and her team will be glad to find your daughter, Kathryn," Rosie says.

"Yeah, no sweat. The folks in the hospice facility are on their way out, anyway. What's a few more?" I grumble.

"That's enough, Blake."

I sigh and glare at Rosie resentfully as I take out a fresh notebook and grab a pen. I go through some basic questions with the Congresswoman, getting the names of friends, phone numbers, addresses, and any computer passwords she might know. It all seems so pointless to me to expend our resources on a girl who's likely off on a bender. It's all rudimentary, and I'm just going through everything by rote. When I'm done, I close my notebook.

"Is it possible your daughter simply skipped town with some friends?" I ask. "That she's on a beach somewhere living her best life?"

"Selene has always been—troubled—but the one thing she has never done is skip town without telling me in advance," Hedlund tells me. "As difficult as she can be, the one thing she's always been is considerate of my feelings in that regard."

"That's very thoughtful of her," I say sardonically. "When you say she's difficult and troubled, how do you mean that?"

Hedlund sighs. "Her friends are not who or what I would hope they'd be. If you're as thorough as they say, I suppose you'll find out, anyway," she says, as if she's justifying something in her own mind. "Selene has had difficulties with alcohol and drugs. She's been through rehab twice, and it doesn't seem to stick. Not for long."

For just a second, the icy, iron-woman façade drops, and I see a real human being underneath Hedlund's exterior. For just the briefest of moments, I see a mother worried for her child. The moment passes quickly, though, and the walls go right back up around her. She looks at me with dead, expressionless eyes. She's defiant and is daring me to say something derogatory about her or her daughter.

I don't say anything, though. I simply frown as the pieces start to fall into place in my own mind. This case—if you can call it that—is starting to reek even worse. It makes me even more sure this wasn't an abduction and that we're going to find dear Selene Hedlund lounging on a beach somewhere, mai-tai in hand. Either that or in a flop house stoned out of her mind. Or the worst-case scenario—and the one I'm sure the Congresswoman would prefer to not consider—on a slab in the ME's office after overdosing.

"I see that look on your face, and let me assure you that Selene did not go willingly. She isn't off on a bender, as you'd say," Hedlund snaps. "She has her issues, but my daughter would not do that. She would not just up and disappear without so much as a text message."

I give Rosie another look, pleading with my eyes to kick this so-called case down to missing persons. And although I can see the frustration and understanding in Rosie's gaze, I also see her resolve. She fully intends for my team to take our marching orders from the Congresswoman. I'm smart enough to know when I've been beaten—usually—and let out a quiet breath of frustration.

"Fine. I'll need a number where I can reach you if I have any follow-up questions," I relent.

"I would also like regular updates on the progress of your investigation," Hedlund says, as she hands me a business card.

Rosie cuts me a frosty glare and the sarcastic reply I had loaded up and ready to fire withers and dies on the tip of my tongue. I close my mouth and sit back in my chair. When I was young, my mother taught me that if I have nothing nice to say, to say nothing at all. I'll admit, sometimes that's really, really hard to do. But I manage.

They both stand up and start to walk out of my office, but Hedlund stops and turns back to me. "I know you and I have our differences, Agent Wilder, but I hope you won't let your personal feelings interfere with doing your job to the utmost of your abilities," Hedlund says, her voice cold.

I stare at her with disbelief on my face. That quickly morphs into a wave of anger that burns deep in my belly, spreading that heat to every corner of my body. I'm just about to lay into her when Rosie, apparently sensing the impending Krakatoa-like explosion, steps in.

"That's enough, Kathryn," Rosie says, her voice equally as hard. "Blake is a professional and she'll do her job to the utmost of her ability as she always does, regardless of her personal feelings. I won't tolerate any suggestions that she would do otherwise. Not even from you."

Hedlund's expression darkens, but she nods. "Please find my daughter, Agent Wilder."

And with that, they both sweep out of my office, leaving me to stew in my aggravation and pure dislike of the woman.

"This is garbage," I mutter.

THREE

"WAIT, she actually used the word 'bailiwick'?" Astra says with a laugh.

I nod. "Yeah, she really did."

"Sounds as if somebody got an *A* in Pretentious 101 in school. I mean, who in the hell says 'bailiwick'?" she adds with a laugh. "Between that and her policy positions, I kind of feel as though I woke up in the Middle Ages this morning. What's next? Repealing the Nineteenth Amendment? Claiming women as property again?"

"I think that's on next term's agenda," I quip.

"Personally, I think 'bailiwick' is a great word," Rick pipes up from his workstation. "It's not used nearly enough anymore."

"Of course, you'd say that," Astra groans.

"So that was the infamous Kathryn Hedlund, huh?" Mo asks. "She looks different than she does on TV."

"They digitally alter the horns and forked tongue," Astra tells her. "That's probably why you didn't recognize her."

"She's definitely twice as mean without her handlers there to massage the conversation and smooth things over for her," I add. "I mean, I get that she's got to be hard to get by in that world she operates in, but I kind of think she just likes being that way."

"It certainly gives her an excuse to let her true personality shine," Mo notes.

"So, we really have to go looking for her daughter, huh?" Astra says.

"Apparently," I grumble. "Rosie volunteered us."

"That's awesome."

I pace at the front of the room feeling agitated. Angry. "I just can't believe Rosie is going to use our team, pulling us off a real case, just to do a solid for her old sorority sister."

"I can't believe Rosie is friends with somebody like her," Mo says. "I mean, the SAC always struck me as kind of—feminist—in her views."

"And Congresswoman Hedlund is more like Phyllis Schlafly on steroids," Astra replies.

Mo nods. "Yeah. Pretty much."

"Never underestimate the power of the sorority sisterhood," Astra says dryly. "It unites people and makes them do some really dumb things."

"Hedlund has some strong views and isn't afraid to speak her truth. Maybe Rosie respects that about her," Rick states. "Just because they differ politically doesn't mean they can't be friends. I mean, I'm more of a Marvel guy and my best friend is all DC, all the time. If we can be friends, seems reasonable Rosie and Hedlund can be."

Astra looks over at him, a sneer curling her lips. "Okay. One, your comparison blows. And I'm going to do you a favor by ignoring the fact that you just equated women's rights with comic books. I really should come over there and slap you stupid for that," she tells him. "And two, until you have somebody trying to strip you of your agency and your rights, you don't get to have an opinion. Got it?"

"Fair enough," Rick mutters, quickly turning back to his computers.

"Rick, do me a favor and run Selene Hedlund's financials," I tell him. "Debit card, credit cards—the works. And when you find the plane ticket to the Caribbean or the Mayan Riviera, forward that to Congresswoman Hedlund with a note from me that says, 'I told you so.'"

"On it," he calls back.

"Mo, I want you to comb through her social media," I say. "Facebook, Twitter, Instagram—whatever the kids are using these days. See where she's posting."

"Yes, ma'am," Mo says and turns to her computer.

"What about me?" Astra asks. "Want me to stay on Nurse Crane?"

"I'd much rather have you stay on her, but I need you with me on this," I sigh. "The sooner we find Hedlund's wayward daughter, the sooner we can get back to it."

"Not to go full tin-foil-hat on you, but have you ever stopped to ask yourself why, with the full power of the FBI and other law enforcement elements behind her, Hedlund demanded that we take on her case?" Astra asks.

"Yeah, the thought crossed my mind," I reply. "What better way to prove her point that women don't have the same investigative prowess as men than to send us on a case that's doomed to fail from the start?"

"Wow. That's really cynical," Rick remarks. "Even for you, boss."

I turn to him. "I'm not a cynic."

He shrugs. "Yeah, you kind of are."

"Fine," I admit. "Doesn't mean I'm wrong, though."

"We're on the same page," Astra says. "It feels as though we're being set up here. We're a successful, primarily female unit within the Bureau. That doesn't fit with her narrative."

"Which could make her see us as a problem," I add.

"Not to be Little Miss Sunshine or anything. God knows I'm as cynical as you guys," Mo starts, "but I don't think Hedlund would come at us sideways like this. If she were going to take us on, she'd come straight at us. She's always prided herself on being tough and taking people head-on. That's the image she's built, and perpetuating that image is all-important to somebody like her."

"Maybe. But I don't trust her," I say.

"Nor should you. You'd be a fool to trust her," Mo replies. "I'm just saying I think she'd do things in a more direct way."

I walk over to the whiteboard and use the blue dry erase marker to write down Selene's name at the top, then underline it. If we're going to work this case, might as well at least pretend it's a normal case or I'll go crazy with the irritation of it all.

"Okay, so what do we know about Selene Hedlund so far?" I ask.

"She's twenty-three and is working on her Masters in child psychology at Marchmont University," Mo reads from her computer screen. "That's a private college for the one percent of the one percent, in case anybody was wondering."

"Of course, it is," Astra says. "Mommy has more money than God. She inherited most of it—her family founded a tech empire. They make all kinds of expensive tech gadgets."

"According to Hedlund, Selene's father died when she was six," I say, as I jot some notes down on the whiteboard. "Brain aneurysm. Died in his sleep."

"So, she's bound to have some daddy issues," Astra notes.

"Could kidnapping be a possibility?" Mo asks. "Could we be looking at a ransom situation?"

I shake my head. "I doubt it. It's been a little over a week, according to Hedlund, and there's been no ransom demand."

"I think I may have a reason for that," Rick announces.

His fingers fly over the keys at his computer, and on the video screens on the wall behind me, what look like Selene Hedlund's banking records pop up.

"Once a day for the past nine days, the maximum amount was withdrawn from an ATM kiosk just outside the Emerald City Trust bank on the corner of Mercer and Fifteenth," he says.

"Excellent work, Rick. Sounds as if Selene's on a big-time bender," I say. "Can you tap into the security footage from that ATM?"

"It'll take me a minute, but yeah," he says. "I can get it."

"Great. Start with the most recent withdrawal," I reply. "Once we're able to get the photo of Selene taking cash out of her account, we can show it to Hedlund and be done with this farce."

"But what if it's not her?" Mo asks.

"What do you mean?" I ask.

"I just mean—what if it's not Selene making those withdrawals?" she presses. "What if somebody grabbed her and now they're draining Selene's account but still plan on extorting a ransom from the Congresswoman?"

"In most cases of abduction for profit, the kidnappers will usually make contact within twenty-four hours," Astra says. "There's no way they'd risk keeping her for nine days now, taking money out of her bank account, only to come back later to demand a ransom. That's too much risk. Unless our kidnappers are absolute buffoons."

Mo shrugs. "It's not as if we haven't tracked down some buffoons in our time here."

"This is true," Astra admits with a grin.

"Astra's right," I add. "What they're withdrawing from her account is peanuts compared to the big payday they could get from her mother."

"All right, I've got the security video," Rick announces. "I've isolated the picture from the time-stamp when Selene's card was used."

He puts the picture up on the screens behind me, and when I see it, I frown. On the screen is a man with long, shaggy brown hair. He's wearing sunglasses and a hat that's pulled down low. He keeps his hair in front of his face to obscure his image, making it impossible to run him through our facial recognition software. The only thing that's clear is that this is definitely not Selene Hedlund withdrawing money from her account.

"Damn," I mutter. "I guess we're actually going to have to put in some work on this."

FOUR

"What can I do for you, Agents?"

Astra and I are sitting across from the bank manager, who looks exceptionally nervous. He's a tall, thin man with more salt than pepper in his hair these days, pale skin, and a neatly trimmed goatee. He's wearing a three-piece suit that's nice, but not too nice. Definitely not name-brand, nor professionally tailored. It's an off-the-rack special for sure. Wire-rimmed glasses are perched on the end of his nose. To me, he looks more like an academic than a bank manager. I half-expect him to break out a pipe and start lecturing us on the psychological underpinnings of Holden Caufield.

I lean forward and set the folder I'm carrying down on his desk. He pulls it over to him and I simply watch as he flips through the photos with a trembling hand.

"Are you all right, Mr. Nash?" I ask. "You seem nervous."

He gives me an awkward grin. "I'm just not used to having

FBI agents in my office staring at me as if I just tried to kill the President."

"Apologies, Mr. Nash," I say. "We don't mean to look at you in any certain way."

"We're running a routine investigation that has nothing to do with any assassination attempts," Astra adds as she leans forward, staring at him malevolently. "Unless of course, you're thinking about attempting to assassinate the President?"

Nash practically chokes, and I have to keep myself from laughing. Nash is quite obviously a nervous and jumpy man. Some people are when they're confronted by law enforcement. But I don't see him as the Lee Harvey Oswald type.

"I—I'm not," he stammers. "I swear I'm not."

Astra gives him a wide smile. "Great. Then we have no problems."

His face is already nearly purple, so before he can swallow his tongue and choke to death, I jump in and point to the pictures in the file I gave him.

"That man has been accessing the accounts of one of your customers. Selene Hedlund," I tell him. "He's been taking the maximum out once a day for the past nine days."

"And before you ask," Astra jumps in, "Selene Hedlund is in fact, the daughter of Representative Kathryn Hedlund."

"We need to know who he is," I tell him. "Or if you've ever seen him before."

Nash turns as pale as a sheet—something I can relate to. Congresswoman Hedlund has that effect on people. But he looks at the photos again, scrutinizing them closely. He shakes his head and turns to his computer, his fingers flying over the keys as he pulls up some information—likely verifying our story. He looks at the numbers on the screen and frowns as he shakes his head. I can see him already trying to figure out how much trouble he's going to be in once Hedlund finds out.

He looks at the photos again, his frown deepening. "I've never seen him before in my life," he says. "But these were all taken from the ATM outside, which means he hasn't come in here before."

"Don't you guys have a computer program that will alert you when there's suspicious ATM activity?" Astra asks. "I'd say withdrawing the max nine days in a row is a bit suspect."

"Of course, we have programs that will alert us to fraud," he says. He taps a few more keys and nods, a palpable sense of relief crossing his face. "It looks as though we sent a text after the third withdrawal, asking if this was authorized or not, and directing her to our authentication website. Ms. Hedlund affirmed that the transactions were valid."

I turn to Astra. "Or whoever has her phone affirmed the transactions were valid."

She nods. "Seems that way."

"We cannot control it if Ms. Hedlund allowed somebody to use her debit card—"

"Relax, Mr. Nash. We're not trying to jam you up or implicate you in any wrongdoing. I doubt you or the bank has liability here," I tell him. "But given who this is, you might want to consult with your bank's attorneys just to clear up your level of exposure. Just in case."

"Do you have any other security cameras in the vestibule where the ATMs are located?" Astra asks.

"Of course. Yes," he nods. "The monitors are in our security office."

"We'll need to see those," I say.

We all get to our feet and he leads us down to the security office. A large Hispanic man with dark hair, brown eyes, and tawny-colored skin is sitting at a desk behind a bank of monitors. He looks at us as we step inside.

"Ramon, we need you to pull up the vestibule footage from—"

I hand him the picture with the time and date stamp in the corner. Nash hands it to Ramon, who accesses the footage and pulls it up on the large screen in the center of his array. We watch as the man with the long hair and hat comes in. He keeps his head down, his hair in front of his face, as he keys in Selene's PIN number and withdraws a thousand dollars. He stuffs it into his pocket then exits the vestibule without ever having looked up, denying us a view of his face.

"Are there any other angles?" I ask.

Nash shakes his head. "No, we only have the one camera in the vestibule. Combined with the ATM cameras, it's supposed to be enough coverage."

"Clearly not," I mutter.

"He's slick," Astra comments to me. "Knows where the camera is and how to hold his head so we can't see him."

"He's done it before," I observe.

She chuckles softly. "Nine times before."

I shake my head. "No, I mean even before he had Selene's card," I say. "He's too smooth and too practiced for this to be his first go-round doing this. He's a bleeder."

"I'm sorry? What is a bleeder?" Nash asks.

"Somebody who gets hold of another person's credit or debit cards and bleeds them dry, taking out the limit every day until the cards are shut down," Astra explains.

"They rationalize it by saying the banks and credit card companies will cover the fraud and restore the money to a person's account, so nobody really loses," I add.

"Except the banks, of course," Nash says.

"It amounts to almost nothing compared to the compensation your executives make. Pocket change, really," I offer.

"That doesn't make it right. Or legal," Nash replies with a hint of steel in his voice.

"Didn't say it did," I reply. "Just telling you these people see themselves as Robin Hood sorts, because nobody is losing real money in the deal."

"That's preposterous," he grunts.

"I've found that people can rationalize anything away—especially when it comes to their bad acts," I say. "Anyway, I think we've gotten what we needed. Thank you for your help, Mr. Nash. We'll be in touch if we have any follow-up questions."

"Of course," he replies. "We'll cooperate in any way we can."

"Good. The first thing I want you to do is leave Selene's account active. Don't close out the card," I tell him.

"What? I can't do that."

"It might be the only way we can figure out who this is," I say, pointing to the video screen. "I also don't want to tip him off that we're looking at this or that we've gotten this far. Leave the account active, Mr. Nash. It would be active anyway if we hadn't come in here today."

He ponders for a moment but finally nods. "I'll need to notify my superiors, but all right."

"Good. We'll be in touch."

Astra and I walk out of the bank and head for the car. Astra diverts us to a coffee house, though, and after we place our orders and get our drinks, we take a table in the corner. The place is only about half full of a mixed crowd made up of students, soccer moms, and nannies. I pause and look around, letting my mind run with what we've learned so far. Which isn't much, to be honest.

But the one thing that's become abundantly clear is that this isn't going to be as cut-and-dried as I first thought. I'm sure

I'm still right about Selene's being out on some massive bender with her friends, but there are more players on the stage, which is going to complicate things further than I would have liked.

"Hey, are you all right?"

Astra's voice pulls me out of my head, and I focus on her. "Yeah, I'm fine."

"You don't seem it. You've been crabby and irritable lately," she says. "More so than usual, anyway."

I laugh softly. "You suck."

"I'm kind of serious, though. I mean, it surprised the hell out of me that you went after Hedlund as hard as you did."

"She annoys me."

"Yeah, but you typically either brush it off or find a way to be more....diplomatic. I mean, I don't think you've ever gone after Torres as hard as you did Hedlund," she points out.

I frown and give it a little thought. She's obviously right. It was true that I went after Hedlund pretty hard. It's not as if she didn't deserve it. Just seeing her face, knowing the things she's said and done, and knowing what she's trying to do, just pushed my buttons. I didn't consciously rip into her, but once I started, I couldn't make myself stop. I wanted to shut up, but once that train got rollin', I couldn't stop it. All I could do was take the ride to the end. But it was also probably pretty out-of-line for the office. Time and place and all that.

I know what it is that's bothering me. It's something I haven't been able to get out of my head since Brody served it up to me—at my own request, of course. But what he showed me chilled me to the core, and I have no idea what to do with it yet. And until I have some grip on what it is, I don't want to talk about it with anybody.

"Yeah, I've just got a lot on my plate lately. A lot of stuff occupying my brain," I say, hoping it puts her off the track.

"Anything you want to get off your chest?"

I shake my head. "Not just yet. It's one of those things I need to sit with for a while and figure out before I'm ready to talk about," I tell her. "Know what I mean?"

"All too well," she nods. "Just know that when you're ready to talk, I'm always here."

"Thanks, Astra."

"What are best friends for?"

I give her a smile and take a sip of my coffee. I've got a meeting in an hour or so that I need to mentally gear up for.

FIVE

I WALK through the front doors of the Pearl and am immediately bowled over by the stench of cigarette smoke and burning incense. I see that some improvements have been made to the Pearl, and it's been cleaned up. There's fresh paint, new billiard tables, and the layer of grime that built up over the years and coated everything before has been washed away. It's practically sparkling in here now. I guess Fish is trying to make his bar and billiards hall seem like a more respectable place of business. Good for him.

I head through the kitchen to the back stairs that will lead me upstairs to the illegal casino that's being run up there. Everybody is apparently so used to seeing me come through the doors by now that they don't even bother staring, even though mine is the only white face in the whole joint. I'm not sure if it's a good or bad thing to be as closely related to Fish as I am. It's probably bad, I decide.

But, to be fair, Fish is an unusually charismatic and likable guy. He's also the man you want to see if you need something handled quietly and discreetly. Fish has his tentacles into just about everything happening in the Seattle underworld. And now that he's branching out and allegedly going legit, he's got the pulse of Seattle's lawful business world too.

He'll forever be associated with the city's criminal underbelly, though—something he does not bemoan in the least. He enjoys his reputation and the mystery and ambiguity of it all as well. These days, nobody seems to know if Fish is a shady crime boss or a legit businessman. Most think a tiger can't change its stripes, others believe in redemption. It keeps them all on their toes. Nobody is quite sure anymore if saying or doing the wrong thing will earn him a pair of .45 slugs in the back of the head or just a stern talking-to.

They're not wrong to think that. Fish's early career was marked by violence and death—though probably not nearly as much as some people believe. I'm pretty sure his reputation has been overblown in the telling over the years. I doubt he did half of the things he's credited with, and he very likely didn't kill nearly as many people as they say. But Fish is, of course, happy to let it stand. Happy to let his legend grow.

Reputation is everything when you live in his world—and reputations in that world are built on the currency of fear. Fear is the coin of the realm, and the more scared people are to cross or displease you, the better. If they think you're capable of the most monstrous deeds, you've reached the pinnacle of your rarified profession. And Fish has been at the pinnacle for decades now.

And honestly, if you stop to think about it, while the top CEOs in the country may not shoot somebody in the face for crossing them, their attitudes and approaches to running businesses are virtually identical to Fish's. And having spoken with a few of them, I have little doubt some of those CEOs would happily shoot somebody in the face.

I push through the swinging doors and into the kitchen area and am immediately greeted by a man as large as Mt. Everest itself. He's at least six-foot-ten and as wide as he is tall. The guy's hands are so huge he could probably juggle Volkswagens for fun. He's got black hair that's tied into a ponytail that falls to the middle of his back, warm golden skin, and dark eyes.

The man is a frightening sight to behold, but as I've gotten to know him, have found that he's a teddy bear. Unless you provoke him. Do that and he turns into a full-blown Kodiak bear. And again, I'm not sure how I feel about being so chummy with Fish's doorman and personal bodyguard.

"G-woman," he greets me, his voice deep and rumbling.

I smile. "Hello, Bai. How's it going today?"

He shrugs. "Can't complain. How about you?"

"Can't complain."

"Then life is good."

"Well, it's not bad, so I suppose you're right. That's a good way to look at it," I say with a small laugh. "Fish upstairs?"

He nods and presses a button on the wall beside him. There's a loud buzz followed by the loud clunk of the door unlocking. I open it up and give him a smile.

"Thanks, Bai."

"Anytime, G-woman."

I make my way up the narrow staircase, then to the steel door at the end of a short hall. I give a wave to the camera mounted high in the corner and there's another loud buzzing sound. Pulling the door open, I step into the large room that is Fish's casino. I know that I should have this place shut down. It's illegal, after all. But I just can't bring myself to make that call. It's mostly because I like Fish as a person. But it's also because he is a valuable resource.

The man knows everybody and everything going on in the Seattle underworld. And he has provided some premium intel when I've needed it—intel that's helped me crack a few big cases. We make deals with criminals all the time. The better their information, the sweeter the deal. It's the grease that keeps the wheels of the justice system working. At least, that's how I justify it to myself.

I catch a few odd, furtive looks as I walk across the room. Most of the people seem to recognize me; as with downstairs, they don't bother me. A few are staring at me, though, as if they can somehow sense that I'm a Fed. They might considering bolting, fearing a raid is coming. I tip a wave to a couple familiar faces, who whisper into their friends' ears. That seems to calm them down as they turn away and go back to their games.

The door to Fish's office opens before I even get there, and he greets me with a warm smile and a hug.

"It's good to see you, Agent Wilder."

"It's nice to see you, too, Fish," I reply.

"Please, step into my office."

The nickname Fish is a nod to his days as a fishmonger on the docks after he immigrated here as a kid. That was how he got started building his sprawling criminal empire. His real name is Huang Zhao, and nobody knows his true age. Based on things he's said, I'd guess that he's in his mid-to-late fifties, but he takes care of himself and is in such good shape, he could easily pass for ten or fifteen years younger.

Fish is tall and lean, with stylishly cut dark hair that's starting to show a little bit of salt among the pepper. He's got dark eyes and perfectly smooth, tawny skin. The man is a martial arts master in several disciplines, leaving him with a fit, toned body. He's also one of the most intelligent people I've ever met. Fish is one of those people who seems to know a little about a lot of things. He hones his mind every bit as much as he does his body. Fish has said he believes his mind is his most dangerous weapon.

He offers me one of the plush wingbacks in front of his desk as he sits down behind it. Fish's office is immaculate and stylishly furnished. It's a reflection of the man himself. He's wearing an expertly tailored dark, pinstriped three-piece suit. It's actually tame for him. Fish is a bit flamboyant and often enjoys wearing odd-colored suits that have metallic sheens to them. The only nod to that quirk of his personality now is the electric blue tie and pocket square that shimmer in the light.

"Did you have to go to a funeral today?" I ask, gesturing to his suit.

He laughs softly. "Unfortunately, no. A funeral would have been far more enjoyable than what I had to suffer through today," he says. "I had to meet with the city council today to discuss a business proposal. I can now see why people hate politicians."

My meeting with Congresswoman Hedlund flashes through my mind and I nod, a small laugh passing my lips.

"I can't say I disagree with you there," I say.

"We haven't spoken for a little while, so I haven't had a chance to apologize for not having been able to serve Stephen Petrosyan up to you," he says, sounding genuinely remorseful. "I know you were trying to make a case against him—"

I purse my lips and look down at my hands. Petrosyan is the head of the Elezi crime family—the Armenian mob here in Seattle. He ordered one of his men, Azad Mushyan, to kill a promising young medical student named Ben Davis. They chopped him into pieces and stuffed him into a barrel, all because Petrosyan didn't want his daughter to date a black man. Ben and Petrosyan's daughter Chloe had plans to run away together, and when he got wind of it, Petrosyan murdered him.

We built a solid case against Petrosyan and thought we had him dead to rights. But then his high-priced mouthpiece, a dirtbag named Palmer Tinsley, dropped a bombshell on us and offered up Petrosyan's bodyguard, Mushyan, instead. Had a signed confession and everything. Then Fish gave us the final nail in Mushyan's coffin—security video showing him shooting Ben in the head. It was incontrovertible, but I know beyond the shadow of a doubt that Petrosyan ordered the murder. Unfortunately, that's not something I can prove, so that scumbag is still walking free.

"It's not your fault, but thank you," I say. "Besides, you gave us what we needed to get a murderer off the streets. Petrosyan may have ordered it, but Mushyan pulled the trigger."

"Well, it's a disagreeable situation all the way around," he replies. "But let's not delve into old unpleasantries. What is it I can do for you, Agent Wilder?"

"I need your help, Fish."

"Another big case?"

I shake my head. "No, actually this is personal."

He leans back in his chair and steeples his fingers in front of him, an enigmatic smile touching his lips.

"Personal. How intriguing. It's so rare that you give me a glimpse of your personal life," he says. "So, tell me, Agent Wilder, how can I be of service?"

I let out a quiet breath. I've thought long and hard about asking Fish to get involved with this, simply because as much as I like him as a person, I know there's a limit to how much I can trust him. And giving him this sort of access to my personal life comes dangerously close to crossing that line. But Fish has the sort of reach I need for this, and it keeps those closest to me out of the line of fire. Fish is a man who knows how to take care of himself. He has an army around him, so I know I have less to worry about when it comes to him. As it is, I worry about Brody, who is the one who gave me this information to begin with. And I'd rather not endanger him any more than I already have.

I pull the file Brody gave me out of my bag and slide it across the desk to Fish. He picks it up and flips through the pages, then looks up at me, an expression of curiosity on his face.

"Mark Walton—this is your boyfriend, is he not?" he asks.

"No, he's not my boyfriend anymore. Nor is he Mark Walton, apparently," I explain. "That's all the information I have, but it shows that Mark Walton is a fiction. His information is backstopped for ten years, but prior to that, he didn't exist. I need to know who he really is. And who he works for."

"Fascinating," Fish says. "So, he was deliberately inserted into your life."

"It seems that way."

"For what purpose?"

"Because I've been looking into the murders of my parents," I admit. "I believe the organization responsible for their deaths inserted Mark into my life to keep tabs on my investigation."

I pause as my thoughts turn to Gina Aoki and how she was brutally murdered after meeting with me. Mark was one of the few people to whom I'd mentioned that meeting, and as uncomfortable as it is to think about, I can't deny that there's a piece of me that thinks he might have done it. If he's cold-blooded enough to insert himself into my life and pretend to care about me, what else is he capable of? It would take a monster to do something like that. And that kind of monster would be more than capable of cutting a woman's throat, I have no doubt.

"That sounds like a very interesting story," Fish says. "What is it your parents were involved in? I believe you said they worked for the government."

"That's a story I'm not ready to share yet. My investigation's nowhere near complete."

Fish looks at me for a long moment, that enigmatic smile still on his lips. And judging by the way he's looking at me, I already know what he's going to ask.

"That's a story I would very much like to hear," he says. "So, that is my price for getting this information for you. When your investigation is complete, I want to hear all about it."

I hate being right all the time. But it seems a small price to pay in the grand scheme of things. There's nothing he can do with that information to leverage me after I've finished my investigation and exposed all the conspirators. If anything, having somebody else know—especially somebody like Fish— might provide me with an added layer of protection.

"Deal," I say. "When I find out who killed my folks and have brought them all to justice, I'll tell you everything."

His smile is wide and wolfish. "Then I look forward to hearing all about it," he says smoothly. "I'll tell you the moment I have any information to pass on."

"Thank you, Fish. I really appreciate it."

"It's my pleasure, Agent Wilder," he grins. "In fact, cooperating with the FBI can only help my public image as I go legit."

Well, at least we're both getting something out of it. Win-win situations are so rare in life.

SIX

"What do you have, Rick?" I ask as I step to the front of the room.

"Nothing good," he states. "Other than the bleeder's taking money out of her main bank account, none of her credit cards and secondary bank accounts has been touched in the last ten days. No lunches, no coffees, no fill-ups at the gas station —nothing."

"Maybe that means she's living off the money the bleeder's taking?" Mo offers.

"It's possible," Astra agrees.

I shake my head. "I don't think that's it," I say. "I think the bleeder's working for himself. I just don't think he'd hand all that cash over to somebody else. That just doesn't feel right to me."

"But it's something we need to keep in mind," Astra says. "Something we can't rule out entirely right now."

"I agree," I nod.

"There is also no evidence that she went anywhere. No plane tickets, no bus tickets, and no receipts from gas stations," Rick adds. "She left zero paper trail. As far as I can tell, she never left town."

"She couldn't have just disappeared," Astra muses.

"No, she couldn't have," I mutter.

"It certainly seems as though this case just got a whole lot more complicated," Astra says.

"Guess she's not off on a beach somewhere on a bender," Mo adds.

"We still don't know that for sure," I caution. "There are a lot of ways she could have gotten out of town without leaving a paper trail."

"Wow. You're usually open to any and all theories but you seem pretty locked in on this one," Astra says. "Are you maybe letting your dislike of Hedlund bleed over into this?"

I step back and take a beat, letting Astra's words sink in. And I realize that despite Rosie's assurances to the Congresswoman, I haven't been behaving like a professional. I have indeed let my own bias and dislike of Hedlund color my view. I wouldn't have handled any other case the way I'm handling this one. I still think Selene, troubled and difficult, is probably off on a bender somewhere. But that shouldn't have affected how I handled this case—or rather, mostly dismissed it. The fact is, she's missing, and we've been tasked to find her. So, whether she's on a beach in Mexico or somewhere else, it's our job to find her.

Looking up at Astra, I give her a small smile. "As much as it pains me to admit it, you might be right," I say. "Mea culpa."

"I'd think you'd be used to that feeling by now," Astra quips.

I glance at the whiteboard and the notes I'd hastily

scrawled there, giving myself a moment to wrap my head around it all. Then I turn back to the team.

"All right. We're going to have to start from square , and I'm sorry for that," I say. "So, let's reset. What do we know so far?"

"We know that Selene has been missing for roughly ten days or so," Mo starts. "We know that other than the bleeder's draining her account, there's been zero activity on her financials. Likewise for her socials—zero activity since the day she went missing."

Looking at things through this new paradigm in my head, even I have to admit that's a bit chilling. Kids these days—and as a twenty-three-year-old who grew up pampered and sheltered, she's still very much a kid—are connected to their social media accounts. They're constantly posting to Instagram and Tiktok, no matter how mundane or simple the thought. They live on social media as if they're afraid they'll be forgotten instantly if they don't post continually. It's as if that's their only real connection to the world.

"Is it possible she's got secret social accounts we don't know about?" I ask.

"Not likely," Rick throws in. "I ran her IP address against socials and didn't turn anything up. I mean, it's still possible, of course. But I don't think it's likely."

I nod and look at the whiteboard again, feeling a vague sense of unease growing and spreading through me.

"Can we track her phone?" I ask.

I hear Rick clacking away at his keyboard for a minute before he shakes his head. "Phone was shut off days ago. Last activity was the confirmation text message from the bank."

"What was the last location it pinged?" I ask.

"It was at her school," he replies. "Last ping comes from a coffee house at Marchmont University."

"That jibes with her last social media post on Instagram," Mo says as she starts tapping at her keyboard. "On the screens."

We all turn and look at the monitors on the wall. It's a selfie Selene took in what looks like a coffee house, which lines up with her last ping. She's a pretty girl and resembles her mother in a lot of ways—especially around the eyes. Selene has the same cornflower blue eyes in a face that's smooth and youthful, and honey blonde hair that she's got pulled back into a simple ponytail. Her expression is pensive. Nervous. But at the same time, there seems to be a sparkle in her eye that almost looks —excited.

"The only way to be truly free is to let go and live in the service of something greater than yourself," Astra reads the caption below Selene's selfie.

"Well, that's not cryptic or anything," Mo comments.

"It almost sounds as though she's taking a vow of poverty and joining a convent," Rick says.

I stare at the caption, reading it through several times. Rick's right in that it almost sounds like a goodbye. As if she's choosing to drop out of society and go join a convent or something. But then, we also live in an age when people jot down what they think are their most profound thoughts and put them on display for the whole world to see. This could be Selene's saying goodbye or it could be nothing. It's an interesting point to ponder, but it's hard to say if it actually means anything right now.

"What are you thinking, boss?" Mo asks.

I shake my head. "I'm not sure just yet. I'm not totally convinced this is pertinent to the investigation. It could just be nonsensical ramblings posing as profound thought."

"Some people do chase internet clout by doing that," Rick points out.

"Yeah, I know. I've seen your socials," Astra says sardonically.

"I don't need to chase clout anymore. It comes to me," he fires back with a grin.

As they laugh with each other, I stare at Selene's face and read her caption again, trying to get into her head. What was she thinking when she posted this? What does she mean by letting go and living in service to something greater than herself? Does it mean anything at all? Or, is it as Rick suggested, a girl chasing internet clout by posting a cute picture and something she thinks makes her seem deep and contemplative?

"What about her car?" Astra asks as the thought occurs to her. "Has she gotten any tickets? Can we trace the car's last known location on her GPS?"

Mo consults her computer screen for a moment then turns back to us. "The car was dropped off at Tony's Auto six days ago. The GPS went dark after that."

I look at Astra and raise an eyebrow as the ominous feeling inside me continues to grow. She frowns as she looks at me, and I can tell that Astra is having the same dark thoughts that are rattling through my brain. This is starting to look bad.

"What is it?" Mo asks.

"Tony's is a chop shop. If Selene's car went in there, it's not coming out," Astra explains.

"Ready to take a ride?" I ask.

"If we're going to Tony's, let me just grab a Kevlar vest and a shotgun."

"Not a bad idea."

"Rick, do me a favor and run a search of the GPS coordinates on both her phone and car before they went dark," I tell him. "I want to know the places she visited most often."

"On it, boss," he chirps.

As Astra starts putting her things together, I turn to Mo and step closer to her workstation.

"I'd like you to hit Selene's socials harder," I say. "Look for anything else that might point to the meaning of her last post."

"Will do," she nods.

"And about that special project—have you had any luck?" I ask, pitching my voice lower. Mo gives a nod over to my office, and we silently walk over there and close the door behind us, just to have some privacy.

"I'm still gathering information, but what I can tell you preliminarily is that I see there are a number of cases involving large corporations that were ruled on one way in the past, but the Court has reversed its position with the addition of Justices Havers, Pearce, and Witkowski," she explains quietly. "I don't want to say too much right now—not until I have specifics. And those I'll have for you in a little while. But just based on what I've seen so far, I think it's safe to say that some rich people were very happy with the rulings and got even richer as a result of those rulings."

"Those specifics—will you be able to get me names of the biggest beneficiaries of those rulings?"

She smiles. "I'll have their shoe sizes for you."

"Excellent," I say. "Thank you. And watch your back, Mo. If this is what I think it is, there will be people with vested interests in not letting this information get out."

She gives me a grin. "I told you when you asked me to look into this that I can take care of myself," she replies. "I know the risks. But this is too important to let it go by the boards. I'm actually grateful you asked me to help with this."

"I don't know that you should be grateful for my putting you in the line of fire."

"The only way to truly be free is to let go and live in the service of something greater than yourself," she replies, giving me a dramatic rendition of Selene's quotation, which makes me burst into laughter.

When my fit of giggles subsides, I give her a shoulder squeeze and a smile, still feeling guilty for dragging her into this. Mr. Corden and Gina Aoki paid for my investigation with their lives. But they knew what they were getting into. I haven't yet told Mo some of the specifics of what I'm asking her to do, but I know I'll have to—and soon. Mo's got the expertise in finding patterns and rooting out irregularities. She's got an understanding of the complex system of high finance that I'll never have. I need her on this with me, but if something were to happen to her, I don't know that I would ever forgive myself.

"Well....watch your back, anyway," I tell her.

She nods. "I will."

"We going?" Astra pokes her head in the door.

"We're going," I reply.

As Astra and I head out of the shop, my stomach churns as I turn Mo's information over in my mind and it brings me back to something Gina Aoki said the day we met—at the root of all of this, it's nothing but greed and power. And it's starting to look as if my family was blown up just so somebody could add a few more zeroes to his bank account.

SEVEN

Tony's Auto Repair, Othello District; Seattle, WA

THE OTHELLO DISTRICT in Seattle has traditionally been thought of as one of the roughest areas in the city. Filled with a lot of low-income housing, plus street gangs and other assorted criminals, it's far from the kind of upper-class sheltered suburb that someone like Selene Hedlund would normally frequent. Unlike other neighborhoods in Seattle, Othello has been steadfast in not allowing gentrification.

The city has tried to improve the area, incentivizing businesses and developers to move in. But the residents always push back on them, so nobody's been able to gain a foothold here. While I obviously don't agree with some of the methods being employed, I'll admit I can sympathize with the residents here who aren't exactly thrilled with deep-pocketed big-wigs trying to horn their way in and drive them out.

We pull through the open gates and into the cracked and pitted asphalt parking lot of Tony's Auto Repair and shut off the engine. We get out of the car, and I'm immediately assaulted by the stench of gasoline, oil, and a host of other, less pleasant, odors. The four bays of the shop contain cars up on hydraulic lifts, and another half-dozen cars are sitting in the parking stalls waiting for their turns. There's also a large warehouse set off to the side, with the steel roll-down door closed up tight. That's where the less-than-legal activities take place, I'm sure.

The office is painted a washed-out shade of blue that looks years overdue for a refresh, and has a large plate glass window in the front that's scratched up and has a couple of cracks that are being held together with silver duct tape. There are four or five guys in blue coveralls buzzing around, working on the cars up on the lifts. Heavy metal is blasting from a set of tinny speakers overhead, almost sounding hollow.

"Nice place," Astra notes. "Very....rustic."

I give her a smile. "Don't be a snob."

She shrugs. "I am what I am."

We walk into the office and find a twenty-something Hispanic girl behind the counter. She's about five-three and trim, with dark hair, dark eyes, and russet-colored skin. I can see the outline of a tattoo just below the neckline of her coveralls, and a couple more on the backs of her hands. She's on the phone and holds up a finger to tell us to give her a minute.

She's dressed in blue coveralls like the guys in the garage and has her hair pulled back into a tight ponytail, with a red handkerchief tied around her forehead. The patch over her breast pocket says, "Letty," and she has a smudge of grease on her cheek. She's clearly not just the receptionist, but works in the garage as well.

The walls are all cinder block painted the same shade of blue, and are just as in need of some touch-ups. Half a dozen plastic chairs are lined up against the wall in the small waiting area, where a battered old coffee pot sits on top of a nicked and scarred credenza alongside a newer-looking flatscreen TV, which is currently tuned to a soccer match. There are posters for tires and different engine parts on the walls and a calendar depicting a bikini-clad brunette model standing next to a Lamborghini—from 2018.

She finishes up with her call, then hangs up the phone and jots something down on the clipboard in front of her. When she's done with that, she looks up at us with a smile.

"What can I do for you, officers?" she asks.

I give her a rueful laugh. "That obvious, huh?"

"You just have that cop look," she shrugs.

Astra and I badge her. "SSA Wilder and Special Agent Russo."

Her eyes widen slightly, and she licks her lips nervously. "Cool," she says, trying to sound casual. "And what could a couple of Feds want with us?"

"Well, we're looking for Tony," Astra says.

Her eyes narrow and she suddenly looks defensive. "What do you want with him?"

"We need to ask him some questions about a car he might have—worked on—recently," I tell her.

She purses her lips and cuts her eyes through the small window that looks out into the garage to her right. I can see that she's grappling with a decision in her mind. Letty finally sighs and runs a hand over her face, and I get the feeling she's chosen the wrong path. She's going to lie to us.

"Tony ain't here," she says. "I don't know where he is or when he's comin' back."

Astra steps forward, her eyes locked onto Letty's. They stand with their faces a foot apart, the waist-high counter the only thing between them. I can see Letty starting to get nervous. She swallows hard and shifts on her feet.

"You don't want to go this way, Letty," Astra starts. "You don't want to start off by telling us lies. Trust me on that."

"I ain't lyin'," she protests. "Now, you two need to go. I got work to do."

"Letty," I say and step up next to Astra. "You really don't want to lie to us. Look, we're not interested in your chop shop. We're only interested in one single vehicle in there."

"I got no idea what you're talkin' about," she snaps.

"You do," Astra presses. "And you really don't want to lie to us again."

"If this is the path you want to take, I can have a warrant drawn up that will shut this place down while we search it," I say. "And when we find all the stolen cars in that big building over there, we'll seize this place and prosecute everybody—including you. Do you understand?"

Letty shifts on her feet and looks away. She gnaws on her bottom lip, and I can see the torment on her face. She's torn and feels cornered. I need to give her a way out of this.

"Listen to me," I start. "As far as I'm concerned, your shop is a matter for the local PD. I couldn't care less about it. What we're doing is looking for a missing girl, and we know for a fact that her car is in that warehouse. Or at least, it was."

"We only need to see that car," Astra says. "We'll probably be so focused on that, we won't even see anything else."

"We're not looking to jam you up, Letty," I tell her. "All we need is to get a look at that car and then we'll be on our way."

She looks at me with her wide, dark eyes. "You promise? All you need to see is one car?"

"I give you my word," I nod. "Once we get a look at it, we're gone, and you'll never have to see us again."

She hesitates another moment but finally nods. She reaches below the counter and pulls out a leather Mariners fob that's got a pair of keys on its ring. Letty nods and silently gestures for us to follow her. I can feel the eyes on us as we cross the parking lot and head for the warehouse. When we get to the door, I see the mechanics have all come out of the garage and are lined up, staring at us. A couple of them are holding large wrenches, another one is holding a baseball bat, and all of them are glaring hard at us.

Astra and I both push our coats back and put our hands on the butts of our weapons at the same time. Letty, who had apparently been oblivious to it all, looks at us then at the line of men and scoffs.

"What are you idiots doing?" she snaps. "You really gonna try to kill a couple of Feds with a crescent wrench? Seriously?"

A man steps forward, his eyes shifting from us to Letty. He's tall, thick, and looks like a man familiar and comfortable with violence. He's completely bald but sports a thick, dark beard that's shot through with gray. He's got a pair of teardrop tattoos under his left eye and more showing from beneath the rolled-up sleeves of his coveralls.

"What are you doin', Letitia?" he snaps. "Why in the hell would you be openin' that door for a couple of Feds?"

"It's not your business, Emilio," she barks at them. "You all go back to work. Now."

"Letty—"

"I said 'now'," she snaps, her voice loud and hard. "Get back to work or I'll fire you right here, right now."

I look at her, surprised not just by the steel in her voice, but by the fact that she's the one in charge. More than that, I'm surprised that the men, all of them hard and vicious-looking, listen to her. Casting baleful glares at us, they turn away and drift back into the garage. Except for Emilio. He still stands there, crescent wrench in hand, a look of pure hatred on his face. Letty stiffens and steps closer to him, her eyes fixed on his.

"Don't think I won't fire you, too," she hisses. "And when I tell Tony why I fired you, he'll agree with me. He might even beat your ass for being so stupid. That what you want?"

"This ain't right," he grumbles. "You shouldn't be the one makin' calls—"

"But I am. Tony put me in charge because he knows I'm smarter than any of you fools," she cuts him off. "Now get the hell out of my face and get back to work. Or you can leave now and not come back. It's your choice."

Slowly and grudgingly, Emilio turns away, grumbling under his breath. He walks back to the garage, but not before angrily kicking an empty box across the parking lot. Letty turns back to us, a sheepish smile on her face.

"I'm sorry about him. He's an idiot," she says. "Tony only puts up with him because he's the best mechanic around."

I nod. "We all have to work with some idiots now and then. I get it."

"Don't worry, no offense taken," Astra says with a mischievous grin.

Letty unlocks the door and pushes it inward. The overhead fluorescents come on automatically, with a loud snap, and we find ourselves standing in a warehouse that holds a dozen cars, all of them in varied states of deconstruction.

"So, Tony put you in charge?" Astra asks.

Letty smiles softly. "He's my uncle. He taught me everything I know. Been workin' on cars since I was ten. I can tear down and rebuild any car you can think of," she says with a note of pride in her voice. "Emilio is better than me with some things, but I'm smarter than he is, so it all evens out. That's why my uncle put me in charge."

"And where is Tony?" I ask.

A frown crosses her face, and she looks down. "He's got cancer. He probably ain't got much longer left," she says, her voice thick with emotion. "But that's part of the reason we're runnin' this shop—money for his treatments. His insurance denied his care. We fought but they won't do nothin', even though he's paid his premiums. Never missed a single one in years. And this is how they do him?"

She bites off whatever she was about to say and looks down. But not before I see her eyes shimmering with tears. My heart goes out to her. She sniffs them back and angrily wipes at her eyes before finally looking back up to us.

"I know it's not legal, but it ain't like we're gettin' rich off it. We're just tryin' to hold onto him because the insurance company did him so dirty," she says quietly. "I mean, if we can extend his life even a couple of months and have that time with him—we have to try, right?"

While I obviously can't condone what she's doing, I'm not going to crucify her for it, either. Her story is one I've heard way too many times. It breaks my heart for people when they're forced to make some very hard decisions because of the endless greed of corporations who care more about their profits than the actual lives of human beings. I hate that somebody like Letty has to gamble with her life and her freedom just to keep her family alive a little while longer.

"There it is," Astra points. "Tesla Model 3."

"Check it out," I tell her. "See if you can find her phone or anything useful."

"On it."

As we watch Astra head over to the car, Letty clucks and shakes her head, a pained grimace on her face.

"Yeah, we haven't been able to figure out what to do with that. None of my guys knows how to take it apart," she says wryly. "We've been trying to part it out, but these parts aren't exactly a hot commodity right now. I wanted to slap Emilio stupid for takin' this one."

"Do you know where he got it?"

"Said some guy called the shop out of the blue," Letty replies. "Served it right up. Didn't want money for it. Said he just wanted it off his hands."

"Did you see the guy?"

She shook her head. "Emilio said the guy gave him an address to pick it up and left the key on the wheel," she tells me. "He never saw the guy."

"But he called the shop?"

She nods. "Yeah."

"Found her phone. It's turned off and smashed to pieces, though," Astra announces, handing me a plastic bag with an obliterated iPhone in it.

"Not that it matters, considering all this," Letty says, "but we didn't do that. It was in the car just like that."

"It's all right," I tell her.

"Forensics would be a nightmare. I'm sure there are prints all over the car," Astra says.

I nod. "Yeah, I don't want to call a team out, anyway. We'll just let it be."

A look of relief floods Letty's face and she gives me a grateful smile.

"If I were you, though," I start, "I'd get rid of that thing ASAP. If we found it here, others can, too. Cut your losses and dump it somewhere. Also, clean it. Wipe off all the prints so it can't be traced back to you or your guys. Trust me when I say it needs to be absolutely immaculate, Letty."

She nods. "I understand. And—thank you."

I give her a small smile and a nod. "Good luck to you. And to your uncle."

EIGHT

"How'd things go with the car?" Mo asks as we walk back into the shop.

"No joy," Astra says, prompting a frown from Mo.

I walk to Rick's workstation and hand him the bag with the iPhone. He looks at it, then up at me, with a crooked grin on his face.

"Gee, thanks?" he raises an eyebrow. "I've always wanted a destroyed iPhone."

I flash him a grin. "I'm not sure if there's any magic you can work on that, but if you can get into it and see if there are any pictures or messages—anything you can do."

"You realize everything on this piece of garbage is probably stored in the cloud, right?" he asks.

"It dawned on me, yes. And I want you to access her cloud," I say.

"You don't even know what the cloud is, do you?" he responds with an amused smirk on his face.

"Don't make me shoot you. I don't want to have to fill out all the paperwork," I tell him. "I do happen to know what the cloud is. But I also happen to know there may be things on the phone that might not be there as well. Hence, my request for you to wave your little wand and make some magic happen with this."

"I, for one, have no desire to see him waving his little wand," Astra says with a laugh, earning Mo's agreement.

"All jokes aside, I don't know that there's much I can do with this," Rick says. "It looks as if they beat it with a sledgehammer."

"I know it's a long shot, but give it a whirl, please."

"I'm on it," he nods. "Don't expect any miracles, though."

I walk back to the front of the room and fold my arms over my chest as I pace, trying to come up with my next move. I turn to Mo.

"I need you to dump the LUDs for Tony's shop. Give me the past twelve days of their phone records," I say.

Mo nods. "On it."

"What are you looking for?" Astra asks.

"Letty said that Emilio took a call from somebody who offered him Selene's Tesla—"

"She drives a Tesla?" Rick asks.

"She did," Astra replies. "Pretty sure it's a pile of burning scrap right about now."

"Why couldn't I have been born rich?" he groans.

"Anyway, Letty said the call came out of the blue," I go on. "I want to see if we can narrow it down and figure out who our mystery caller was."

"Smart," Astra says. "That must be why they pay you the big bucks."

I look up and see Rosie standing at the doors of the shop

and she waves at me to come out into the hall with her. Astra grins.

"Looks like Hedlund wants one of her progress reports," she says.

I groan. "I hate politicians."

I head out into the hall, making sure the door is closed behind me before turning to Rosie.

"What's up, boss?" I ask.

"Where are we with the Hedlund case?"

"Wow, I'm great, thanks. How are you today?" I respond, the sarcasm dripping off my tongue.

"Blake, I'm not in the mood," she says. "I don't mean to be so brusque, but I'm getting squeezed here."

"Hedlund?"

She nods. "You can't be surprised."

"I'm not," I say. "But it's only been a couple of days. Did she really expect me to pull her daughter out of my magic hat like a rabbit?"

"So, I guess Selene's not on a beach in Mexico drinking mojitos, then?"

I grimace, feeling the sharp sting of my words being thrown back in my face. I can't say I like it very much.

"Yeah, it's gotten more complicated," I say. "I wouldn't lay money on it just yet, but it's starting to look as if she's been taken. Or maybe she went off with somebody of her own accord. We're still trying to put all the pieces together. The only thing we can say with a fair amount of confidence is that she's not off on a bender."

Rosie frowns and nods her head. "I was afraid of that."

"Yeah, and now I stand before you with egg on my face."

"Not the first time and it won't be the last time," she says, approaching the first bit of good humor I've seen from her in a couple of days.

"What is it with you and Astra and your constant need to drill me about my failures?" I ask with a laugh.

Rosie shrugs. "Somebody has to keep you humble."

"Clearly," I say.

I fill her in on everything we've uncovered so far—doing my best to dance around Tony's chop shop. I doubt Rosie would care, thinking it's small fish and not worth our time or notice, but if she let it slip to Hedlund, I could see her going full Godzilla on the shop, stomping the life out of Tony and Letty in the process. And that's not something I want to see happen. Especially after I gave her my word that I wouldn't jam her up.

"So, in essence, we've got nothing," she says.

I shrug. "It's early days. You know how these things go," I tell her. "But once we start building some momentum, we can close this pretty quickly."

"I understand it," she replies. "I'm afraid Kathryn won't. She wants immediate results."

"Unfortunately for her, that's not the way the world works," I say. "I'm still waiting for that pony I never got as a child."

A rueful smile crosses her lips. "Kathryn has always been difficult. Always been a little bit unreasonable," she says. "I remember a time back in college when she broke up with her boyfriend because he didn't say he loved her soon enough. Broke up with the next one because he said it too fast. Kathryn's always wanted things done her way, on her schedule."

"How can you be friends with her?" I ask. "She seems to stand opposed to everything you're for."

"We're not exceptionally close. But we've been friendly for a long time now. Bonded by our sorority," she says. "And believe it or not, she does have some redeeming qualities.

When she's not wearing her Congresswoman's suit, she's quite charming. Funny."

"Honestly, I have a hard time imagining that woman as ever being funny," I tell her.

"All I'm saying is that there are more facets to her than you realize."

"And she still opposes most of the things I'm for. I somehow doubt we'll be on each other's Christmas card lists anytime soon."

A small, sad smile crosses Rosie's lips. "She wasn't always this way, you know. The things she believes have—changed— over time. Back in the day, she was as wild and free as the rest of us. These traditional values she goes on and on about—she never had them back in school," she tells me. "Watching this transformation has been—well, disturbing, if I'm being honest. Part of me thinks it's all just schtick to get people in her district to vote for her. They eat up what she spouts with a spoon."

"I don't know about that," I reply. "She seems pretty committed to it."

Rosie shakes her head. "All I know is that Kathryn has some real influence in Congress. She sits on the Judiciary Committee, which, as you know, oversees the Bureau, among other things."

"Which could make our lives more difficult."

"Not to mention she's got some influence over the budgeting committees," she says. "It would only take a few words from her to see our budget cut to the bone—"

"Which means extraneous units like mine might be deemed expendable."

"Now you're seeing the big picture," Rosie says dryly. "And why it's important we keep her as a friend."

I grit my teeth and ball my hands into fists. "Where does it end? We're supposed to operate independently of political pressure," I say. "Are we just supposed to dance every single time she calls a tune for fear of losing our jobs?"

"You know as well as I do that we've never operated free of political pressure."

"But we're not supposed to be one representative's personal police force, either," I counter. "Hedlund's pressuring us into looking for her daughter, threatening us with having our funds slashed if we refuse, really walks that fine line of misconduct."

"It's the way of the world, I'm afraid," Rosie sighs. "All we can do is play the game."

I know it's not Rosie's fault. She didn't set the rules of this game and she's simply trying to keep us all safe from an out-of-control politician who thinks we live to serve her.

"And what happens the next time? What happens when she threatens to cut our budget if we won't cross a line that shouldn't be crossed?" I ask.

Rosie sighs again. "I understand where you're at, Blake. I really do. And trust me, I'm caught between the same rock and hard place you are," she says. "Regarding your question, we'll cross that bridge when we come to it. Let's just solve this case, find her daughter, and hope that she goes back to forgetting we even exist."

"Until she needs us to do something for her again."

"Until then, yes. And we'll figure out how to proceed then," she says. "But for the moment, we have a legitimate case, so let's solve it. Find her daughter."

I frown and shake my head. There is nothing I hate more than feeling as if I'm being used. That some puppet master is pulling my strings and I have no choice but to dance.

"I'll do my best, Rosie," I tell her. "But I'll tell you right now, I already have a bad feeling about this case. I don't see a happy ending here."

She sighs. "Well, let's hope you're wrong."

"I hope so," I say softly. "But I don't think I am. Not this time."

NINE

"WHEN WAS the last time you saw her?" I ask.

"Gosh, it's been a little over a week I guess," she replies.

"And you haven't called anybody to report her missing?" Astra asks, arching an eyebrow. "It hasn't alarmed you that your best friend and roommate has been missing for eleven days?"

Brooke Dawes is the living embodiment of what I assume Selene Hedlund is—a narcissistic, shallow, self-absorbed, trust fund brat who honestly believes the world revolves around her. She's got platinum blonde hair that falls to her shoulders, green eyes, and a fair complexion. She's a physically attractive girl but has a vapid personality that's really off-putting, to be honest. We've spent ten minutes with her so far, and I'm more convinced than ever that if this is the future generation of leaders, we're all doomed.

"Alarmed? No. I wouldn't say Selene disappears for days at a time on the regular, but it's also not an uncommon occurrence," she says with a bubbly giggle. "You know how it is, you meet somebody new, get caught up in all the feels, and the next thing you know, you're taking off to St. Kitts for a few weeks of fun in the sun, if you know what I mean."

"Safe to say neither one of us knows what you mean," I say.

"No? Huh. Interesting," she frowns. "But like, if you haven't gone to St. Kitts or someplace like that in the Caribbean on a whim just for fun, have you ever even really lived?"

I blow out an irritated breath and look around the student union and shake my head, fearing that the entire student body is like Brooke Dawes.

"So, you say it's not uncommon for Selene to just take off like this?" Astra asks.

"Not uncommon, no. She does it at least once a quarter," she shrugs. "She meets somebody, falls in love, and jets off to wherever for a weekend. But then that turns into a week— sometimes more—then she comes back and says it just wasn't destined to work out."

"So, she doesn't have a regular boyfriend," I say.

"Oh, actually, she has a few of those as well," she replies. "She's a popular girl."

Astra and I exchange a look, and I can see the same irritation in her eyes I'm sure is in mine as well. Getting information out of this girl is like pulling teeth.

"Was there anybody in particular she was serious with?" I ask.

"Ummm... You can talk to Ryan Bancroft, Miller Hurley, and Edwin Gates," she says. "I think she was fairly serious with them. At least, she was for a while. Honestly, I haven't seen them around in a little while."

"Was she acting differently before she went missing?" I ask, as I jot down the names she gave us.

"Different how?"

"In any way," Astra clarifies. "Did her personality or behavior change at all before she went missing?"

She laughs and looks at us as if we're idiots. "You guys keep saying she's missing. I'm telling you, she's not missing. She's probably vibing on the beach with some hottie and a raspberry mai tai."

"I appreciate your input, but we still need to do our job. And until we find her, whether she's on a tropical island, a mountain chalet, or wherever, we have to proceed as if she were missing," I tell her. "Now, about Agent Russo's question—was she acting any differently when you last saw her?"

Brooke screws up her face and gives it some thought for a moment, and when she turns her eyes back to us, she looks a little less smug.

"You know, now that you mention it, I remember thinking she was acting a little weird," she says. "She didn't want to go out the last week or so before—before she went missing, as you say. She wouldn't meet us downtown. She wouldn't come to the Sigma Phi mixer. She didn't even want to go to this crazy—"

"All right, so she wasn't partying as much," interrupts Astra. "From what you said, that sounds like a major personality shift."

"Well....it's not like she wasn't going out. She was. It's just that she wasn't going to the big events. She was a little more serious," Brooke recalls. "I remember thinking at the time that she'd actually met somebody. As in, somebody she wanted to be serious with. I figured it wouldn't last very long and that she'd be back to normal in no time."

"Why's that?" Astra presses.

"Because that's just not Selene," she tells us. "She doesn't want to get serious right out of school. Her mom wants her to settle down, and it's just like, *ugh*. But she's not that kind of girl.

She's the live-deliberately-and-suck-the-marrow-out-of-life kind of girl. You know that poem, right?"

"Of course," I reply dryly. "They do teach Thoreau at schools other than Marchmont."

"They do?" she raises her eyebrows, sounding genuinely surprised.

I look down at my hands and silently count to fifty as Astra clears her throat.

This question is standard in missing persons cases, and considering Selene's background, and given the nine days' worth of bank withdrawals, it's critical. "Brooke," I say, "Was Selene using drugs or alcohol?"

Brooke hesitates a second. "Well....I mean, we partied a bit, but nothing heavy."

Astra comes in with, "Define 'heavy.'"

"We'd do a couple shots and a few beers sometimes, maybe a little pot, but that's all. And please don't tell Selene's mother. She'd kill both of us."

I study Brooke for a moment, and decide that if she's keeping anything back here, it's not much. We seem to be done with her at this point.

"Can you think of anybody else we can talk to?" Astra asks. "We're looking to fill in some of Selene's background and just need to get as much information about her as we can."

"Yeah, you can probably talk to Dr. Crawford," she says. "He's a philosophy professor and is also Selene's faculty advisor."

"Great. Thank you," I say, handing her one of my cards. "If there is anything else you can think of that might help, or if you hear from her, please call me right away."

"Sure thing," she chirps and slips my card into the case on her phone. "Is there anything else I can do for you?"

"No, I think we've gotten what we need," I say.

"Awesome. I've got a spin class to get to," she replies.

We watch as Brooke gets to her feet and flounces off, completely oblivious to the fact that her supposed best friend is missing, and for all we know, has ended up like Ben Davis—cut into pieces and stuffed in a barrel. The simple fact that her best friend is missing and she's casually playing it off as nothing more than some spontaneous trip and isn't worried in the least tells me what kind of person she is. A real friend and a good person would have called it in. Would have let the police know to begin looking. Or at least, when confronted with this news, would have been worried. But Brooke is acting as though Selene is going to come waltzing in any minute.

"What do you think?" Astra asks when Brooke disappears from view.

"I think that we're all in trouble if these kids are going to be running the show in a few years," I reply.

"God help us all," she mutters.

"You're not kidding," I say and get to my feet. "Come on. Let's go have a chat with Dr. Crawford and see what his story is. We'll check out Selene's apartment later."

"Sounds like a plan."

TEN

WE STAND in the corridor on the fourth floor, home of Dr. Silas Crawford's office, watching the parade of undergrads stepping through the door. I lean against the wall behind me with my arms folded over my chest, just shaking my head.

"You notice anything about the students going into his office?" I ask.

"If you're talking about the fact that they're all gorgeous young women, then, yeah, I noticed," Astra replies.

"Not a single male student to be seen," I remark.

"Maybe there aren't many boys taking philosophy this quarter," she offers.

"Maybe," I admit. "Or maybe Prof here has got something to hide."

"Could be that, too," she notes.

I look at the line forming outside his office door and groan.

We've already been standing there for the better part of forty-five minutes, and the line is still ten girls deep.

"I'm tired of waiting," I say.

"I was hoping you were going to say that."

"We have badges."

"Why not put them to some good use?"

"My thoughts exactly," I reply.

We both pull out our creds and step to the doorway. The girls standing there groan and object when we start to push our way through to the head of the line—a few of them look as though they want to scratch our eyes out. I hold my badge up for them all to see.

"FBI," I call out. "We're here on official business, so you'll have to come back for office hours later."

This prompts another bout of groaning and muttered remarks. But amidst all the eye-rolling and other histrionics, they all drift away. Once they're all gone, I knock on the office door and step inside. Dr. Crawford is sitting behind a large oak desk, reclining in his seat with his hands behind his head, the perfect picture of repose. The girl sitting in the chair in front of his desk jumps as if we'd just caught her in the middle of something. Crawford looks over at us and flashes us a million-dollar smile.

"I'm sorry, perhaps you didn't see the sign on the door that says I'm in session with a student?" he says, his voice smooth with a pleasant timbre to it.

Astra and I both badge him. "SSA Wilder and Special Agent Russo," I announce. "We apologize for interrupting your session, but we need a minute of your time."

The girl's eyes grow wider as she jumps to her feet, and even Crawford looks startled for a moment. He recovers quickly though and turns to the girl.

"We'll pick this up tomorrow," he says. "Until then, read

from the list on your syllabus and jot down your thoughts. We'll go over the interpretations of the subtext tomorrow."

"Thank you, Silas."

"Of course," he replies.

The girl practically sprints from the room, leaving us alone with him. He gestures to the two chairs in front of his desk.

"Please. Have a seat," he says.

We take the chairs and I casually look around his office. Everything's done in a dark wood that's polished to a mirror shine. The wall behind him and the wall behind us have bookcases, the shelves lined with textbooks, classical literature, a range of philosophy texts, and even some newer genre and self-help titles. The wall to our right holds the door but the wall to the left is almost completely glass, letting a flood of natural light into the room. The lighter hardwood floor is covered in a Persian rug that looks expensive. The office is tidy and clean yet still somehow has that smell of an old bookstore, which I love.

Crawford himself is just as neat and tidy—though I can't confirm that he, too, has the smell of an old bookstore about him. He's got sandy blond hair that's parted on the right and trimmed short. He's clean-shaven and has a bit of a baby face, with blue eyes that sparkle in the light. Even sitting down, he looks tall—if I had to guess, I'd put him around six feet or six-one. He's lean and fit, with a strong jawline and a proud, patrician face. He reminds me of that actor, Cary Elwes. I'm almost tempted to ask him to say, "as you wish," just to complete the picture.

"You look surprised," he says.

I shrug. "I suppose I was expecting a professor of philosophy to have a ponytail and dress like a beatnik," I say. "Not look like a corporate banker."

He laughs softly. "An unfortunate stereotype."

"You seem to have quite the following," I comment. "Standing in that hall, I thought we were backstage at a Justin Bieber concert or something."

He offers us a sheepish smile. "I'm afraid the Beebs beats me in attendance every day of the week and twice on Sundays."

It's a nice bit of self-effacing deflection, and when I cut a glance at Astra, I can see she picked up on it as well. We usually encounter that sort of behavior when somebody is trying to hide something—though I'm not sure what it is Crawford could be hiding behind his false modesty. He's obviously a god among his students—the female students at least. But all the girls in his classes are of age, so even if he were sleeping with them, we couldn't touch him. The school might have something to say about it, but legally speaking, he's in the clear.

"So, Agents, I have to admit to being curious," he starts. "What could the FBI possibly want with a dusty old lit professor?"

I sit back in my chair and cross my legs, folding my hands in my lap. "We're here about one of your students—Selene Hedlund."

He cocks his head, looking somewhat concerned. "Yes, I noticed she hasn't been in class all week. Is she all right? Did something happen to her?"

"That's what we're trying to find out," I reply. "She's missing right now and we're trying to get some background on her. See if we can figure out what happened."

"Missing. That's awful," he murmurs.

"We heard that you're her faculty advisor," Astra says.

"Yes, that's correct," he nods. "She's an incredibly bright girl. And when she's focused, she is a force of nature, that one. That girl will go places if she can keep herself together."

"We've heard that she's done this before—disappeared without a trace," I say.

He frowns. "Every once in a while, yes, she'll drop off the radar," he tells us. "She says it's because she needs to recharge her batteries. And that, I understand. I mean, who doesn't need a little sabbatical now and then? Especially somebody under as much pressure as she is."

"Pressure?" Astra raises an eyebrow.

He gives her a look that says the answer is so obvious she shouldn't even have to ask the question. But he quickly smooths out his features and gives her a small smile.

"The daughter of Representative Kathryn Hedlund is expected to be perfect in all ways, as I'm sure you can imagine," he tells us. "Her mother is hard on her. An A is not good enough, she should be getting A-plusses. That sort of pressure on a young person is incredibly tough to deal with. It's not surprising she acts out sometimes."

"And how *are* her grades, then?" I ask.

"Very good, actually. For as unfocused and undisciplined as she can be, she comes through when it counts," he replies. "As I said, she's incredibly bright. A—"

"Force of nature when she's focused," I cut him off. "Got it."

"Right," he says with a smile.

"We've also heard that she's—popular—with the boys," Astra says. "Do you know if she had any problems with any of them?"

He sighs and runs a hand through his hair. "I'm aware of her reputation. But you need to understand that although Selene is a wonderful girl, she is a bit—troubled," he says reluctantly. "I'm no psychologist, but I'd assume many of her problems stem from losing her father at such a young age. Combine that with a life of pampered privilege and the incredible amount of pressure her mother puts on her, and it can become a toxic stew."

He's not wrong, and it's a very insightful observation to make—more insightful than I would have given a philosophy professor credit for. It almost sounds as if he's familiar with psychology, if only vaguely. His observations could have come straight from a textbook.

"You seem to know your students very well," I say. "You seem to have a very personal connection to them."

He shrugs. "I take an interest in the lives of my students," he says, giving me a pointed look. "All of my students."

"Back to my original question: did she happen to mention any problems she was having with anybody she was seeing?" Astra asks. "Or with anybody else, for that matter?"

He shakes his head. "No, she didn't mention anything to me," he replies. "Nothing that stands out."

"Did she happen to mention why she might need to get away for a little while?" I ask.

He shakes his head. "No. Not to me, I'm afraid."

"What about where she might go?" Astra presses. "Do you know of any place she might go to take a little sabbatical?"

"I'm sorry, but I don't. When you have the resources Selene Hedlund has, you can take a sabbatical anywhere in the world," he replies. "We were close—as close as a teacher and student can be, anyway. But there was a lot I didn't know about her. A lot she didn't—or wouldn't—tell me about her personal life."

"So, she never told you where she liked to go to, as you said, recharge her batteries?"

He shakes his head. "No, I'm sorry. I don't," he replies. "She liked to travel and experience new places. She's as likely to be in France as she is to be in Iowa."

I frown and look down at my hands. I'd hoped that, as her faculty advisor, he'd have something for us. But it's looking like another dry hole. But then he cocks his head and looks at us as if he's had a thought.

"There was one guy she mentioned she was having an issue with," he says. "Spencer—Paul. Spencer Paul, that was it."

"What sort of problem was she having with him?" Astra asks.

"She'd said she got together with him a couple of times and he got too clingy. Wouldn't leave her alone," he replies.

"Stalking?" Astra asks.

"Not exactly stalking," he says. "More like just turning up at weird places and following her around. Not taking a hint that she didn't want anything serious with him. I seem to recall that she didn't think he was dangerous or anything. Just annoying."

I nod and jot his name down in my notebook. "That's good. Thank you, Dr. Crawford. That gives us somebody to talk to."

"Of course," he nods. "I want to help any way I can. I want her back home safely as much as you do."

"And one last question, Doctor. Did you get any read as to whether Selene was doing drugs or drinking?"

He answers right away, "No, not at all. Naturally, being a college student, she undoubtedly attended the occasional kegger or club, but I never saw any indication of frequent usage of either drugs or alcohol." I think he's answering me to the best of his knowledge.

I slide my card across his desk. "If you can think of anything else that might help, don't hesitate to give me a call."

"I will. Thank you, Agents," he says. "And please....find her."

"We'll do everything we can."

Astra and I head out of the building and walk across the campus. Our plan is to run down Selene's stable of boyfriends. I don't anticipate they'll have anything of value. I don't have the feeling anything at the school is at the center of her disappearance, but you never know. In any investigation, things can turn on a dime.

"What's your read on the good doctor?" Astra asks.

"I honestly don't know. He's tough to get a read on."

She nods. "But he looked pretty startled when we first walked in."

"I think he was just worried we were going to shut down his co-ed pipeline," I say with a laugh.

"That guy is living the dream of every middle-aged man out there," she replies. "Unlimited access to gorgeous co-eds who treat you like a rock star."

I shrug. "Well, he's an intelligent, good-looking guy who's charismatic as hell. That's like catnip to college girls, especially ones with daddy issues," I tell her. "I remember having a crush on one of my psych professors back in school."

"You know what's messed up? How come 'daddy issues' is always used as an insult against women when it's usually the man's fault for having treated them poorly, or not having been in their lives?" Astra points out. "It's totally sexist. Of course, that experience will give you 'issues'."

"You know what, you're right," I admit. "I never thought of it that way."

"Point, Russo."

"Anyway, guys like Crawford can always pick those girls out of a crowd and foster those issues," I say. "Guys like him make better profilers than we do sometimes."

"You ain't lyin'," she says with a laugh.

"Come to think of it, didn't you tell me once about that English pro—"

"Blake!" Astra cuts me off with a playful slug to my shoulder. "You promised you wouldn't bring that up anymore." Her eyes are lit up somewhere between irritation and laughter. "I'll admit that some of my choices in the past were never exactly....wise."

"That's putting it mildly," I chuckle.

Astra raises both hands as if in surrender. "All right, I'll admit it. There was a time in my life when I'd have been right there in that line, too."

"Point, Wilder."

I laugh as we head into the registrar's office to see if we can get a fix on Selene's boyfriends. I just have the feeling these guys are going to be a lot like Brooke Dawes, meaning this is going to be a very long day.

ELEVEN

Lecture Suite 231, Holbrook Hall, Marchmont University;
Seattle, WA

USING the school ID photo we got from the registrar, we watch the crowd of students flow out of the room. We've struck out on the first three guys on the list. None of them had anything very interesting or useful to say. What's clear was that they were all narcissistic, sexist pigs who think women exist only to be their playthings. It's not an unusual mindset for the sons of wealthy CEOs and elites. And soon enough, they'll be running board-rooms of their own. The thought makes me want to vomit.

The upshot of what we got from them is that they liked to party with Selene—and they definitely enjoyed sleeping with her. They were all shocked and upset to hear she'd gone missing—mostly because it meant they wouldn't get a chance to sleep with her again. They weren't interested in her as a person. They were only into her for what she could do with, and for, them behind closed doors.

None of the guys we've spoken to so far has been what I'd

consider a decent guy. That's why I'm not expecting to get much from Ryan Bancroft—he's very likely just another one of these spoiled rich kids with little-to-no regard for anybody other than himself.

When the classroom clears and he still hasn't come out, Astra and I wander into the room. We see him talking to the professor at the desk in the front of the room. I double-check the photo the registrar gave us, then give Astra a nod.

"That's him," I mutter.

She nods in return, and we wait until the professor says goodbye to Ryan. He gives us an odd look on his way out the door. Ryan is loading things into his backpack and doesn't seem to realize we're standing here.

"Ryan Bancroft?" I ask.

He turns and gives us both the elevator eyes, a smarmy smile on his face. "That all depends on who's asking."

Astra and I both flash our badges, and the smirk on his face slips for a moment. But he quickly recovers as he slings his backpack casually over his shoulder. To me, Ryan Bancroft is average. At best. He's about five-nine with pale skin, short dark hair, and green eyes. Other than his dressing in high-priced designer brand-names, there's really nothing all that special or distinctive about him. He's nondescript. The sort of guy you'd forget five minutes after meeting him. Or at least, I would.

And yet, he's brimming with this self-possession and sense of confidence that seems totally at odds with his physical appearance. He's thin and kind of stringy looking; he's definitely never going to be an underwear model or pro athlete. But he carries himself with the kind of conviction that says he's the best thing since sliced bread. I'm sure it's a confidence born of the wealthy lifestyle he grew up in, having everything handed to him on a silver platter, with nobody's ever saying no to him. It's kind of impressive in a way.

"Agents Wilder and Russo," I say in my best authoritative voice.

"Well, what can I do for you ladies?" he asks.

"Selene Hedlund," I say. "We understand you were seeing her."

His grin widens. "Oh yeah, the Omniwhore," he says with a chuckle. "Yeah, I was seeing her. If you want to call it that, anyway."

"The Omni—what?" I ask, anger flashing through me.

He laughs as though it's the funniest thing he's ever heard. "I have no idea who coined it, but it fits," he says. "The simple fact is Selene got around. She slept with anybody—guys, girls, it didn't matter. Certified freak, seven days a week, that's for sure. So, somebody nicknamed her the Omniwhore. You know, it's a play on the word 'omnivore'—"

"Yeah, I got that," I cut him off. "I'm just disgusted by it and don't see the least bit of humor in it at all."

Ryan's smile slips slightly, but he stands up straight and looks me in the eye. "I admit, it's a little lowbrow as far as humor goes, but regardless, it's a fairly accurate description."

"Tell me something," Astra starts. "Why is it a guy like you can sleep with however many women he wants and be considered a stud, but when a woman has a healthy sexual appetite, she gets hit with a foul and disgusting nickname like that?"

That seems to stop him short. He opens his mouth to reply, but then closes it again without saying a word. He doesn't seem to know how to respond to that.

"You know, maybe if you didn't act like such a repugnant, spoiled little rich kid who thinks he's God's gift to women, you wouldn't have to rely on your family name and money to pressure a troubled woman into bed," Astra growls at him.

"Whatever," he mutters, his expression darkening. "You don't know me. You don't know anything."

I cut Astra a look, telling her to take it down a couple of notches. We want to push him a bit, but not too hard. We don't want him storming out of the room until we've gotten answers to our questions. He frowns and looks at us as if a thought only just occurred to him. Frankly, he's so self-absorbed, I'm surprised he had a thought that wasn't about himself at all.

"Wait. Why are you guys asking about Selene?" he asks.

"She's missing," I say. "We're investigating her disappearance."

"Missing?" he replies. "What do you mean she's missing?"

"We mean she's missing. Not here. Possibly abducted," Astra says. "You wouldn't know anything about that, would you?"

His face pales and he suddenly seems to realize what we're asking him. Ryan clears his throat and tries to smooth his features and gather himself again. His success is limited.

"You don't think I had something to do with her disappearance, do you?" he asks.

"Did you have something to do with her disappearance, Ryan?" I ask.

"No. I did not. I wouldn't," he says, his voice quavering. "I —I like her. A lot."

It's a surprising admission—and to me, it sounds sincere. He actually looks rattled by the fact that she's missing. His whole smarmy-rich-kid persona is scrapped for the moment.

"You like her and you call her names like that?" I ask. I know I just told Astra to cool it, but I can't help it.

Ryan makes a sort of non-committal grunt sound and looks away, covering his mouth but not answering the question.

"Do you know if she was having trouble with anybody?" Astra asks.

He meets her gaze and shakes his head. "If she was, she never mentioned anything to me."

"Do you know of anybody who threatened her? Anybody who would want to hurt her?"

"No, of course not," he replies. "She was well-liked."

"Yeah, you made that abundantly clear," I say.

"No, not like that," he snaps, sounding defensive. "People genuinely liked her. As a person. She was nice. Kind. She got along with most everybody."

"Enough for people to call her the Omniwhore?" I raise an eyebrow.

Again, he covers his mouth and looks away without answering.

"Was she acting any differently lately?" Astra asks. "Any personality changes?"

He pauses for a moment, but then nods. "Now that you mention it, yeah," he replies. "She was a bit quieter than usual and didn't party as often. And when she did, she never went home with anybody. That was pretty unusual."

"And what did you make of it?" I ask.

Ryan shrugs. "Honestly? I kind of thought she found somebody she was being serious with. As in, an actual boyfriend, instead of a friend with benefits. It started a few weeks back. She didn't want to hang out with me—or anybody. That and she started disappearing at odd hours," he says. "At least, that's what Brooke said. She told me she'd wake up in the middle of the night and find Selene gone. If she ever bothered coming home in the first place."

I couldn't help but hear the twinge of jealousy in his voice. The façade he keeps up is beginning to crumble. It would be adorable if not for his other less cute, more toxic traits.

"A boyfriend instead of somebody like you. Somebody who could scratch her itch, huh?" Astra says. "That must have burned your butt."

He hesitates but then nods. "Yeah. Somebody like me. And

no, it didn't burn my butt," he says, regaining a little bit of his swagger. "There are plenty of women on this campus who would give anything to bed me."

"Hate to burst your bubble," Astra says. "But when you're sleeping with them, they're actually thinking about all the money your family has. Not you."

He frowns and looks down at the ground for a minute. I can see that Astra's words are striking their target and Ryan is feeling pretty low right about now. Good. I hope he feels really, really low. He deserves it.

"All right, well, do you know of anywhere she might go if she wanted to unplug and get away from everything for a while?" I ask.

He gives it a little thought then shakes his head. "I don't. We weren't exceptionally close," he says. "I mean, what we had wasn't really—deep. Or meaningful. It was just two people scratching an itch without much conversation. You know?"

"Yeah," Astra says. "I'm hearing that a lot."

"So, you don't know of anybody she had a beef with. Nobody who wanted to hurt her. And you don't know where she might go to unplug," I say.

"No idea whatsoever," he says. "You're going to find her, right? She's going to be okay, isn't she?"

"We hope so," I say. Then, "OK, Ryan, as you seem to know Selene so well, let me ask: what about booze and drugs?"

"She wasn't a druggie, if that's what you mean," he says. "I saw her drink a bit in the clubs a couple times a week, maybe a little weed, but she wasn't any worse than anyone else on campus, and not as bad as most."

He sighs and continues. "Listen, all that stuff I said....I didn't really mean it," he says. "As I said, I really like her. I just....when you're a guy in my position—"

"Save it. I don't care what position you're in," I say. "Being as disrespectful and as horribly sexist as you've been is a choice. Treating Selene like you have is a choice. It doesn't matter who you are or what position you think you're in. You wake up every day with the choice to either be a decent person or not. That's up to you."

"Make better choices," Astra adds.

We turn and walk out of the lecture hall. We've gotten everything we're going to get from him, which, sadly, isn't much —other than the bit about Selene's personality changing. The thought that she was seeing somebody a little more seriously. It jibed with what Brooke thought, which lends a little more credence to it in my mind.

But we still haven't been able to track down Spencer Paul, and I want to talk to him before we head over to Selene's apartment and then back to the shop. Based on what we've gotten from Selene's boyfriends so far, I'm not expecting much from him. But we need to cover all our bases and do our due diligence.

We're in that frustrating stage of the investigation right now. All we have are disparate parts, with no clear direction of how to put them all together. I'm anxious to find a focus to our investigation, but we're just not there yet. It's exasperating to be sure, but it's as I told Rosie—it's still early days. All we need is to find the one thing that will point us in the right direction. And I'm hoping against hope it'll be back at the shop when we get there.

TWELVE

The Olympic Luxury Condominiums; Seattle, WA

THE DOORMAN HOLDS the door for us, and I give him a nod of thanks as we step into the lobby of the luxury condo building Selene called home. The pristine floor is a very expensive-looking marble, and the lobby has a distinctive art deco motif. With the zig-zagging lines along the ceiling, the geometrical shapes all around us, and the vibrant colors, it's something straight out of the 1920s. Period art hangs on the walls all around us, making the lobby almost look like a show gallery. It's beautiful, actually.

Astra whistles low. "Wow. This place is something else."

"Sure beats the dorms."

"You're not lyin'," she says with a small laugh.

"May I help you?"

We both turn and see a thirty-something woman with short, dark hair cut in a bob, dark eyes, and cool, pale skin. She's dressed in a simple black pantsuit with a cream-colored blouse beneath the jacket, and is standing behind a marble desk that's topped with a dark oak counter cut in smooth, flowing lines. Astra and I walk over to her and flash our badges. She's wearing a golden, oval-shaped nametag that announces her as Missy.

"We're with the FBI—SSA Wilder and Special Agent Russo," I start. "We need to see Selene Hedlund's condo, please."

She clears her throat and gives us an awkward smile. "I hate to sound so dramatic, but do you have a warrant to enter her premises? The privacy of our residents is of the utmost importance to us. I'm sure you can understand."

I nod. "I do understand. And we don't have a warrant, but we do have the permission of Representative Kathryn Hedlund, who is the papered owner of the condo, to enter the premises. If you'd like, I can get her on the phone and let her explain the situation."

The woman goes even paler, and an expression of near terror crosses her face. She's obviously dealt with the Congresswoman before and is having some sort of a PTSD-fueled flashback. I can't say I don't understand.

"Of course," she says. "That won't be necessary—calling her, I mean."

She picks up the phone and punches a couple of buttons. I glance over at Astra, who's stifling a smile. The woman turns her back and speaks in a low tone, making it difficult to listen in, but she turns back around and hangs up the phone, a trembling smile on her face.

"Rodrigo will meet you at the unit to let you in," she tells us. "It's unit twelve-oh-four. Just take the elevator up to the twelfth floor."

"Thank you for your help, Missy."

She nods and gives us a courteous smile as we turn and walk over to the bank of elevators. We step into the car, and I hit the button for the twelfth floor.

"You were pretty quick to name drop the good Congress-woman," Astra remarks with a chuckle as the doors slide shut.

"Some situations require a surgical scalpel and others require a blunt sledgehammer to get things moving," I shrug. "I use whatever tools I happen to have."

"Well, you just dropped an atomic bomb on that poor woman."

"Sometimes that's what the situation requires."

We get off at the twelfth floor, and there's a man in dark green coveralls standing beside the door. He's about five-five, with thinning dark hair, russet-colored skin, dark eyes, and a warm, friendly smile.

"Rodrigo?" I ask.

He nods. "Yes ma'am," he says. "The Bureau, huh? What'd Miss Hedlund do this time?"

"This time?"

He shrugs. "I'm not one to talk out of school..."

That's usually the phrase people use right before they talk out of school. That's fine with me, though. I happen to like chatty people. Especially when the subjects of their gossip involve my cases. You just never know what you'll learn.

"You didn't hear this from me, of course," he says.

"Of course," Astra confirms.

"Well, Miss Hedlund is a bit of a party girl, if you know what I mean," he goes on. "People in and out of here all the time. Lots of men. She's even had the cops called on her a few times when the party got too loud. Most of the other residents don't like her much. They've been trying to get her thrown out, but she owns the place, what can they do, y'know?"

"You said the cops have been out a few times," Astra says. "She ever been taken in?"

He scoffs and shakes his head. "A girl like that? With that kind of background?" he says. "She ain't gettin' arrested for a noise complaint. Or much of anything else. All those problems tend to just go away, if you know what I mean."

I nod. I do know what he means. When you're rich and well-connected, crime somehow doesn't ever stick to you. It's like magic.

"Anyway, I should let you in," Rodrigo says.

"Thank you," I say. "We appreciate it."

He nods and unlocks the door for us. Astra and I step inside, and she closes the door as I walk down a short hall, passing the door to the kitchen and into a living room that seems about twice as large as my whole apartment. The space is richly appointed. Opulent, really. To my left is a spiral staircase that leads up to what looks like an informal den of sorts. The living room is done in black and white, the floor beneath us solid marble.

A pair of plush sofas sit across from one another on a richly colored rug, separated by a glass coffee table that could pass as a piece of art. The entire rear wall of the condo is glass, and there's a balcony just outside. The view is absolutely stunning. Downtown Seattle sprawls below her condo, and in the distance, I can see the peak of Mt. Rainier. The wall to our right holds a gas fireplace that seems to be more for show than functionality, and beyond the staircase is a hallway that I assume leads back to the bedrooms.

"This place is—wow," Astra comments. "I would have loved to live in a place like this when I was in school."

"Right?"

We both pull black nitrile gloves out of our pockets and snap them on as we spread out and start searching the front rooms. We don't find anything too useful, though. I go up the narrow spiral staircase and into the den. There's a large flat-screen TV on a stand against the wall and a sofa that's got a pile of pillows and neatly folded blankets in front of it. The wall opposite the television is one large bookcase, and I scan the various titles. They mirror the inventory I saw in Dr. Crawford's office—lots of classics and literary fiction. But I also come across quite a few books on philosophy and simpler, cleaner living.

I recognize some of the titles on simpler living from some of the prepper compounds we've raided. People big on getting back to nature and living off the land and all that. Also, those who want to be prepared for the fall of the government, civil unrest, general national—if not global—chaos, and in some cases, the zombie apocalypse. These books are almost a guide to off-the-grid living, which makes me wonder about Selene. Did she drop out on purpose? Is she living in some prepper commune now?

Taking one of the books with me, I head back downstairs and find Astra in Selene's room, going through some boxes on her desk. She looks up as I enter, and I toss her the book. She looks down at it and frowns.

"*Living Clean, Living Free,*" she reads the title. "Where'd you find this?"

"Upstairs." I nod my head back toward the other room. "It looks as if Selene spends a lot of time up there. She's almost nesting up there."

The bedroom is immaculate. Like everywhere else in the condo we've looked, it's pristine. The bed is perfectly made, and there's not a speck of dust to be seen anywhere. I'm sure there's a maid service, but this bedroom doesn't feel lived in. Not the way that upstairs den did. You could practically feel Selene in that den. But I don't feel her here.

"Nesting?" Astra asks.

I nod. "Pillows and blankets on the sofa. Seemed as though she was sleeping up there."

"Why would she do that?" Astra asks.

"No idea," I reply.

Astra picks up a small wooden box. The rich, red wood is intricately carved. She opens the lid and frowns. Without a word, she hands it to me, and I see that it's filled with a small baggie of pot and some other paraphernalia. I also see a couple small glass cylinders that are filled with a fine white powder.

"Want to take bets on what that powder is?" she asks.

"I'm pretty sure it's not baking soda."

She frowns and puts her hands on her hips. "Something about this is bothering me. Why would she go off and leave her party kit?" she asks. "If this were some, 'I'm going to go live off the land for a while' kick she was on, you think she'd take her goodies."

I shrug. "Unless they're serious about that living clean thing."

"Yeah, maybe. It still doesn't quite pop for me though."

I don't disagree with her. It's a flaw in the argument that she just dropped out of society. Somebody doing that will usually either use up her existing stash as a last hurrah or will give it away. It doesn't make a lot of sense to me that she would just leave her drugs right there on her desk. I check her closet and her dresser and see that they're full. Her clothes are still neatly folded and hanging. But then, most of her stuff is club-wear. Probably not so useful out on some off-the-grid prepper compound.

As I try to imagine her living with people like that, though—so paranoid or isolated that they cut themselves off from society—I just don't see it. The image falls apart for me. Granted, I don't know Selene at all. But what I do know of her, along with the image I have been able to construct based on what we've found so far, doesn't mesh with that kind of life. I just can't see her voluntarily dropping out of the world to live out in the dirt. Maybe I'm wrong and she's become somebody totally new, but that image just does not ring true for me.

"Hey, check this out," Astra calls over.

I turn and walk over to the desk. She's holding a loose picture of Selene with a young man—early twenties, I'd say—dressed in khakis and a blue polo shirt. In the photo, he's got his arm around her shoulder and she's leaning into him. Judging by the way she's looking up at him, her eyes locked onto his, there seems to be a mutual affection between them. Far more affection than you'd expect to see from somebody who changed partners as often as Selene supposedly did.

"What am I checking out?" I ask.

Astra taps the logo on the guy's shirt—the emblem of the local aquarium. It's then I see what she's really showing me. She wanted me to see the nametag on the shirt. It says Spencer.

"Looks as though we might have found our missing man," she says.

"Well, then, how about a day trip to the aquarium?"

"Thought you'd never ask."

I still don't have a lot of hope that Spencer will have anything too useful for us, but you never know. People can surprise you. I'm already surprised by the fact that Spencer is not one of the rich Marchmont kids. He actually has a job—a job most of the trust-fund brats at Marchmont would consider menial. And yet, the way Selene looked at him in that picture makes it appear she was entirely besotted with him.

It's something that doesn't quite fit in the picture we're constructing. And it's those puzzle pieces I always find the most interesting.

THIRTEEN

The Pacific Emerald Aquarium; Seattle, WA

"No offense, but you don't look like the typical Marchmont kid," I say.

He quirks a grin. "No offense taken. Actually, I'll take that as a compliment."

We're sitting with Spencer at a table near the outdoor cafe adjacent to one of the shark enclosures. He's a tall, lean kid with an unruly mop of dark curls, green eyes, and the tawny skin of somebody who spends a lot of time outdoors. He's one of the aquarium's docents—he gives tours and lectures mostly about the sharks they have in captivity. We learned that he's got a degree in marine biology and is pursuing a Master's in the subject.

He's smart. Articulate. And obviously passionate about his field, given that he spent the first fifteen minutes of our introduction explaining the difference between the blue shark and the brown cat shark to us. It was the longest biology lecture I've had since college. He's immensely likable. That much was clear from the start. So, too, was his affection for Selene.

"How long has she been missing?" he asks.

"Almost two weeks," I answer honestly.

He seems to deflate, and there's an expression of agony etched upon his face that's heartbreaking to see. I can see how much he cares for her.

"How did you two meet?" Astra asks.

A wan smile touches his lips. "This aquarium is owned by the Hedlund Foundation. Selene's mother likes to come out for photo ops now and then, and Selene was with her for one of them. We started talking and hit it off."

"And how long did you two date?" I ask.

He shrugs. "Six months, maybe? She really was unlike anybody I ever met before. She's a—force of nature," he says. "She really can do anything she sets her mind to."

Astra and I share a glance, recognizing the phrasing Crawford used to describe her. It could be coincidental. I mean, there are only so many ways to describe somebody with as big a personality as everybody says Selene has. And I'm honestly not picking up on a creepy, stalkerish vibe from him. He seems like a decent guy so far.

"Why did it end?" Astra asks.

"That's....complicated."

"Explain it to us," I say.

He sighs heavily, and I can see a sadness in his eyes. "Well, as I got to know her better, I discovered her life up at March-mont—the drugs, all the guys—all of it."

"And I take it that didn't sit well with you?" I ask.

He shakes his head. "No. I'm not about that kind of life. It surprised me. When we were together, she was so down to earth. Calm. Fun. We'd have a few drinks, but we wouldn't go out clubbing or partying. She didn't do drugs or anything like

THE LOST GIRLS   99

that. At least, that's what she always told me," he says. "It was a shock when I found out what she was like at school."

"And how did you find out?" Astra asks.

"Somebody sent me a video. Anonymously, of course," he says. "In the video, she was drunk or high—I couldn't tell. But she was—she was with a couple of guys. They were..."

His voice tapers off, but he doesn't need to say it. I can guess where he was going with it. I frown and take a drink of the soda I grabbed from the kiosk nearby.

"You have no idea who sent it to you?" Astra asks.

He shakes his head. "I didn't even know anybody at Marchmont knew we were together. I'd never met any of her friends from school."

"And what did you do when you received the video?" I ask.

"I confronted her about it," he replies. "She and I argued about it, and she broke it off."

"We've been led to believe that you're still a part of her life," Astra says.

He shrugs. "Not really. We still talked and all. She wanted to get back together, but I wouldn't do it. Couldn't do it," he tells us. "I mean, she said she wanted to change and that she didn't want to live that life anymore. But how could I trust her when she hid that side of herself from me? If I'd known what she was really like, I probably wouldn't have pursued her to begin with. I'm just not about that life. Never have been, really. I'm a simple, quiet guy who's passionate about fish."

I laugh softly at his last line, earning a small smile from him. There's a sadness in his eyes more profound than I would have expected from somebody whose relationship lasted about the length of a hockey season. But then, I'm not one to judge. When it comes to matters of the heart, I'm about as skilled as I am at ice skating—and I've never been ice skating. As if he's reading my mind, he looks up at me.

"I know you think I'm too torn up about a six-month relationship," he says. "But as I said, she's different from anybody else I've ever met. It sounds utterly ridiculous to say out loud, I know. But I really thought she was the one. Or at least, I thought the side of her personality I was falling for was the one."

Astra clears her throat. "Tell us something Spencer....we were also led to believe that you had—difficulty—letting go. That you may have been turning up in places you weren't expected—"

His laughter cuts through her words, drawing a surprised expression from Astra. He shakes his head and runs a hand through his thick curls.

"Stalking her? Is that what you were going to say?" he asks.

"Well—yes."

"No. I was not stalking her. If anything, it was the other way around," he says. "Selene would show up at places where I was. She came by here a lot. She texted me, begging me to give her another chance."

"Do you still have those texts?" I ask.

He shook his head. "No, I deleted them all and eventually blocked her," he sighs. "It was just too painful for me." A wry smile crosses his face. "Not that she let that stop her. She got another phone and started texting me again. She was determined. But I just ignored her after that."

"When she showed up places, what happened?" I ask.

"She'd beg me to take her back and give her another chance. She'd make a scene. She got me into trouble here a couple of times, to be honest," he admits. "I had to have my boss' boss call her mom and have Selene barred from the aquarium."

"Ouch," I wince.

"Yeah."

A strained silence descends over us as we sit there, and I can see the pain he's in. I can see his regret.

"Didn't you think she could change?" Astra asks gently.

"I don't know. All I know is she broke my trust by not being straight with me from the start," he tells us. "The fact that I found out through some anonymous video that she's got this double life—that hurt, Agent Russo. That hurt a lot. I really thought she cared for me as much as I cared for her."

"Do you know if she was having any difficulties with anybody, Spencer?" I ask. "Did she mention having troubles with anyone?"

He shook his head. "No, not at all. But she didn't tell me much about her life at school. Obviously," he says. "The last time I saw her was—a couple of weeks ago. I was out to dinner with a few friends, and she showed up with a pack of people from Marchmont, I assume. She was drunk and made a big production of hanging over the guys in the group. Making a spectacle of herself. I knew she was trying to get under my skin, so I ignored her. Tried to, anyway. I left early and she ran me down in the parking lot, screaming at me. Some older guy who was with her group had to come out and pull her away. He apologized for her and got her back into the restaurant."

"Older guy?" I raise an eyebrow. "Do you know who it was?"

He shook his head. "No idea. I didn't ask."

Astra holds up her phone, showing him a picture of Professor Crawford. "Was that him?"

He nods. "Yeah, that was him," he says, his eyes widening. "Do you think he did it? Do you think he abducted her?"

"We don't know yet, Spencer," I say calmly. "We're still trying to get all of the background right now. Trying to figure out who the players are."

I hand him a card. "If you can think of anything else, or remember anything, just give me a call. Please."

He nods. "I will."

Astra and I leave him sitting there, wallowing in his misery. It's hard not to feel bad for the kid. I'd like to say I can't imagine falling in love with somebody only to find out that person isn't the one you know. But that's a story that's all too familiar and hits way too close to home for me right now.

We head across the parking lot and get into the car as a million different thoughts swirl around in my head.

"Interesting that Crawford didn't mention that incident," Astra mentions.

"It is. But it also could simply be that it didn't come up in our chat."

She shrugs. "He was quick to point the finger at Spencer when he knew it was Selene doing the stalking."

"Maybe. But it also could be that he misinterpreted the situation. Or that Selene told him something completely different," I offer.

She sighs and runs a hand through her hair, but concedes my point with a nod. As I drive away from the aquarium, I can't help but see that haunted look of grief in Spencer's eyes and wonder if it's also in mine. The things that are easiest to see in other people are often the most difficult to see in ourselves.

FOURTEEN

"Please tell me you've worked some magic for me," I call out as we enter the doors.

"I've pulled street cam footage around the bank from the last withdrawal from Selene's account and have something interesting," Rick tells me. "I'll put it up on screen."

I turn to the screens and fold my arms over my chest as I watch the grainy footage. In it, I see the bleeder who's been draining Selene's account stepping out of the bank's vestibule. He walks over to a man leaning against a car parked at the curb. The car looks like an older Lincoln Towncar, a pretty nondescript, anonymous vehicle that can be had cheap for the most part. From the distance of the camera, I unfortunately can't see any distinctive markings or anything that makes it stand out.

The man leaning against the car is tall and thick. He's wearing jeans and a hoodie with the hood pulled down over his head. I can see the brim of a ballcap sticking out from under it, but can't make out his face. The distance and his natural camouflage make it impossible. I let out a grunt of frustration. The bleeder walks over and hands him what could be the cash he withdrew. It's too grainy and far away to make out for sure, but it's a safe bet that's what it is.

"Can you zoom in on that?" I ask. "Can we see what's being handed off?"

"Unfortunately, no. This isn't like how they do it on TV. I zoom in, the images just get more pixelated," he says. "There's something over the license plate—mud maybe—that's obscuring it. Keeping me from getting the tag numbers. Crooks who know about the street cams do that."

"I'd say it's the cash he took out of the ATM," Mo adds.

"So would I. But I'd like to have some actual proof," I tell them. "Any defense attorney is going to argue that because we can't see it, it could be anything. Drugs. Tickets to the Mariners game. The Hope Diamond."

In the video, we see Hoodie hand Bleeder something that he quickly tucks into his pocket. Probably his cut. They seem to exchange a few words before Hoodie jumps into the car and drives off. Bleeder walks away, seeming to be in a chipper, upbeat mood all of a sudden—no doubt off to get his next fix.

"Okay, so we've got a widening scheme," I announce. "We have somebody running the bleeder for a cut of the proceeds."

"Looks that way," Astra says. "I can also guarantee the dude in the hoodie is not our dreamy philosophy professor."

"You guys met a dreamy professor?" Mo raises an eyebrow.

"Very dreamy. Even Blake was into him."

"I was not," I protest.

"She totally was," Astra grins.

"Why don't I ever get to meet guys like that? All I ever seem to get are killers and crackheads," Mo complains, drawing a laugh from me.

"How about I take you out there if we get to arrest him?" Astra asks. "I'll even let you frisk him."

"Deal," Mo says with a grin.

"Okay, so, if you guys are done violating about every word of the sexual harassment section of our HR handbook, I have something to share," Rick says.

I turn to him. "Please. Share with the class."

"So, I pulled the phone records from Tony's Auto the way you asked. I narrowed it down to three days—one day before and one day after that day you asked me to run," he says. "Then I filtered out all of the legitimate numbers—businesses, known associates, the works."

"You know you don't have to go through these long, tedious explanations every single time," Astra quips. "We can all stipulate that you're the smartest guy in the room if it makes you feel better."

"I wouldn't go that far," Mo says.

"Anyway," Rick goes on, "I've got a list of numbers that have not been accounted for. But on the day in question, during that nine-to-ten hour you specified, I've got six numbers that are not accounted for—all of them burners."

"Makes sense, given the business they run out of the shop," I nod.

"This is true. But I then cross-referenced the numbers against previous calls—you said the call to drop off Selene's Tesla was a one-time event, right?" he asks.

"That's what I said, yes," I reply.

"Then applying that filter, we now have just one number. Also, a burner," he says proudly.

"And? Do we have a name to go with the burner yet?" I ask.

"Well, it's a burner, so no. I'm trying to track down the location it was purchased from," he says.

"So, you actually have nothing new to share, right?" Astra asks dryly.

He gives her a smile. "I will. I just wanted you all to know I've been putting in some work, too."

I laugh softly and shake my head. "I work with clowns," I mutter, then look up. "That's good work, Rick. Stay on it and let me know when you have the purchase location."

"I knew this degree from Clown College would come in handy someday," he cracks. "I'll get right on it, boss."

"Okay, so where are we with theories?" I ask. "Let's start throwing them out. Nothing's too outlandish at this point—unless you're going to pitch that Selene was abducted by aliens. Do that and I'll slap you stupid."

"Well, I'm out, then," Rick says.

"I think we're looking at a girl who is desperately seeking love. And validation," Astra pipes up. "It explains her behavior —she's trying to find her value in others. In men."

"And from what you've said so far, her value to them seems to only be in bed," Mo adds.

"But the one guy who breaks that trend is Spencer," I note. "He was actually repelled by her behavior and obviously didn't value her in that way. Or at least, valued her for more than that. He valued her as a person, whole and complete."

"Which could explain why she was so desperate to win him back," Astra says. "He gave her a taste of a different life and she wanted more."

"But then we have Crawford," I say. "What's his role in all of this?"

"Maybe, as you said, he doesn't have one. Maybe he just misread the situation between her and Spencer that night," Astra offers. "Maybe he's nothing more than he seems to be—a horny, middle-aged teacher who is enjoying his endless buffet of entirely snackable co-eds."

"That's just living the dream," Rick calls from over his shoulder as he types away.

Astra arches an eyebrow at me. "See?"

I give her a grin. "I'm thinking that's right. Unless we can find a connection between Crawford and the bleeder."

"We already know the hoodie isn't Crawford. At least, it's a solid educated guess," Astra says. "Hoodie doesn't look as if he's more than five-seven or five-eight."

I nod. "And Crawford is at least six feet."

I look at the whiteboard and see the notes I've jotted down as I think about Selene's psychological makeup. She's fiercely intelligent but is a party girl. Promiscuous. Issues with authority stemming from lack of a father figure and friction with her mother. Seeks acceptance and attention, even when it's unhealthy. But then I factor in what we learned from Spencer. She's got a serious side. Has a desire for stability and settling down—at least, that's what I take from her dogged pursuit of him.

It seems that Spencer may have brought that out in her. Maybe she realized that there was a better way because of him. He loved her for who she was and not for what she could do for him. He didn't value her simply as a sex object, but for the person she was. That had to be a massive paradigm shift for her. Coming to that understanding made her want to cling to him even harder—hence her almost stalkerish behavior.

I realize I'm relying on Spencer's account of things and that it could be faulty. It could skew the whole profile and invalidate it. But I saw a sincerity in him that made it difficult for me to believe he was making it all up. I believe him. But as I ponder it, that nagging voice in the back of my head still won't let me totally take his side.

"Rick, I need you to crack into Spencer Paul's phone. I need his text messaging history with Selene," I say.

"On it," he calls.

"What are you thinking?" Astra asks.

I flash back to Selene's apartment. We didn't find anything useful, but some things were suggestive. At least from a certain point of view. The fact that her party kit was left behind, along with the clean-living books she had, could suggest a woman who wants a fresh start, the party kit a symbolic gesture of leaving her past behind. It's suggestive of a woman who could be seeking a simpler life than she's lived—one that might line up more with the life Spencer Paul lives.

It's a huge leap of logic. I'm making a whole lot of assumptions, I know. And not a lot of it is lining up for me. There are massive plot holes everywhere I look. How do all these different pieces connect? Do they actually connect, or am I simply trying to jam square pegs into round holes?

I shake my head. "There are just so many moving parts, but we seem to be trying to put a puzzle together using two different sets," I say. "There are so many things that just aren't adding up. Nothing about this is making any sense."

"To be completely honest, we don't even know if she was abducted or if she left on her own," Mo offers. "I mean, the fact that Hedlund said her daughter was abducted doesn't make it so."

"She's right," Astra adds. "It could be that Selene got tired of all the pressure her mother was piling on and decided to walk away—and not for a booze-soaked bender on a tropical beach somewhere."

Astra throws my first assumption back in my face and flashes me a grin. She knows how much I love that. I follow Mo's and Astra's words and nod along with them, though. It's all technically true, but it still doesn't quite fit right. It's like trying to squeeze myself into a sweater that's a few sizes too small.

"But why not just go withdraw all of her money at once?" I ask. "Why have a bleeder come in and do it piecemeal? And then add another layer with the guy who's running the bleeder? Why not just take it all at once and disappear?"

"Given how much is in her bank account, she could afford to live in style for a while," Rick notes. "Speaking of which, the account got hit again today. I ran the cams and the picture's no better. Nothing good enough for facial rec."

Astra nods. "That's a hole in the theory."

"A big one," Mo concurs. "I didn't even think about it."

I close my eyes and draw in a deep breath, letting it out slowly as I let myself see all the disparate parts in my mind, struggling to see a connection among all of them. But no matter how hard I try, I can't seem to find one. There isn't one bright line that runs through all the different points, connecting them all.

I grit my teeth in frustration, but quickly force myself to relax. At times like this, when nothing is making sense or adding up, I have to remind myself to think simply. To shut out all the background noise and focus on the basics. Focus on the things that do make sense and build out from there. My first impulse may not be the right one, but it feels closer to pointing us in the right direction than anything else we've come up with so far. It makes sense in ways everything else hasn't.

"Okay, let's cut out all the noise and background chatter. Just shut it all out," I say. "When I tell you we have a missing girl, a bleeder who's draining her account, that her car wound up in a chop shop, and she's completely off the grid, what would be your first thought?"

Astra puzzles over for a moment but nods, seeming to pick up what I'm putting down. "My first thought would be that she was snatched and possibly trafficked."

"Not to be a wet blanket, but we haven't seen any evidence of trafficking," Mo says.

"You usually don't," Astra tells her. "Girls who go missing are trafficked all the time. And they usually leave no trace behind. But a lot of them have those same characteristics."

"Okay, we need to find the bleeder," I say. "And from there, we find the hoodie. That should give us all the information we need."

It's still a shot in the dark, but at least we have a direction to run in. It's not much, but it's something. And right now, with not a whole lot about this case making sense, I'll take it.

FIFTEEN

The Emerald Lounge; Downtown Seattle

THE EMERALD IS a gem of a little bar a few blocks from the shop Astra and I discovered a little while ago. It's a nice, quiet place to come to have a drink and a conversation. It's built from red brick and light oak and has that charming, timeless feel of an old-fashioned speakeasy. The place is about half-full when we walk in, and soft instrumental jazz is drifting through the speakers hidden discreetly overhead, which doesn't hurt, given my love of jazz.

Tonya, the owner and head bartender, gives us a wave when we walk in and take a seat in a booth near the back of the place, giving us a view of the whole bar. One of her waitresses comes over and drops off our usual drinks—an old fashioned for me, a martini for Astra—then bustles off with a smile. I take a sip of my drink and sit back against the padded booth, trying to unwind from a long day.

"So, are you going to tell me what's going on with you?" she asks.

"What do you mean?"

Astra takes a sip of her drink, eyeballing me over the rim of her glass. She sets it down, then looks up at me again, concern etched into her features.

"Something's not right with you, Blake. You've been on edge for awhile now," she says. "You hide it pretty well, but I can see through you. You're my best friend. I know you inside and out. Hate to break it to you, but you're not that big a mystery to me anymore, babe."

I laugh softly. "If I'm not that big a mystery to you anymore, then you tell me," I reply. "What's wrong with me?"

"That's a long, long list," she replies. "But in this particular case, I don't know because you won't tell me. I mean, if you don't want to talk about it, that's fine. Just say that. But don't walk around thinking you're fooling me. You're definitely not."

"Clearly," I note.

"So? Going to tell me?" she asks. "Or are you just going to keep pretending that I can't see through you?"

I sigh and drain my glass, then signal Tonya for another round. "We're going to need more drinks."

The waitress brings our round over and I take another sip to fortify myself. Then I launch into my story, telling Astra everything that's going on—including everything I've learned about Mark. Or whatever his name really is. She sits back and listens to me over the course of an hour and a couple more drinks. When I'm done, she lets out a loud breath, as if she's been holding it in.

"Jesus," she mutters, then looks up at me. "Why didn't you tell me any of this? You shouldn't be trying to carry this all on your own."

I shake my head. "The fewer people I pull into this garbage, the better. The last thing I want is to see any of you hurt," I reply. "I'm already feeling guilty as hell about asking Mo to look into all of it. I wouldn't have, but she's the best I know about detecting financial patterns. If anybody can connect all the dots, it's going to be her. And I hate that it is. Dealing with a group who may have murdered not just my parents and their working group, but three sitting Supreme Court Justices, is no joke."

"No, it's definitely not," she replies, her voice serious. "This is big and nasty, Blake. You're going to need help. Have you spoken with anybody about it?"

"God, no," I say. "Aside from you, Pax, Brody, and Mo, I have no idea who I can trust. I have no idea who's running this thing."

"Huge slam on Rick," she cracks, which draws a laugh from me. "But you have to trust somebody."

"I trust you. And the others I mentioned. And Rick, I guess. But that's it," I say. "I mean, if I can't trust the man I've been sharing a bed with and confiding all my secrets in for awhile now, how am I supposed to trust anybody?"

She purses her lips and looks down, nodding. "I see your point." She takes another sip of her drink, then looks up again. "But I'm not following something—what do the three Justices who died have to do with any of this?"

"First, they didn't die. They were murdered," I tell her. "Second, they cast votes in certain cases that wound up costing some big corporations a lot of money. We're talking billions—"

"So, those Justices are replaced by ones who have a more corporate-friendly reputation," she finishes.

"Exactly. Those three Justices give them the votes necessary to push through some radical ideas that will benefit very few people. I mean, there may be other objectives, but Gina told me it was mainly for money and power," I say. "That's what I have Mo working on—collecting the cases they've decided and finding out who was behind them. If we can figure that part out, we'll have a suspect pool."

"This is—complicated," she says. "And you think your folks stumbled onto the idea and they were killed for looking into it?"

I nod. "Definitely. Between what I learned from Mr. Corden and from Gina Aoki, I have no doubt that's why they were killed. None whatsoever."

"And it's this group, this—"

"The Thirteen."

"Right. The Thirteen planted Mark in your life to keep tabs on you?"

I nod. "That's the working theory. Who in the hell else would insert somebody into my life like that?" I ask. "And I'm convinced the woman who broke into my place and beat the hell out of me was sent by him—not Torres—after all. I guess you were right about that."

"Well, I was wrong about who sent her," she mumbles.

She looks away and drains her own drink, then signals for a fresh round. It arrives a couple of minutes later, but all the while, I've watched her. The wheels are spinning in her brain. And I hate that they are. The last thing I wanted was for Astra to become involved in this. And simply knowing about what's happening—or what I believe is happening—is enough to get her killed. It's why I haven't wanted to tell her.

"So, you have no idea who Mark really is?" she asks.

I shake my head. "I don't even know if he's a real doctor," I reply. "Brody gave me a file that shows me that all of his personal information was faked. Ten years ago, Dr. Mark Walton didn't exist."

"Jesus," she says again, starting to look pale and stricken. "Does he know you know?"

I shake my head. "I don't think so. But he knows I've been pulling away from him," I reply. "I just don't think he knows why. Every time he brings it up, I change the subject. And I don't see him often."

"If he was put into your life to watch you, I'm worried about what happens when he finds out that you know. Or even if you just want to break up with him," she says. "I mean, does he have orders to kill you?"

I shake my head. "I really hope not. But I have no idea."

"We need to get you out of there. Away from him," she says. "The Bureau has safe houses—"

"Absolutely not. For all I know, there are members of this Thirteen inside the Bureau," I cut her off. "If they get wind that I'm onto them, it wouldn't be very difficult for them to find out where I am, then come for me. Or even worse, come for the people I love most."

She runs a hand over her face and looks at me with genuine fear in her eyes. I give her a wan smile and a shrug.

"This is why I didn't want to tell you. We're playing some high-stakes poker right now," I tell her. "But I have no choice. I have to play out the hand I've been dealt."

"To be honest, I'd rather know than be left in the dark," she says. "If somebody's coming for you and possibly me, I'd rather have a heads-up so I can be ready."

"It's going to make you paranoid."

"A little paranoia isn't a bad thing," she shrugs.

"I suppose not."

We sit in silence for a couple of minutes as the sounds of Coleman Hawkins' saxophone wash over us. I watch Astra as she tries to wrap her mind around the enormity of it all. She's struggling with it, which is something I can relate to. I still have difficulty with it, sometimes.

"That's a lot," she finally says.

"Yes, it is," I reply. "So how about we talk about something else? Give you a chance to process it all."

"Good idea," she responds. "Do you really think Selene Hedlund was trafficked?"

I laugh out loud, not expecting her to go there. "Not one for light, cheery, vapid conversation tonight, are you?"

Astra grins. "After doing this job for as long as I have, I'm not sure I even know how to do that anymore. I mean, it's not as though I watch reality TV or anything, so that's out."

"I think we suffer from the same disease."

She nods. "We do. But at the same time, there's nothing else I'd rather be doing," she says. "And I know you feel the exact same way."

"I do," I reply. "And to answer your question, I think there's a very strong possibility that Selena was snatched and trafficked. She's a very pretty girl. I'm sure somebody else noticed that, too. But I take it you're not convinced."

She shrugs. "Honestly, there's part of me that thinks she simply walked away. Yeah, given what we have to work with right now, it looks like a trafficking situation," she says. "But if you change your vantage point of the situation, it can also look as if she simply got tired of her life and decided to cut ties with it. I think Spencer helped her see just how toxic her life was, and there's part of me that thinks she wanted a fresh start somewhere else—somewhere she isn't Selene Hedlund. She was just Selene. Even if she couldn't have that life with Spencer, I think she wanted it all the same."

I nod. "That is entirely possible. And you're right. From a different perspective, it can definitely be that. I think we're going to know more once we track down the bleeder. We get him, we can get to Hoodie, and from there—I hope we'll have the answers."

She raises her glass. "Then let's nail these guys."

"Hear, hear," I say and tap my nearly empty glass against hers.

SIXTEEN

Emerald City Trust Bank, Capitol Hill District; Seattle, WA

WE'RE STANDING on the sidewalk just outside the bank, looking at the crowd flowing by. There's some small part of me that hopes the bleeder just stumbles into our arms, but I know it's not going to be that simple. Nothing ever is.

"Does your head hurt this morning?" Astra asks.

"Not anymore," I reply. "I had half a dozen Advils in my coffee this morning."

"Smart," she groans. "When did we get so old, Blake? I can't put 'em away like I used to."

"I think you've lost your pro card," I tell her. "You are officially relegated back down to the rank amateur drinking league."

She puts her sunglasses on and nods. "Yeah, sounds fair."

"This is what happens when you get all happy and cozy in a relationship," I go on. "You're not out at the bars pounding every night. You lose your stamina."

She laughs softly. "I think it's a fair trade-off. I'll trade the hangovers and Advil coffee for what I have with Benjamin."

"That's so sweet, I think I'm about to slip into a diabetic coma," I say.

"We need to find you a good man, Blake Wilder."

"Given my recent history, I'm going to pass," I reply. "But when I'm ready to brave those piranha-infested waters again, I'll settle for a guy who's not a spy for an organization that wants to murder me."

"That's a pretty high bar. But I'll see what kind of magic I can work."

"Deal," I reply and point to a pizza shop across the street. "Over there."

We cross the street and walk over to the pizza shop. Incredibly loud and fast punk rock is blasting through the speakers at such volume that I wonder how anybody can hear over the music. When we get to the counter, we flash our badges to the kid behind the counter. He pales as he looks at us.

"Wh-what can I do for you?" he asks.

"We need to speak with your manager," I say.

"And we need for you to turn the music down as well," Astra adds.

I give him a smile as he turns and dashes through the swinging doors that lead to the back of the shop. A moment later, the music is turned off. The air in here is thick with the smell of garlic and cheese. It smells delicious, actually. There are half a dozen small tables against the wall behind us, but other than that, the rest of the seating is outside. The glass case on the counter in front of us displays several different pizzas under the heating lamps. My stomach rumbles and I'm just about to order a couple slices of pepperoni and pineapple when a tall, heavy-set man walks out of the back room.

Yeah, I like pineapple on pizza. Sue me.

The manager is roughly six-and-a-half feet tall, with one stripe of blue hair down the center of his otherwise clean-shaven head. He's got so many tattoos that I can't actually see the skin on his arms and neck. He's got a black goatee and a nose ring that's connected to his ear by a gold chain.

"He's pretty," Astra says quietly.

"That's—that's a look," I whisper back. "But I gotta say, not exactly my type."

"Take a walk on the wild side, Blake," she grins furtively.

"I'm Devin Wilkes. I'm the manager here," he announces. "What can I do for you, Agents..."

"Wilder and Russo," I introduce us. "And we'd like to ask you about those security cameras outside the shop."

He nods. "Yeah, we had them installed a few months back. Kids kept breaking the windows," he says. "Vandalism's gone down since we installed them."

"That's good," I say. "And how long do you store your footage?"

"Indefinitely."

"Excellent," I nod. "Then may I ask for you to show us the footage from a certain time and day?"

"Uhhh....don't you need a warrant or something?" he asks.

"The whole world watches *Law & Order* and now they're freaking experts," Astra mutters. I have to suppress a grin.

"We can certainly come back with a warrant, Mr. Wilkes," I tell him. "But we're not interested in anything happening in this shop. I notice a couple of your cameras are pointed across the street—those the ones I need the footage from."

He shifts on his feet. "So, that's all you need?" he asks. "You're not interested in anything here?"

I give him a smile. "I have absolutely no interest in whatever side business you're running here, Mr. Wilkes. And because, as you so astutely pointed out, I don't have a warrant, nothing I happen to see—assuming there is something to see—would be inadmissible, anyway," I tell him. "But I assure you, all I want is the footage from those cameras pointed toward the bank."

"Somebody rob it or something? The bank, I mean," he asks.

"Something like that," I say. "So, will you help? Or will I need to get a warrant?"

He hesitates a moment and I can see he's torn. Which tells me he's got something really cooking in the back of his shop. Something he doesn't want us to see. I guess I'm going to have to give him a nudge.

"Mr. Wilkes, if you're more comfortable, I can go get a warrant," I start. "But when I do, I will have to leave Agent Russo behind to keep an eye on things to make sure nothing—goes missing. And when I come back with a warrant, anything and everything we see will be very much admissible in court."

"Please, come on back," he says almost immediately. "Just—excuse the mess."

"Of course."

We follow him behind the counter and to the back of the shop, where we find somebody weighing out weed and putting it into various sized baggies. There are different tubs for the different weights sitting on a table against the wall.

"Weed is legal here, you know," I point out.

"Yeah, but some folks don't want to go out," Wilkes shrugs. "So, we deliver it to them with a piping hot pie. You get your weed and something to munch on when the craving strikes. We're like a one-stop-shop."

I laugh. "You know, for a punk rocker, that's quite a brilliant capitalist invention."

"I prefer to think of it as providing a service for the community. Cutting out the middleman."

I laugh. "You're not wrong."

We step into a small room in the back. A flat-screen computer monitor is mounted to the wall above a desk, and the lone office chair groans in protest as Wilkes drops down into it. Astra and I are practically standing shoulder to shoulder behind him as he logs in.

"So, what was the date you wanted?"

I give him the time and date, telling him to run it five minutes before the allotted time. He does and blows up the first screen, giving us a clear look.

"This camera is so much better than the city's cams," Astra notes, and I nod.

"There. Freeze it, please," I say.

On the screen are Hoodie and Bleeder. Hoodie's back is to the camera, so he's a total loss. But the bleeder is perfectly visible.

"That's got to be good enough for facial rec, right?" Astra asks.

"You don't need facial rec," Wilkes pipes up. "That's Crackhead Burton. He's a homeless vet who's usually high on smack or meth—whatever he can get his hands on. Sad story, really. He's always rummaging around looking for food and stuff. I usually float him a pie when he comes around every few days."

I have to say, I'm surprised by the kind and generous gesture. It's a really nice thing to do for a guy who can't take care of himself.

"Burton—is that his first or last name?" Astra asks.

He shrugs. "Not sure. He's got an Army jacket that has the name Burton on the patch. That's just what everybody calls him," Wilkes replies. "Well, that and Crackhead Burton, of course."

A patch on a military jacket makes it his last name. "Can you print out a few copies of that frame for me, please?"

He nods. "Comin' right up."

There's a high-pitched whirr as copies of the still picture slide into the printer tray. Wilkes hands them to me. I take one and hand the rest to Astra, then study the man's face for a moment, committing it to memory.

"You wouldn't happen to know where we can find him, would you?" I ask.

He shrugs. "Not for sure, no. He did mention once that he crashes at the shelter over on Westinghouse. You know that one?"

"No, but I will," I reply. "We appreciate your help, Mr. Wilkes."

"So, you know, about—you know," he stammers. "I mean, I helped you out, so we're cool and all, right? I mean—"

I give him a devious grin. "Give us a couple slices of that pepperoni and pineapple pie up front and we'll call it even."

"Comin' right up," he says with a wide grin.

SEVENTEEN

Hope Harbor Shelter, Capitol Hill District; Seattle, WA

"I'm not seeing a lot of hope in Hope Harbor," Astra remarks.

A frayed and faded banner hangs on the façade of the building bearing the name Hope Harbor Shelter. One of the corners has come loose, flapping wildly in the soft breeze.

"You're not kidding," I reply.

Sitting behind the wheel, I look at the shelter and finish off my slice of pizza. I wipe my hands on a napkin, dropping the refuse into a brown paper bag on the seat beside me. The building itself is a converted church. The outside of it, once white and pristine, is now a dull, dingy gray. The paint is peeling in plenty of spots, revealing the cinderblocks underneath. The grass and bushes along the front are all overgrown, most of them already dried and dead.

"Shall we go?" I ask.

"Let's," she replies. "Maybe it gets better on the inside."

"I wouldn't hold my breath if I were you."

We get out and walk across the street. I can feel the eyes on us as we walk toward the front doors. As we mount the cracked brick steps, a few men who were sitting off to the side of the porch turn and look at us, sizing us up. They're hard-looking men, wearing clothing that's little better than rags at this point. They're dirty and grimy, with long, bushy beards, unkempt hair, and looks of pure desperation about them. Unfortunately, the last few years have seen an uptick in people living on the streets in Seattle, due to a combination of rising housing costs and the city government's utter lack of care. I feel for them.

It's especially a shame when the homeless person is a vet like Burton. Thousands of men risked their lives to serve their country and were left disabled—physically or mentally—with crippling PTSD or addiction, and all the slimy politicians who claim to support them simply see fit to just sweep them under the rug. Congresswoman Hedlund included.

We step through the doors of the former church and find ourselves in a large room that's been sectioned off by large rolling and retractable walls. Three-fourths of the room is dedicated to sleeping quarters. Cots are lined up in rows that remind me of a military barracks. It looks as if they can hold about a hundred people or so in here. The space is currently empty. A large sign plastered on the wall says that nighttime accommodations will begin at eight o'clock.

The remaining quarter of the room is the soup kitchen. A long row of folding banquet tables fronts a small kitchen. Tables have been set up in front of the food line. A quarter of them are already occupied with people talking, playing cards, or just sitting there staring off into space as they wait for food to be served. Through the pass-through window, I can see people cooking in the kitchens. The air is saturated with the smell of baking bread and other spices.

"Smells like chili night," Astra says.

"Good nose."

"Good afternoon, may I help you?"

We both turn quickly and find a man in black pants, a black, short-sleeved shirt, and a white clerical collar. He's about five-ten, with brown hair, brown eyes, and a kind, friendly face. He looks youthful, but his eyes tell a different story. He's a man who's been around and has seen some things, but he still exudes an air of calm, peace, and warmth.

"Hello. I didn't mean to startle you," he says. "I'm Father Tobias. I oversee the shelter."

We both badge him, and I see a look of concern flash across his face. "Special Agent Russo and SSA Wilder," Astra introduces us.

"FBI," he frowns. "Has something happened?"

"We're actually looking for somebody," I say, unfolding the picture Wilkes printed out for us. "His last name is Burton?"

Father Tobias nods, a frown touching his lips. "Yes, that's Leonard Burton," he says. "Former Army Sergeant Leonard Burton."

I pull out a pen and jot the name down on the back of the picture quickly, then tuck the page and the pen both back into my pocket.

"Is Sergeant Burton in trouble?" the priest asks.

"Unfortunately, he is, Father," Astra says. "So, we'd like to find him before it gets any worse for him."

"May I ask what he's done?"

"I'm sorry, we can't comment on an ongoing investigation," I tell him. "But I can tell you it wasn't anything violent. It's something I'm hoping we can clear up with him."

"You wouldn't happen to know where he is, would you?" Astra asks.

Father Tobias shakes his head. "No, I don't. Our unhoused population here is perhaps the literal definition of 'transient'—

they come, and they go," he says. "And you never know where they are in between."

"When was the last time Sergeant Burton was here? Do you recall?" I ask.

"Of course. He was here last night. He had a scuffle with one of our other guests. Unfortunately, we had to expel them both for the night," he tells us. "Fighting and violence are not tolerated on Hope Harbor grounds. We have to have a zero-tolerance policy—you fight, you lose your bed for the night. And with so many people who need shelter, there is no shortage of people who will gladly take your spot."

"Do you know what Sergeant Burton's story is, Father?"

He shakes his head. "It's a tragedy. After everything he sacrificed for our country...," his voice trails off for a moment. He frowns but continues. "Anyway, my understanding is that he suffered a tremendous personal loss in Afghanistan. And when he came home, the only way he could cope with it was by turning to drugs. It's an awful story."

I nod. "It really is."

"I've tried to get him to check into the VA's rehab program. It will not only help wean him from his addiction, but it will also provide counseling, a roof over his head, and three squares a day. It's a better deal than he can get out here on the streets," he says sadly. "But he's resistant. He won't go in on his own."

"Father, does Sergeant Burton have any friends here? Anybody you see him talking to regularly?" Astra asks.

"There are a few people he speaks with—I don't see them right now—but for the most part, he keeps to himself," he says. "After supper, he likes to sit somewhere quiet and read. He always manages to find books to read."

I nod. "What time does he usually come in to claim a bed, Father?"

"We don't allow line-ups until seven. He's usually here right around then," he says.

I glance over at Astra and see her give me a nod. Father Tobias seems to catch on and he shakes his head, a worried expression on his face.

"I would ask that you don't do what you're thinking about doing. Not on Hope Harbor grounds," he pleads. "It will upset our guests, and we don't need that sort of turmoil here, Agents. I'm sorry, but I have to insist that you don't attempt to arrest him."

"We might not have a choice, Father. If we can't find him by other means—"

"I really don't wish to quarrel with you," he says. "But if you attempt to arrest him on Hope Harbor grounds, I will grant him sanctuary."

"You know that's not legally binding, right?" Astra points out. "Sanctuary in a church might have worked in the Middle Ages, but it's not really a thing in the twenty-first century."

"No, of course, it's not legally binding," he acknowledges. "But believe me when I say it will not go well for you or for the Bureau if you're viewed as brutalizing or oppressing unhoused residents at a shelter. The church has an excellent legal and PR team, and we will make use of it if forced to."

"So, you're blackmailing us?" Astra raises an eyebrow.

"I hate the word—it's so ugly and has such terrible connotations—but in essence, I suppose you could say that. Yes," Father Tobias says firmly. "Who do you believe the public will side with? The downtrodden veteran taking shelter at the Church? Or the Bureau, trying to strong-arm him into a cell?"

"I can't believe we're being blackmailed by a priest," Astra mutters. "Isn't there some passage in the Bible that forbids that?"

"Actually, there's not," Tobias counters. "And I am very

sorry. I mean no disrespect, but I will do whatever is required of me to protect my flock. And this flock needs more protection than most. I have no desire to see them disturbed."

I nod. "That's all right, Father. I get it," I say. "We'll find other means."

"Sergeant Burton is a good man. He's simply troubled," Tobias tells us. "Troubled and has a terrible addiction. He can't help himself."

"I understand. And we'll do all we can to help him," I say.

I had him my business card. "If you can think of anything that might help us, please give me a call, Father Tobias."

"I will," he replies.

We watch him walk away and I turn to Astra, who's laughing softly to herself.

"I can't believe a priest just hard-balled us," she says. "It's actually kind of hot. I never had bad-boy preacher fantasies until now."

"You are so going to hell."

"My ticket was booked long ago."

We share a laugh as we turn and walk out of the shelter. As we pass through the hard-eyed scrutiny of Father Tobias' guests, an idea occurs to me. I walk over to the small knot of men who'd been eyeballing us when we came in. They all get to their feet as I approach them, their faces like stone—if stone could be angry, anyway.

"Gentlemen," I start. "Would anybody be willing to answer a couple of questions for me?"

None of them says anything at first. They simply continue glaring at me as if they think they can shoot lasers from their eyes and burn me to a crisp on the spot.

"I'll give the one who talks to me twenty bucks," I announce.

"Make it fifty," counters the man on my left.

"Done."

He gives his friends a shrug, then walks off with me. Astra and I lead him across the street, and I lean against the car. His dirty blond hair is limp and greasy. It looks as though it hasn't been washed in weeks. Same with his clothing. And I have to breathe through my nose—short, shallow breaths—to avoid taking in too much of his aroma at once.

"What's your name?" I ask.

"Just call me Bobo," he replies. "Everybody does."

"All right, Bobo," I say, pulling the picture out of my pocket. "Do you know Sergeant Burton?"

He shrugs. "A little. Ain't like we ever talked much before."

"That's fine. I have to ask you something very personal now," I say. "Do you use drugs? Meth or heroin? Anything?"

He shrugs again. I can see the wariness in his eyes. I hold my hands up in a half-surrender gesture to keep him from bolting.

"I'm not looking to jam you up. What you do is your own concern. I'm not here for that or for you," I tell him. "I just need a little general information."

He clears his throat. "Well....yeah. I sometimes need somethin' to take the edge off. Sure. But it ain't like I do it regular or anythin'. Just sometimes."

"Okay, that's great. But was there any place special you might go to....partake?" I ask, doing my best to speak carefully. "Was there some place you'd go after you scored where you felt safe enough to partake of your purchase?"

"You mean like a flophouse, right?" he asks with a gap-toothed grin.

I laugh softly. I guess maybe there was no need for all the carefully coded words.

"Yes, Bobo. Is there a flophouse nearby?" I ask.

He nods. "Sure. There's an abandoned house over on

Mulberry. Lots of us use it," he says. "It's safe as anywhere, I guess. That guy in the picture you showed me? He been there most of the last week or so."

"He has?"

"I mean, he came for food here last night, but he's been buyin' a lot of stuff and hangin' out at Mulberry for most of the last week like he came into some money or somethin'," he tells us. "He floated me a bump the other day. Got me well. I appreciated it."

"And do you think he's there now?" I ask.

He nods. "Probably. Been higher than a kite for days."

"Do you know how he came into this money?"

Bobo shakes his head. "Nah. Ain't my business to ask," he says. "Out here you learn to mind your own business. Askin' too many questions is a good way to get dead."

"That's fair."

Out of questions and with a solid lead now, I dig into my bag and pull out a hundred dollar bill then hand it to Bobo. He looks at it with wide eyes and looks at me.

"I ain't got change to break this," he says.

"I don't want you to. What I want is for you to not put that in your veins, Bobo. I want you to go get a good meal," I tell him. "You need some food."

He gives me an awkward smile. "Thank you. It's been a while since I had a real good meal."

"Well, go have one," I say. "And thank you for your help."

He turns and walks off as Astra and I get into the car. I start the engine and pull away from the curb. I feel the full weight of the human tragedy we just witnessed inside the shelter settle down over me—people with nothing to their names, nowhere to go, and despite the name of the shelter, no hope for anything better. It's a feeling of crushing despair, knowing you can't help everybody. But at least I might have been able to help somebody today.

We ride in silence for a moment before she turns to me. "Think he'll actually get food?"

"Yeah. Yeah, I do."

EIGHTEEN

Outside 4387 Mulberry Street; Capitol Hill District; Seattle WA

"You THINK we should call in a SWAT team?" Astra asks. "I'm kind of thinking we should call in a SWAT team."

I laugh softly. "By the time we get authorization for the team and take the time to plan a proper op, Burton might be long gone."

"If he's even in there," she says. "I mean, we're relying on intel from somebody who likely wasn't entirely sober."

I shrug. "He seemed pretty straight to me. But if you don't want to go, you don't have to. Either way, I'm going in to have a look around and pull Burton out if I can," I reply. "I mean, it's a house full of people so strung out they probably can't even get on their feet. I just think a SWAT team would be a little heavy-handed."

She sighed heavily. "Fine. You're right."

"I'd think you'd be used to that by now," I smile as I throw her words back at her.

"Funny. She got jokes now."

We get out of the car, and I take a look at the neighborhood around us. It's run down, and most of the buildings are dilapidated. Lights glow behind the steel bars and curtains that cover the windows in some of the houses, but the one we're looking at is something out of a Halloween landscape. It's a two-story structure that might have been Victorian in design at some point in its past. The windows have been boarded over—though most of the boards have been broken off. There are holes in the walls and the roof. There aren't many, but the shingles that are left on the roof are all dried up and cracked.

I slip my weapon out of its holster, but hold it down at my side as we cross the street. Astra does the same. The steps that lead to the porch creak and groan ominously as we climb them. It looks as though somebody went straight through a large hole in the center of one tread. We manage to make it to the porch without going through, and I say a silent word of thanks.

We step to what's left of the door and push it open. It swings inward with a sharp squeal and bumps against the wall behind it. I pull the flashlight out of my pocket and click it on. Even though night has not yet set in outside and the world is still clothed in the deep purple and blue hues of dusk, the interior of the house is black as pitch. Blankets, old sheets, clothes, and even newspapers have been plastered over the busted-out windows, blocking the light from outside and leaving the interior cloaked in shadows and gloom.

"Jesus, it smells awful in here," Astra whispers.

I nod but don't say anything, not wanting to take the stench into my mouth. It's the smell of human waste combined with a powerful haze of body odor and the unmistakable miasma of drug smoke. It seems as if this place has been used as a flop house for a good long while, judging by how pungent the odor is. I'm suddenly wishing I'd thought to bring breathing equipment along. This can't be good for us.

There are three people in the living room, all of them doped to the gills. Or maybe they're dead—I can't really tell. We move from the living room deeper into the house. I sweep my flashlight back and forth, the bright beam of light cutting through the darkness. Trash is piled up against the walls everywhere and the floor is covered in food wrappers, old syringes, used condoms, newspapers, and more, all of it crunching beneath our boots. I shudder to think what's sticking to the soles right now.

"I'm burning these boots when we're done here," I comment.

"You're buying me a new pair."

"That's fair."

In the first bedroom, we find half a dozen people scattered about on the floor. A couple of them are propped up against the wall, the others are sprawled out, all of them in the blissed-out daze of people who are stoned out of their minds. None of them is Leonard Burton, though. We continue through the bottom floor of the house, searching each room, but come up empty. A few of the people opened their eyes and groaned at us, but most of them didn't even realize we were there. Yeah, a SWAT team would have been way too heavy-handed. I give a nod to Astra, and both of us holster our weapons.

"That leaves the upstairs," I say.

"Awesome," she replies.

The air in the house is still. Fetid. It hangs heavy and is so silent, it's as though we're walking through a vacuum. Or a morgue. We walk gingerly up the stairs, sticking close to the wall rather than walking in the middle of the treads. The stairs groan and creak and several times, I'm sure we're going through. But we make it to the second-floor landing without incident and continue our search. We check two of the four rooms upstairs and come up empty and I'm starting to get the sinking feeling that we're not going to find Burton here after all.

Astra checks out the third bedroom and I enter the last one. I sweep the light around the room and pause when the beam falls on his face. He's wearing the green military jacket Wilkes described, and the name patch above the pocket reads *Burton*.

"Jackpot," I whisper.

"Isn't a jackpot usually something good?" Astra mutters.

Burton's eyes flutter and then open. I watch as he slowly starts becoming aware of himself and everything around him. His high looks is beginning to ebb. He stares at me, and I watch his eyes narrow and his jaw clench. Knowing that look well, I hold my hands up to show I'm unarmed.

"Sergeant Burton, I don't want to hurt you," I start. "I just have a couple of questions, and I need you to come with me to answer them."

With a wordless howl of rage, he launches himself at me. I spin to the side and let him blow right by me. He turns back around and pulls a knife. The edge of the blade gleams coldly in the glow of my flashlight, and his face is twisted into a mask of fury. Behind him, I see Astra slip out of the bedroom and into the hall. I raise my hands further, taking a step back.

"Sergeant Burton, I don't want to hurt you," I repeat. "Please put the knife down."

"You want to kill me. You all want me dead," he growls, tapping his head with his other hand. "I know you want me dead. I know too much."

"I assure you that I don't want to kill you, Sergeant," I say. "I don't want to hurt you—"

The floorboard squeaks loudly, revealing Astra creeping up behind him. Perhaps it's his military training, but even cracked out like he is, Burton is fast. He spins and slashes with his knife and my heart drops into my stomach when I hear Astra cry out. He turns back to me, and as I see Astra crumple to the ground, I see the edge of his blade coated in red.

I'm temporarily distracted by the sight of Astra's blood, and he seizes the advantage, lunging at me with a wild, maniacal gleam in his eyes. But my own instincts and training take over. I deflect his arm, turn his blade aside, then drive my fist straight into his throat. He lets out a choked gasp and drops the knife, clutching his wounded throat. Grabbing the back of his head, I pull him down as I bring my knee up with force. The sound of the crunch echoes through the hall. Burton goes limp, crashing heavily to the ground.

I let out a breath of relief when I see Astra sit up. She's looking at the slice through the arm of her jacket and the spreading crimson stain. She looks up at me.

"Add a new jacket and blouse to those boots you owe me," she says, looking down at the ground she's sitting on. "Scratch that. You're buying me a whole new suit."

A laugh of relief bursts from me as I cuff Burton's arms behind his back. That done, I scramble over to her and check out her arm, shaking my head.

"It's not horribly deep but you're going to need some stitches," I tell her.

"Just wrap it up with a bandage. It'll be fine," she shrugs. "No, I don't need stitches."

"Yeah, you do. And that's an order."

Burton groans as he starts to wake up. I help Astra to her feet and we both reach down, grabbing hold of him. It takes a little doing, but we manage to get him up on his feet. I look around and notice that a couple of the other people in the room are sitting up, looking at us, still high but half-interested, with a dash of annoyance.

"Dude," one of them calls over. "Can you take that outside? You're killin' my buzz, dude."

"Yeah, don't worry. We're gone," I tell him.

"Hey," says another, her voice slow and thick. "Can you give us what he's got in his pockets before you go?"

I roll my eyes and turn away. Astra and I head downstairs to put him in the car and take her to the hospital to get patched up.

NINETEEN

"So, who am I looking at?" Rosie asks.

"That is Sergeant Leonard Burton," I tell her. "Otherwise known as Crackhead Burton to the residents of Capitol Hill."

We're standing in the observation pod, looking into the interrogation suite. The tech is sitting at the board, checking her instruments, making sure everything is functioning properly. She looks back at me.

"We're good to go here," she says. "Whenever you're ready, Agent Wilder."

"Thanks, Toni."

"How is Astra?" Rosie asks.

"A few stitches," I say. "I sent her home and told her to take tomorrow off."

"Yeah? How'd she take that?"

I grimace. "About as well as you'd expect."

"Do I need to blackball her at the gates?"

I laugh softly, remembering that Rosie had literally deactivated my badge, preventing me from getting into the field office, while I was recovering from being attacked in my own home.

"No, I think deep down she's looking forward to spending a day off with Benjamin," I tell her.

"So, what's the story with Burton?" she asks.

I fill her in on what we've found to this point, and I see her expression darken. She frowns and purses her lips, suddenly looking concerned. In her place, I'd probably feel the same way. I wouldn't want to have to give that sort of status report to Congresswoman Hedlund. She runs a hand through her hair and blows out a loud breath.

"So, I guess Selene isn't on a beach somewhere, huh?" she asks.

I shake my head. "Unfortunately, no," I say. "It's looking as if there's a strong possibility she was snatched and then trafficked."

"My God. What am I going to tell Kathryn?"

"Nothing yet. It's not a certainty," I say. "We're still in the middle of our investigation. There are still a lot of moving parts that could break a dozen different ways."

She turns to me, her expression hard. "What does your gut tell you?"

I frown. "My gut tells me she was trafficked. But I still have a lot of questions. There are still a bunch of things that aren't adding up," I say. "So, if Hedlund is pressing you for a status report, I'd just tell her we're working the case and a lot of things are still in flux."

"She's not going to accept that."

I shrug. "She's going to have to," I tell her. "I mean, there's no use in getting her all bunched up and then having things break differently. I think she'd crucify us more for that than if we tell her the case is still in progress."

She looks in at Burton again and seems to be thinking about it. She finally nods, then turns back to me.

"Yeah, you're probably right," she says.

"You want to come in and talk to Burton with me?"

Rosie shakes her head. "No, I need to get to a meeting. I'll read the transcripts later," she says. "Squeeze him hard, Blake. Do what you have to do to get him to give it up."

"I will."

Rosie heads out of the pod, leaving me alone, staring through the window at Burton. I'm not quite sure how to approach him just yet, so I'm hesitating. He's sitting at the table, a chain running from a bolt in the middle of the table attached to the shackles around his wrists. His head is lowered and he's muttering to himself, but it's too low for me to make out the words. He might not even be speaking English for all I know.

The man is clearly unstable; I have no idea what I'm going to get out of him. Or if it's even going to be useful at all. But I need to try. I need to see if I can get through that drug-induced haze and the layers of psychosis to pull something—anything—out of him. Gritting my teeth, I push open the door and step from the pod into the interrogation suite, then close the door behind me.

Burton looks up and seems to be having trouble remembering who I am as I take the seat across the table from him. He looks exhausted. Wrung out. He looks like a man who's had the life squeezed out of him. His bloodshot, red-rimmed eyes are a dull shade of blue. His iron-gray hair is limp and greasy, his cheeks sunken, his skin sallow.

I believe he was once a proud man—a soldier. But now he looks like a man who's utterly defeated. He looks like a man who's had the pride—and the life—beaten out of him, leaving him a hollowed-out shell of a human being. And as I look at the man, my heart goes out to him.

"Sergeant Burton, I am Blake Wilder with the FBI," I start. "I know this must be a little confusing and disorienting for you and I apologize for that. But I have some questions to ask, and I need you to answer them for me. Can you do that, Sergeant?"

He stares at me with vacant, lifeless eyes. Burton doesn't say a word. I honestly don't know if it's because he doesn't want to or if he's incapable of understanding me. I frown and look down at the table for a moment, giving myself a second to collect my thoughts.

"Sergeant Burton, we know you've been withdrawing money from accounts that aren't yours," I continue. "That's fraud. And fraud is a serious felony, Sergeant Burton. You could be charged not just with state crimes, but federal crimes as well."

He still doesn't say anything. He just sits across the table from me with that dead-eyed stare. I look deeply into his eyes and don't see anything happening beyond them. He just seems totally checked out of reality.

"Sergeant Burton, I want to help you. I really do. I know you were only doing what you were asked to do. Only doing what you could to make a little money," I press. "Tell me who the man in the hoodie is. Tell me the name of the man who put you up to it. Tell me that and I can help you. We can work something out so perhaps you don't have to go to jail. We can get you some help. Get you into a facility."

We sit in silence for several long minutes. I'm not getting through to him at all. Whether it's because he's still strung out on his dope, or his mental issues are preventing him from engaging, I don't know. All I do know is that this is pointless right now. I'd have a better chance of getting through to a brick wall.

My cell phone buzzes with an incoming text, so I turn it over and see that it's from Mo in the shop. I call up my texts and quickly scan it.

Need you in the shop, ASAP. 911.

I close my phone and look up at Burton again. He hasn't moved a muscle. I'm not sure he's even blinked the entire time we've been sitting here.

"Okay, Sergeant Burton, I'm going to give you a little time to think about things," I say, just in case there's some brain activity happening inside. "And I do need you to think about what I said. I need you to take this seriously."

I give him a moment, then get to my feet and walk back into the pod, closing the door behind me.

"Toni, I have to get down to my shop. Can you please call Wagner and have him take Burton down to a holding cell? We'll leave him there overnight," I say. "Let him get some rest and sleep it off. Hopefully, he'll be a little chattier next time I see him."

"You got it," she nods.

"Thanks, Toni."

I walk out of the pod and head down the corridor toward the elevators, moving as quickly as I can. Mo wouldn't text me 911 unless it was important, which piques my curiosity. I make my way through the warren of corridors, then down to the basement floors to the CDAU.

The doors open with a pneumatic hiss as I step through to find Mo and Rick standing at her workstation with Burton's bag opened and spread out on the desk in front of them. I step over and look at what they've pulled out of the bag. There are some dirty clothes, some books that are dog-eared and have torn covers. He's got some magazines and a few other assorted odds and ends, but nothing I see seems very important.

"What's the 911 about, Mo?" I ask.

She and Rick exchange an uneasy glance, and then she hands me a plastic evidence bag. I take it from her and look at the contents and frown, not sure what the emergency is.

"All right. So, Burton had more ATM cards than we thought," I say.

"That's twenty-one ATM cards," she explains. "Twenty-two, if you add in Selene Hedlund's card."

"So, he's been bleeding people for a while. I'm still not seeing the emergency here, Mo."

She turns to Rick. "You want to tell her?"

Rick lets out a deep breath. "We ran the names on the cards," he says, brandishing a sheet of paper. "Every single name on each of those twenty-one debit cards corresponds to a girl who's turned up missing over the last five years."

I stare at them both for a long moment, my eyes growing wide as the realization of what they're saying sinks into my brain.

"Are you sure?" I ask.

Rick hands me the sheet of paper and I read it over, picking cards out of the evidence bag at random and matching them up against the list Rick put together. When I get to the end of the stack of cards, I set the sheet down and put the cards back into the bag, giving myself a moment to process it all.

"Twenty-one missing girls," I say softly.

"Twenty-two, if you count Selene," Mo says.

"Jesus," I groan. "What is going on here?"

"Bad stuff, boss," Mo says. "A lot of very bad stuff."

TWENTY

I'M SITTING at the desk in my living room, my laptop open, sipping from a glass of Chardonnay as the guitar acrobatics of Django Reinhardt wash over me. I've been doing some research on the twenty-one missing girls. Obsessing over them, really. Ever since Mo and Rick dropped that on me yesterday, I haven't been able to get them out of my head. The fact that Burton had the debit cards of twenty-one—no, twenty-two—missing girls, seems to reinforce the human trafficking theory.

I've gone over the list a thousand times already, digging up all the information about the missing girls I can find. I've looked up their socials and read every newspaper article I could get my hands on. I looked into the police reports about their disappearances, but there wasn't much to see. I don't even know how vigorously their cases were pursued, honestly. But none of them was very high-profile, so knowing the SPD as I do, I'd guess the officers who caught the cases didn't expend a whole lot of energy.

I've been looking for some nexus between them and Selene, and other than Burton, I haven't found anything. They all just vanished without a trace. And apparently, Burton has been bleeding their accounts—presumably on the orders of the man in the hoodie. But who in the hell is he? That's the question that needs to be answered. That guy is going to be the key to all of this. If we can track him down, I have a feeling we'll be able to crack this case wide open.

I take a sip of my wine and sit back in my chair, closing my eyes and letting the music soothe me. My shoulders are tight with tension and I'm having trouble relaxing. This case is really getting under my skin. I've gone from thinking that it was a case of a spoiled rich kid jetting off on an impromptu vacation to thinking it's something bigger. And something much, much darker.

The knock on the door startles me, and I jump up, very nearly spilling my glass of wine. I set the glass down on my desk, grab the holster I'd set down next to my laptop, and slide my weapon out. I wasn't expecting anybody tonight. As I said, a little paranoia is a good thing. Keeps you healthy and above ground.

Holding my weapon down at my side, I make my way to the door and look at the monitor that displays the picture from the doorbell camera I had installed, and freeze. An ice-cold chill sweeps through me when I see Mark—or whatever his real name is—standing on the other side of my door. I give brief thought to simply not answering, but I just get the feeling he knows I'm home. After all, what kind of spy would he be if he didn't know, or couldn't get, basic information like that?

With a sigh, I unlock the door and open it to him, trying to put on the best smile I can muster. There's a strained tension in the air between us. He shuffles his feet.

"Hey," I finally say.

He gives me a warm smile. "Hey yourself."

We remain where we are on opposite sides of the doorway, staring at each other for a long, awkward moment before he chuckles softly.

"So, are we just going to stand here gawking at each other all night, or may I come in?" he asks. "I just wanted to talk to you."

"Ummm..." I hesitate. "Yeah, sure. Sorry. Of course."

I open the door wide and let him pass by. I know I need to pretend that everything is fine. That I don't know he's a fraud, somebody whose job is to get into my life and make me fall in love with him. All for the sole purpose of getting into my head. Keeping tabs on me. And reporting back to the puppet master who's pulling his strings—and is trying to pull mine.

"Have a seat," I say.

As he sits down on the long sofa, he notices the weapon in my hand as I slide it into the holster. He arches an eyebrow at me.

"Expecting trouble?"

"I wasn't expecting anybody," I tell him.

"Well, given everything you've gone through, I suppose it's understandable that you'd be a little keyed up."

Everything I've gone through? No, it's everything I'm *still going* through. But I let the words turn to ash on my tongue. I drop down into the chair across from him and cross my legs, folding my hands in my lap. The air between us is tense and strained. A host of emotions is swirling through his eyes.

"It's been a while," he says.

He says it with what sounds like genuine hurt in his voice. Mark, for lack of an actual name to call him, is a very talented actor. I know I need to keep my cool. I need to keep pretending that everything is fine and there are no problems here. I'm conscious that my apartment is actively being surveilled as well. I don't doubt they have people breaking in regularly— just to maintain the illusion, I move things around my war room and move things around to make it look as though I'm still investigating but not getting anywhere new.

That's the simple part. The window dressing. When it comes to dealing with people, face-to-face contact, I've never been a very good liar and I'm definitely not an actor. Pretending that everything is just hunky-dory when it's not isn't really in my repertoire. I have to learn how to do it on the fly, though, or risk tipping my hand. And I really don't want to see what happens if Mark or the Thirteen find out how close I'm actually getting to them.

"Yeah, I've been busy. I'm working on a missing persons case that just turned into something much bigger," I tell him. "I haven't had much time for social events."

"I can tell," he replies, looking at me closely. "Are you all right?"

I run a hand through my hair and nod. "Yeah, I'm fine," I say, knowing I need to give him more just to throw him off my scent. "When this case started, I was dead certain it was one thing—a spoiled rich kid running off to the Bahamas or something. I was positive."

"But it's not," he says.

I shake my head and do my best to sound abashed. "Not even close. I was just so wrong from the jump, and I'm scared that I cost this girl her life because I was following the wrong path—the path my own biases and prejudices led me down."

Mark looks at me with an inscrutable expression. He seems to be trying to probe me and see into my depth to determine if I'm telling the truth. It helps that that part of the story is actually true. I don't actually believe I cost Selene her life. By the time Hedlund brought us the case, the chances were good that Selene either was already dead or was actively being trafficked and only wishing she were dead. But I'm still kicking myself for letting my biases cloud my judgment.

"That's rough," he says. "But I think you're taking too much of it onto your shoulders. You always do. You personalize everything, Blake."

"I think that's one of the things that makes me good at my job."

"Perhaps," he replies. "It's also one of the things that leads to a heart attack and an early grave if you're not careful."

We both fall quiet again, and the tension in the air between us only seems to be growing thicker. I don't know if he's buying my excuse or not, so I know I need to divert the subject and get us talking about something else. Anything to draw his scrutiny away.

"So, what brought you by tonight?"

A small smirk curls the corners of his mouth. "Other than the fact that I haven't seen or heard from you in a couple of weeks?" he asks. "It almost feels as though you're ghosting me. But I thought we..." he pauses. "I thought we were beyond that."

"I'm not ghosting you," I tell him. "Things have just been really crazy at work. The missing girl I'm looking for? She's Representative Kathryn Hedlund's daughter. So, it's been an all-hands-on-deck sort of thing."

He nods and looks at me as if he understands. And maybe on some level, he does. I don't know. I can barely look at him. The very sight of him is making me sick to my stomach. To think that I shared so much of myself and my life with this man, only to have him turn out to be a spy ordered to keep tabs on me, makes me want to throw up. And I'm having a really tough time trying to keep that sentiment out of my expressions and my voice.

"I know. You've got a busy job. And I promised that I wouldn't get on you about it," he says. "It's just—I miss you, Blake. I miss you a lot. I've never enjoyed somebody's company more than I do yours. And nobody has ever been able to make me laugh like you do. I miss that."

I hear the sincerity in his voice. It pulls at my heartstrings, and I have to remind myself for the thousandth time that spies are trained to make you believe anything. They're sociopathic in their abilities to mimic emotion.

"I know. Things have just been crazy," I tell him.

"Are you sure that's all it is?"

I cock my head. "What do you mean?"

He lets out a long breath. "I guess I'm just asking if this—thing—between us, this relationship has run its course for you?"

And there it is. We've finally come to that crossroads where I need to decide what's going to happen here. Do I cut him loose and assume all the risk that comes with it? I mean, knowing what I know about him, I have to believe that if I cut things off, there will be repercussions. Maybe his employers will think I cut him loose because I know what he is. Maybe if they think they can't keep tabs on, or control, me anymore, they'll give him a green light to take care of me once and for all.

Like it or not, keeping him in my life might be the only thing keeping me alive. He's in my life watching me every bit as much I'm watching him. And if I know where he is and what he's doing, I have some assurances that neither he nor the Thirteen is making a final move on me. As much as I hate to say it, keeping Mark in my life might give me the chance to get all of my pieces on the board arranged, so that when I'm ready to make my play, I'll be able to strike fast and hard.

"No, Mark, I don't feel that it's run its course," I tell him. "Again, things have been—"

"Crazy at work. I know," he interrupts me. "But even beyond that, it just feels as if there's a chasm between us. It feels as though you're holding me at arm's length."

I make a show of frowning and looking as if I'm thinking hard about what he said. After taking a few beats, I nod and look up at him.

"And I'm sorry for that. There's just been—a lot going on in my head lately and I'm in a really weird space right now. I'm sorry you're caught in that crossfire," I tell him. "I'm getting nowhere with my parents' murder investigation, so it's been frustrating me and causing me a lot of pain. I guess I haven't communicated that clearly with you, so I'm sorry for that. I hate to say it, but it's not you, it's me."

He laughs quietly and the expression on his face softens. He looks at me again, but this time, I see something akin to compassion in his eyes and I know that he's buying my story. Excellent.

"I promise I'll make it up to you," I tell him. "Once this case is over and I get the Congresswoman off my back—"

"There will be another case. There always is," he says. "So, be careful with the promises you're making."

"That's fair," I chuckle. "All right, well I'll simply promise you the best dinner at your favorite steakhouse. We'll have a lovely evening out. Just the two of us."

He purses his lips and looks at me for a long moment in silence. But then a slow smile spreads across his lips and he nods.

"That sounds pretty wonderful," he says. "It's a date."

"Great," I say. "I can't wait."

"Me, either."

He stays and we chat for a little while longer before I feign exhaustion and tell him I need to go to bed. I tell him I have to get an early start on the day, which isn't a lie. And it gives me an excuse to get him out of my house. But before he goes, he gives me a kiss that leaves me feeling dirty. Greasy. And I have to rinse my mouth out with mouthwash three times and brush my teeth twice before I can get that taste out.

When I'm done, I lean on the vanity and stare at myself in the mirror for a long minute. My eyes are red-rimmed and there are deep shadows underneath them. I pride myself on being fearless and taking anything and everything head-on. But right now, I look so scared I barely recognize myself. Things are in motion and are picking up steam. The train is rolling and there's no way I can get off now. I know I can either steer the train or keep riding until it crashes.

And right now, I feel so out of control, I can't even see the wheel—let alone grab hold of it well enough to steer it.

TWENTY-ONE

Criminal Data Analysis Unit; Seattle Field Office

"Where are we, kids?" I ask as I step to the front of the room after a largely sleepless night. "Rick, have you had any luck with those phone numbers yet?"

He shakes his head. "Still running them, boss."

"Mo, anything on our missing girls?"

She leans back in her seat and rubs her eyes, looking as if she got about as much sleep as I did last night. Cases like these haunt you. When you know there are twenty-two women out there in the wind, having God-knows-what done to them, it eats away at your soul. It nags at you. I have little doubt that Mo was up all night trying to find the nexus across all of the missing girls. But judging by the look on her face, she didn't find one.

"Not yet, boss," she says. "I'm still looking."

I nod as the doors to the shop open with a pneumatic hiss. Astra walks through the door with a broad smile on her face.

"The prodigal daughter returns," I say.

"Pretty sure you can't say that when I've only been gone a

day," she remarks. "I don't think I can be considered a prodigal anything unless I've been gone more than a couple of weeks."

"So, I should throw out the welcome-back cake I made for you?" Mo asks with a grin.

"I never turn down cake," Astra replies.

"I'll remember that next time I make one," Mo says.

Astra laughs as she drops down at her workstation and gets her computer booted up. She swivels in her seat to me.

"How are you feeling?" I ask.

"As good as I did before you told me to take a day," she replies. "But I did enjoy a nice day off with Benjamin, so thank you for that."

"I thought you might," I reply.

"So, where are we with everything?" she asks. "You've surely solved the case by now and Selene Hedlund is back home safe and sound?"

"Oh, my god, you were only gone a day," I say dryly. "And unfortunately, we're still pretty much right where we were when you went home."

"When you sent me home, you mean."

"Po-tay-to, Po-tah-to," I shrug.

"Burton still hasn't said anything?" she asked.

I shake my head. "I'm going to take another run at him today, but he wasn't exactly—lucid—the last time we spoke."

"Not surprising. I mean, we did pull him straight out of a crack house."

"Yeah, but I had high hopes," I say and pick up the bag with all the debit cards and toss it to her. "There is one important thing we learned, though."

She looks at the cards in the bag then up at us, looking for an explanation.

"Sergeant Burton had all of those in his possession," Mo says.

"And those all belong to girls who've gone missing," Rick adds.

I hand Astra the list Rick put together and watch as her eyes widen as the full scope of what's happening sinks in.

"So, we are talking about a trafficking ring after all," Astra says.

"It's looking that way," I reply.

"All right, so how do we play this?" Astra asks.

"Right now, Mo is trying to find the nexus among the missing girls. There has to be one," I say. "And Rick is still trying to track down where that burner phone that called Tony's Auto was purchased."

Astra flashes me a grin. "Wow. I miss a day and this thing has gotten a lot more complicated than we even imagined."

"Tell me about it," I say. "It makes finding out who the man in the hoodie is that much more important. It's critical, I'd say."

"Yeah, I'd say so. So let's go squeeze Burton," she says.

"Thought you'd never ask," I reply. "Mo, Rick, keep digging. We need to cast as wide a net as we can."

Astra gets to her feet and follows me out of the shop and over to the wing of the building that houses the holding cells and interrogation suites. We stand in the pod watching Burton being brought into the room, his shackles attached to the bolt in the center of the table.

"He looks a little less like a corpse today," I note. "That's encouraging."

"Maybe a good night's sleep and a meal brought him back down to Earth."

"Let's hope."

When the tech gives us the signal that everything is up and running, Astra and I go into the room and sit down across from him. Burton looks at us suspiciously from beneath his shaggy locks. The lines in his face are etched deep, and there are dark bags beneath his eyes, but he surprisingly has a little color in his cheeks. Looks as though Astra is right—a good night's sleep and some hot food might have helped.

I quickly recite the date and time for the record and then give Burton his Miranda warning. When I'm finished I look at him.

"Do you understand your rights as I have read them to you?" I ask.

"Sure."

"I need you to say out loud that you understand your rights as I read them," I repeat.

"Yeah, I understand."

"And would you like to have a lawyer present?" I ask. "I need you to say yes or no out loud for the record."

"No, I don't need no lawyer."

"So, just to be clear, you are waiving your right to counsel," Astra presses.

"Just said that, didn't I?" he states. "No, I don't want no lawyer."

"All right, that's good," I say. "So, how are you feeling, Sergeant Burton?"

"Like hammered crap," Burton grunts. "Who are you?"

"SSA Wilder and Special Agent Russo," I reply. "We met yesterday."

"Why am I in shackles?" he asks, jangling the chain that connects him to the table.

"Because I'm probably going to have a scar on my arm for the rest of my life thanks to that meeting," Astra says.

Burton shakes his head. "I—I don't know what you mean," he says, his voice deep and gruff. "I don't remember much of yesterday."

"Well, that's not surprising, given where we found you," Astra says.

"I don't know where you found me," he says, shaking his head in confusion.

"The house on Mulberry Street," I offer. "The flophouse."

He nods as if he recognizes the street name. I guess he probably would if he spent enough time there. And looking as rough as he does, I have no doubt he's spent a lot of time there.

"Sergeant Burton, you're in some serious trouble," I continue. "You were using a stolen ATM card to withdraw funds from Selene Hedlund's account. We have you on camera doing it. Now, that's not only state but federal charges that you're facing."

He looks away and starts to pick at his fingernails. He's fidgeting in his seat, and I can hear the chains around his ankles rattling as he bounces his leg. I'm pretty sure it's not because he's nervous, though. I have a feeling he's getting antsy because he needs a fix—something that might become problematic for us in the not-too-distant future.

"I—I don't know what you're talkin' about," he mutters.

"Sergeant Burton, you were in possession of twenty-two debit cards that were not yours," I go on. "In fact, those twenty-two cards belonged to women who have gone missing over the last five years. I don't think I have to tell you how that looks for you."

"Missin'?" he gasps as his eyes grow wide. "I don't know nothin' about any missin' girls."

"We want to believe you, Sergeant Burton," Astra says. "But you were in possession of those cards. You drained their accounts. That directly ties you to the missing girls."

"And that means you're not just looking at bank fraud charges, Sergeant," I jump in. "You're looking at kidnapping, human trafficking, maybe even murder charges."

Burton shakes his head, an expression of genuine fear crossing his face. He looks away and remains silent for a beat, trying to wrap his mind around what we're telling him. Burton looks authentically shocked by the news. I believe that he didn't actually have any part in the disappearances of the girls. His role in this scheme was to simply act as a bleeder. To keep using those cards until the river ran dry.

"I—I was only doing my job," he mutters.

"I believe you," I tell him. "But do you see the pickle we're in? The cards were in your possession, Sergeant."

"So, if you really had nothing to do with this, we need to know who your boss is," Astra says. "Who gave you the cards and the instructions to use them?"

He hesitates and looks down at the shackles on his hands, possibly weighing his options. On one side of the coin, he's staring down the barrel of doing serious time in federal prison— likely the rest of his life. On the other side of that coin, he's looking at possibly catching a bullet if he rolls on whoever it was who set him up on this side of the scheme.

"I know you're in a tight spot, Sergeant. I know your options aren't good either way you look at it. There are dangers in going down either path. I get that," I tell him. "But you shouldn't have to carry the full weight of what's coming down. Somebody is going to answer for twenty-two missing women, Sergeant. Do you really want that somebody to be you? Especially if your part was limited to withdrawing money for someone else?"

Burton's gaze is fixed on his hands; he's struggling with his decision. He's still bouncing in his seat and is obviously itching for a fix, but he's managing to hold it together well enough to remain lucid and communicative. For that small favor, I'm thankful.

"I don't know his name," he starts.

"You've been working for him and you don't know his name?" Astra asks.

He shrugs. "It's not that kinda job."

"Walk us through it, Sergeant," I say.

He chews on his thumbnail, his hand trembling. He's bouncing his leg harder, though, and I can feel his grip on himself and his cravings starting to slip. Burton is barely holding on to his self-control, his need for a fix growing by the second, making him desperate.

"About five years ago, I was livin' in McIntosh Park. Well, I'm still livin' in that park. But back then, this guy comes to me. He offers me a deal," Burton stammers. "Says he'll come to me with a card and I'm supposed to take out the max once a day until the card gets shut down. That's it. I swear it. That's all I did."

"Why did he pick you out of the crowd?" I ask. "Why you, when several dozen people are living in McIntosh Park?"

"Said he had a soft spot for veterans," Burton says. "So, we've been doin' this for I guess five years now. He comes to me, gives me a card, and I do it. I get fifty bucks every time I withdraw the money for him."

"And you don't know his name?" I ask incredulously.

He shakes his head. "No. Like I said, it's not like that kind of job," he says. "His name is Bones to me. That's all I know. I swear that's all I know. And I didn't do nothin' to them girls you say are missin'. That wasn't me."

"Can you tell us anything about this guy, Bones?" Astra asks. "Any distinctive markings? Tattoos? Anything?"

"H—he's got a tattoo on the back of his hand," he says. "He's got a skull on the back of his right hand, yeah."

"That's good," I nod. "That helps."

It's not much but it's more than we had a couple of minutes ago. It's a bread crumb but I'm still not seeing the bigger trail it leads to. It's frustrating, but this is the job. We have to build a case brick by brick until an unassailable wall is built around the suspect. I'm just not used to cases moving so slowly. The momentum I usually feel when we start adding bricks to that wall is absent. The pace of our case is so slow we're being lapped by turtles.

"So—can I go now? I helped you. Can I get out of here?" Burton asks.

I shake my head. "Unfortunately, not, Sergeant. We need to look into this before we do anything," I tell him. "You need to understand that you will face some charges for the crimes you did commit. But if your information checks out, we'll do all we can to help you. I give you my word."

TWENTY-TWO

Office of SSA Wilder, Criminal Data Analysis Unit; Seattle Field Office

I DROP into the chair behind my desk and have to keep myself from blowing out an irritated breath as Kathryn Hedlund takes the chair across from me. Seeing her standing in the shop when we got back from questioning Burton was about the worst surprise I could get today. We stare at each other in silence for a moment. I know the tactic is designed to trip me up. Tense silence is a classic power play, but I'm not in the mood and I don't have time for these games.

"Representative Hedlund," I start. "What can I do for you?"

"I'm told you have a suspect in custody."

This time, I can't keep the irritation out of my features. Leaks are the bane of any investigation, and they irritate me more than anything because all they do is complicate a situation. Oftentimes they make situations worse and jeopardize investigations. They never help. If I had my way, we'd be able to put leakers on the rack. Or break them on the wheel—or any of a hundred other medieval torture methods.

"And who told you this?" I raise an eyebrow.

"That doesn't matter," she snaps. "I'm more interested in why I wasn't informed. I seem to recall telling you I wanted status reports and to be apprised if you had any breaks."

"With all due respect, Congresswoman, I do not report to you. I have provided status reports to my direct superior," I say coldly. "As for the person we are questioning, he is not a suspect in your daughter's disappearance. He's a bit player who very likely never met your

daughter."

"I want to speak to him."

"Out of the question," I say. "You're a civilian and have no standing to question anybody we bring into interrogation."

"I am a Member of Congress," she says through gritted teeth.

"But you do not work for the Bureau," I fire back. "You are not a law enforcement officer. You have no standing to speak to people we are interrogating."

"I don't think that's your call to make."

"Fine. Take it up with Rosie," I growl. "I suspect you will find that the bond of sorority sisters doesn't trump FBI protocols or the law."

"You are dangerously close to insubordination," she seethes. "You had better watch yourself."

A small smirk curls the corners of my mouth and I shake my head. "Again, you are not my supervisor, nor are you a Bureau agent. You are a visitor in this building," I say. "Therefore, I cannot be insubordinate to you."

Hedlund's face turns purple, and she looks as if her head is going to explode. I know part of her anger stems from her worry about her daughter. I understand that, and for that reason, I know I should cut her a little slack. I know I shouldn't be too hard on her. I can't imagine what she must be feeling right now. It's not easy, though. My dislike for this woman is so intense, I can't see much of anything outside that prism of loathing.

But I know I need to try. If for no other reason than that making an enemy of Hedlund—or at least, more of an enemy— doesn't serve any purpose. It's only going to make things more difficult for me in the long run. Not to mention the fact that if Hedlund believes I'm keeping her out of the loop, she'll want to get more involved with this case, which complicates everything even more.

"Listen," I start. "Bickering with you is pointless. It serves no purpose and does nothing but waste time—time we don't have."

"Finally. Something we agree on," she says, exasperation in her voice.

"So, I'm going to loop you in on where we are right now," I tell her. "But you need to let us do our jobs, ma'am. I can't take the time out to keep having this same silly argument with you. If you need a status report, go to Rosie. She's looped in on everything that's happening with the investigation. But above all else, stay out of our way and let us do our jobs."

By all rights, I probably shouldn't be telling her any of this at all. But I need to give her something, and hopefully telling her will get her off our backs. She stares at me through narrowed eyes for a couple of beats. Her jaw is clenched so tight, I'm sure she could bite through steel right now. But she finally gives me a firm nod.

"Fine," she says, her voice ice cold.

"And because this is an ongoing investigation, I have to

insist that you keep this to yourself. I don't want to threaten you, but if this information gets out, I will have you charged with criminal obstruction," I say. "Member of Congress or not, if you leak what I'm about to tell you, then I will bring a case against you."

I don't know if I can actually bring obstruction charges against a sitting Representative, but that won't stop me from trying if she leaks what I'm about to tell her. If this gets out and it screws up our case, I will scream so loud they'll be able to hear me up on Capitol Hill all the way from here in Seattle. And I won't stop until either she suffers the consequences for blowing our case or I'm out of a job.

"Tell me you understand," I press.

"I understand."

I lean back in my chair and organize my thoughts. What I have to tell her isn't going to be pleasant. I don't know how she's going to take it. I already have a feeling she's not going to take it well. And all I can do is hope she holds to the terms of our little détente, stays out of our way, and lets us do our jobs.

"We believe that Selene was snatched and then trafficked," I say.

Hedlund holds her hand to her chest and draws in a sharp breath. The look of absolute horror on her face tells me it's even worse than she suspected. I think, deep down, she also thought that Selene had skipped out on some impromptu sabbatical.

"Trafficked?" she whispers, her voice quiet and trembling.

"It looks that way," I say. "She's one of twenty-two women who have gone missing over the last five years—"

Hedlund's eyes widen, and her mouth falls open. I don't know what she was expecting to hear when she walked in here, but this is definitely not it.

"Twenty-two women?" she asks.

I nod. "That we know of so far, yes."

"Have any of them been found?"

I shake my head. "Not as of yet."

Hedlund's eyes shimmer with tears she's struggling to keep from falling. Knowing that her daughter is just the latest in a string of abductions and trafficking victims has to be a heavy weight upon her shoulders, one I know she doesn't know how to bear. When you're not immersed in this world of blood and death the way we are every single day, it can be overwhelming. I think Hedlund is starting to understand that.

"A—and the man you brought in for questioning?" she asks.

"He's only one part of this entire scheme. He's the lowest level on their ladder," I tell her. "He's a homeless vet with a dope problem. An intermediary gave him Selene's debit card— the debit cards of all these women, actually—and paid him petty cash to withdraw the funds every day until the accounts were dry or somebody flagged and deactivated the cards."

She sniffs loudly, then pulls a lacy handkerchief from her bag and dabs at her eyes. "So, who gave him the debit cards?"

"That's the next step in our investigation," I tell her. "We believe if we can get to that person, he'll give us the next person on the ladder."

"You don't think that person is the trafficker?"

I hadn't stopped to give it much thought, but as I talk it out, I come around to the conclusion that Hoodie is not, in fact, the top of the food chain. I don't think the actual trafficker would risk being caught withdrawing the cash. My thought is he would likely keep a buffer between those cards and himself. Somebody loyal. Trustworthy. Somebody who would take a bullet for him before giving him up. And the more I think about it, the more right it seems.

"No, I don't think he is," I tell her. "The trafficker would want to maintain a level of hierarchy to avoid detection. Operations like this are tightly-run syndicates designed to throw law enforcement off the trail. I think the man who gave Sergeant Burton the cards is just another cog in that machine."

She shakes her head, looking green around the gills and absolutely sick to her stomach. Hedlund looks up at me, seeming to be at a loss for words, which is understandable—there really is nothing to be said when confronted with something as unequivocally evil as this.

"Just hold onto hope, Congresswoman," I tell her. "No bodies have been found, which means she could still be out there. All of them might be. We just don't know yet. And I can give you my assurance that we are investigating as diligently and thoroughly as we can."

She dabs at her eyes with her handkerchief again. "What does your experience tell you, Agent Wilder?" she asks, obviously searching for some scrap of hope to hold onto. "Are girls who are trafficked ever found alive?"

I frown and look down. I don't want to lie or give her false hope. I think that would be the cruelest thing I could do. Regardless of how much I may dislike her, I'd never do that to another human being. Besides, I think Hedlund would appreciate the truth—no matter how brutal it might be to hear it.

"To be honest, most of the girls who are trafficked are never found. And those few girls who are found are never the same. They're forever changed. Fundamentally speaking. They're broken," I tell her honestly. "But you know, maybe with enough intensive therapy, they learn to move on. But I think they'll forever bear the scars. You don't go through something like that without having some lasting scars."

She takes a moment to compose herself and dabs at her eyes again. She sniffs again and settles back in her seat. The expression on her face is pinched and pained. Grief is etched into her every feature. It's as if she's already trying to make peace with the idea that her daughter is dead.

"Thank you, Agent Wilder," she says, her voice trembling. "But please....bring my little girl home. I beg you."

"We're doing all we can, ma'am," I tell her. "I promise you that."

TWENTY-THREE

Criminal Data Analysis Unit; Seattle Field Office

THE DOORS SLIDE CLOSED, and we watch Hedlund until she disappears around the corner toward the elevators. And when she's gone, I blow out a long breath of relief and slump into the chair at the vacant workstation next to Mo's.

"Well, that looked like a lot of fun," Astra whistles low.

I look at her and roll my eyes. "That woman has a unique talent for getting under my skin."

"What? You hide it so well," Mo cracks.

I give her a small laugh as I get to my feet and step to the front of the room. Crossing my arms over my chest, I start pacing back and forth, letting my mind work.

"What did she want from you this time?" Astra asks.

"Blood. Firstborn child. Left arm. You know, the usual," I quip.

"So, what did you have to give her to get her to jump on her broomstick and fly out of here?" she presses.

"I read her into the case," I say. "She knows what we know."

"Was that smart?" Mo asks.

"Probably not. But it was expedient," I tell her. "It will hopefully keep her out of our hair for a little while. She took the information hard."

"I actually feel a little sorry for her," Mo says. "I can't imagine what it would feel like to hear your child was possibly trafficked."

"I imagine it sucks," Rick pipes up from his station. "Really, really bad."

"Thank you, Captain Obvious," Mo groans.

"So, we're trusting her to not go running to the cameras with this?" Astra questions. "Or compromise the investigation in any way?"

"I threatened her with an obstruction charge if one word of what I told her leaks," I reply.

"Can we do that?"

I shrug. "I guess we'll find out it if comes to it."

"Well, if nothing else, this will be interesting theater," Astra says.

I keep pacing as I try to think this all through. Try to come up with some other means of finding the man in the hoodie since Burton is a dead end in that regard. My mind keeps going back to the call to Tony's Auto. To the mystery caller who turned Selene's car over to them. Then my mind turns back to the theory I was developing in my office—that the man in the hoodie is the buffer between our trafficker and the street-level operations.

"I'm thinking the man in the hoodie—the one who gave Burton his marching orders—is the same guy who dropped Selene's Tesla off at Tony's Auto," I start.

"What makes you think that?" Mo asks.

"I got to thinking about it, and I'm relatively certain the hoodie is our trafficker's fixer. He does the dirty work like running Burton, getting rid of our victims' cars and whatever other nasty deeds need doing," I say. "He also provides a layer of insulation for our trafficker. Our top dog is at least one step removed from the street-level action. Hoodie keeps him safe that way."

"So, we need to find out who that is, snatch him up, then squeeze him," Astra says.

I nod. "Exactly."

"And how do we find him?" Mo asks.

"That's the million-dollar question," I mutter.

"Rick, I really need you to find out where that burner was purchased," I say. "Drop everything else you're doing right now and focus on that."

"On it, boss," he says.

"And if the burner doesn't pan out," Astra starts, "what's our plan B?"

"We don't have one right now," I sigh. "That's the problem. We need to get creative and figure this out. We need to find a way to track this guy down."

"What about Selene's last location?" Astra asks. "Does anybody know where she was last seen before she got snatched?"

I shake my head. "We don't even know the exact day she was taken," I say. "It's hard to know where to look without even that bit of intel."

"We should still do our due diligence," she replies. "Maybe if we can figure out the last time anybody saw her—and where —we might be able to get a bead on who snatched her."

"You're right. It's a good idea," I say. "So, we need to put together a timeline of her last movements as best as we can. I don't know how we'll verify it all, but we need to give it a shot."

"I'll get on that. I can try to piece it together from her financials," Mo offers. "It might not be complete, but it might give us a decent general idea of her last movements. If we happen to get really lucky, there will be a receipt from the last place she went the night she got snatched."

"That's good, Mo. Really good," I nod. "Excellent idea. Do that."

"You got it, boss."

"And what about us?" Astra asks. "What are we going to be doing?"

"We'll get out and start pounding pavement," I say. "We'll go hit the school again and see what her friends say. Maybe they know where she was the night she went missing."

Astra scoffs. "Betting it's going to be one big dry hole," she says. "Nobody we talked to even knew she was missing."

I frown and nod, knowing that much is true. That's the problem with the sort of wild-child, jet-setting lifestyle she was leading—nobody knows when you're missing because everybody is so used to your picking up and going. If nothing else, though, maybe we can find some consensus on the last day anybody saw her. I have my doubts and reservations, but one can hope, right?

"Uh, boss?" Rick raises his hand with a note of concern in his voice.

"What is it?"

"I've had an open search running to see if any of the names of the missing girls pop up anywhere," Rick explains.

"Okay and?"

"Yeah well, the name of one of the girls just popped up," he tells me. "Stacy Burkett."

I perk up, my curiosity piqued. It's the first hit on any of the twenty-two missing girls we've had. I find myself hoping it will lead to an avalanche of the others. Hopefully alive. I think

THE LOST GIRLS   173

somewhere in the back of my mind I've been hoping these girls all maybe moved to different cities or states and are living good, happy lives. Naïve and foolishly optimistic I know, considering what I do for a living and all I've seen. But sometimes, I need to hold onto that optimism and hope just to maintain my own sanity.

"And where did Stacy Burkett turn up?" I ask.

He looks at me and just from the expression on his face, I know that my optimism and willful naïveté won't be rewarded.

"She's at the King County ME's office," he says, his voice subdued.

I glance at Astra and see her frowning. She'd obviously been harboring the same naïve hopes that I had.

"Well, I guess we're not going back to Marchmont today," I say.

"I find myself in the weird position of suddenly wishing we were going to be spending the day with the spoiled rich kids," she replies with a groan.

TWENTY-FOUR

King County Medical Examiner's Office; Seattle, WA

WE STEP through the door and into the sterile and antiseptic-smelling lobby of the ME's office. I'll never get used to the smell. That stench of bleach will forever remind me of death in all its many horrible forms. The one thing I've learned for sure in all my years in the Bureau is that humans have a limitless capacity for cruelty and inflicting terrible acts of violence upon one another.

We reach the receptionist's desk, which is more of a booth, really. The counter is waist-high but then topped with inch-thick plexiglass all the way up to the ceiling. There's a narrow pass-through for documents. We have to communicate through a two-way speaker system. It's a testament to the times we live in, I suppose.

Astra and I step to the counter and badge the woman behind it. She's in her mid-thirties with her dirty blonde hair pulled back into a tight ponytail. She's got blue eyes, pale skin, and a very dry, humorless look about her.

"SSA Wilder and Special Agent Russo," I say. "We're here to see Rebekah Shafer."

The woman doesn't say a word, just turns to her computer and bangs away on the keys. She reads something off her screen then picks up her phone and speaks quietly into it before hanging up and turning back to us.

"She'll be out in a moment," she tells us. "You can wait in the seating area."

The woman turns back to her computer, clearly done with us. I look at Astra and give her a grin.

"I guess we've been dismissed," I say.

"Clearly, the ME's office isn't hiring based on personality anymore."

I can feel the woman's eyes burning holes into my back as we walk over to the seating area to wait. We stand to the side and I lean against the wall. An older couple is sitting in the hard plastic chairs, their expressions downcast, holding hands. The woman's eyes are red and puffy, her face splotchy. She's obviously been crying. It doesn't take much of a leap of logic to guess they're there to identify a loved one. The smile that had been on my face slips, and I have to tear my eyes away from her.

Rebekah Shafer pokes her head out of the door and waves us back. Astra and I head over, and I cast a glance back at the older woman. The man leans over and murmurs something to her. He pulls her to him and holds her. He's staying strong for her even though his face says he wants to break down himself. I find myself wondering what having that sort of love is like. And if I'm ever going to experience it.

Once we're back through the doors, my mouth falls open in a gape. The first thing I noticed the moment she opened the door was that her formerly rust-colored hair is now a bright shade of pastel pink. Honestly, I'm surprised she got away with it at work. Beks has always been on the edgy side, and back in the day when we were roommates in college, pushed me to lighten up and live a little. Those were some of the best days of my life.

"Hey, how are you, Blake?"

"I'm good, thanks," I say and point to her hair. "That's a....new thing."

"Thanks," she winks. "Just got it done a couple days ago. I like to think it brightens up the place."

"I'm glad I can always count on you to do just that," I tell her. "I'm kind of shocked they let you come to work like that, though."

"Well, I love it," offers Astra. "If I could pull it off at the Bureau, I totally would go maybe, like, teal."

"Oh, that'd look awesome on you!" Beks encourages her. "Come on, let's go back."

Rebekah leads us into her office and closes the door behind us. She drops into the seat behind her desk and offers us the chairs across from her. I lean forward and set the cup of coffee and bag of doughnuts from Fred's—her favorite doughnut joint —down on the desk in front of her.

"Bribery," Rebekah observes with a wry grin. "So you mean to say you're not just here to have a chat about hair color?"

"As always, Beks, you are right on the money."

I give Rebekah a minute to take a bite of her chocolate-sprinkled doughnut and wash it down with a swig of coffee. She groans indecently as she chews her doughnut and slumps back in her seat, a wide smile on her face.

"I'll admit, I do love the bribes," she says.

"It helps to know your audience."

She takes another bite and nods. "So, what is it I can do for you?" she asks around a mouthful of doughnut. "Must be some-thing good for you to be plying me with Fred's. Lay it on me."

"Stacy Burkett," I say. "What can you tell me?"

She takes another bite, then turns to her computer and taps on the keyboard, reading off the information that pops up. Rebekah takes a moment, then turns back to us.

"Stacy Burkett, age twenty-five," she says. "Originally brought in as a Jane Doe, but she was subsequently finger-printed and revealed to be Stacy Burkett. Her mother made the official identification yesterday."

"Cause of death?" I ask.

"Official listed cause of death is internal bleeding caused by blunt force trauma. But it's hard to know exactly which injury caused the bleed," Rebekah says, her chipper expression falling to one more serious. "If I had to guess, though, I'm thinking somebody....beat her with a baseball bat."

Astra and I share a grimace. "Jesus," I mutter.

"This girl was beaten up badly. I'm looking at the photos and it's grim. Broken ribs, fractured arm, fractured leg, she had more abrasions and bruises than could be counted. Frankly, she looks as if she went through a meat grinder. The shapes of some of the injuries I've seen are consistent with a long, blunt object —like a bat," she explains. "But here's the weird thing—she was normal weight and in good health otherwise. In the message you sent me earlier, you said you thought she was a victim of a trafficking ring. I don't see any of the usual signs of that. She wasn't malnourished, her tox screen was perfectly clean—other than being beaten savagely, she was the picture of health."

Rebekah turns the monitor so we can see as she scrolls through the photos, each one of them seemingly worse than the last. Somebody worked her over hard, which doesn't jibe with the picture of the girl's good health Rebekah just painted for us. It's a detail that doesn't make the least bit of sense.

"Where was she found?" Astra asks.

"According to the reports, she was found just off old

Highway 12. Drivers said she just appeared out of nowhere," Rebekah says. "They clipped her but that wasn't what killed her. Her injuries were already pretty severe when she was out on the road."

"And nobody knows where she came from?" Astra asks.

Rebekah shakes her head. "Negative. Not according to anything I'm reading right now," she says. "But my question is, since she's from Seattle, how in the hell did she get all the way down to Highway 12, to begin with? What was she doing down there? And was she down there the entire time she was missing?"

"Those are all excellent questions," I note. "And we will be sure to ask her mother all of them."

"Is there anything else you can tell us?" Astra asks.

"Yeah," Rebekah says, her face growing pale and drawn. "She gave birth recently."

"Not aborted?"

She shook her head. "No, she definitely gave live birth."

"How recently?" I ask.

"Hard to say for sure," she replies. "But it was recent. Probably within the last month."

Astra and I exchange a glance. This whole thing just took on an even darker shade. If there's an infant out there, that just puts a whole new sense of urgency into this investigation.

"Okay, anything else we need to know?" I ask.

She shakes her head. "Nothing I can't text you later."

"Great," I say as I get to my feet. "If you come across anything you think we need to know, please do. Thanks, Beks."

Astra and I get to the door, but Rebekah stops me, and I turn around.

"I've heard some of the cops who come through here talking. There's apparently a pool going around the SPD right now," she says.

"Yeah? What are they betting on?"

"How long it's going to take Deputy Chief Torres to indict you for Gina Aoki's murder," she says. "As it stands, the over/under is thirty days."

"Thirty days? Is that right?" I raise an eyebrow.

"It is," she replies with a laugh. "Which should I bet? The over or the under?"

I give her a devious grin. "Oh, the over," I tell her. "Definitely bet the over."

"That's my girl," she smiles.

TWENTY-FIVE

Residence of Mia Burkett, Crown Hill District, Seattle, WA

"So, are we really not going to talk about Torres and this betting pool?" Astra asks.

I pull the car to a stop at the curb and cut the engine. Before we get out, though, I turn and look at her.

"There's nothing to talk about," I shrug. "You know there's no case there. No matter how hard he tries to imply there is."

"I know that, but if the rank-and-file cops are talking openly like that, it means Torres is gearing up for war," she points out. "He's coming after you."

"Then let him come. All he's got is a bad attitude and a grudge. There's no way he can connect me to a murder I didn't commit," I say.

"That doesn't mean he's not going to try."

"And the worst thing I can do is give it oxygen," I counter. "If I acknowledge it, I give it validity. I give it life it doesn't deserve."

"But if you ignore it, you let Torres shape the narrative. You let him get his story out there and let his minions continue to amplify it."

"So what? Let them talk," I shrug. "I don't care."

"You should care. He's going to wage a PR campaign against you," Astra presses. "These days, you don't need actual proof to tar somebody's reputation. And make no mistake, Blake—he's not doing this with the hope of a criminal conviction. He's trying to smear you badly enough to damage your career. Maybe even tank it entirely."

"Please. The brass isn't going to listen to him," I say.

"You need to be very careful, Blake. This is all politics and theater. It's trial by innuendo," she says. "And Torres is not only very well connected, but he plays the game a lot better than you do."

"It's not going to come to that," I insist.

On some level, I'm more concerned about it than I'm letting on. I know Torres is coming for me. I know he's going to try to hang Gina Aoki's murder on me. He's been trying from the moment her body was found. I know his dislike of me stems from my friendship with Paxton Arrington as much as it does from the fact that the cases my team has broken have made him look bad in the court of public opinion.

But there's not much I can do about it. Torres is going to do what he's going to do. All I can do is fight the battles he brings my way. And that's exactly what I'll do. I will fight tooth and nail. To the bitter end. And when the smoke clears, I know that I'm going to be the one left standing. All Torres has are lies and innuendo. He has no case. I'll let my record speak for itself.

"All I'm saying is that you better start digging your trenches now."

"I will," I tell her. "I'm not going to let somebody like him take me down or tarnish the work we're doing."

"And you know I've got your back. No matter what happens, you know I'm in your corner," she smiles.

"I do. And thank you."

"Anytime."

We get out of the car, and I look around the solidly middle-class neighborhood. Trees line both sides of the street, and the houses are older but are mostly well-tended. The people here seem to take pride in their homes and try to keep them clean and nice. The Burkett home is a one-story ranch-style home that's painted a light shade of blue with white shutters. Both could probably stand a new coat. The lawn is well kept, and a large sycamore tree stands in the middle of the yard.

We walk up the driveway and to the front door. I knock and step back. A couple of moments later, the door opens to reveal a woman who's probably in her mid-forties but looks ten years older. She's got a wild tangle of dark hair that's shot through with gray and looks as if it hasn't been brushed in days. She's wearing a ratty, threadbare housecoat, with rumpled pajamas underneath it.

Mia Burkett is about five-five, pale as a sheet; her eyes are bloodshot, with dark bags beneath them. It's obvious she's been crying and likely hasn't slept for days. She's holding a coffee cup that has more booze than coffee in it—I can smell it from where I'm standing. Given her loss, I can't say I blame her for doing a little self-medicating.

"Yeah?" she asks.

We badge her. "Special Agent Russo, SSA Wilder," Astra starts gently. "We are very sorry for your loss, Ms. Burkett. But we'd like to ask you some questions, if that would be all right?"

"I talked to the cops yesterday," she says.

"I understand, but we're also looking into your daughter's case, and we'd like to follow up with just a few more questions,"

Astra says. "I promise that we won't take up much of your time."

She takes a long swallow from her coffee mug, then shrugs and turns away, walking back into the house. She leaves the door open, though, so I'm going to take that as an invitation. We follow her in, and Astra shuts the door behind her. We find ourselves in a living room. Ms. Burkett is sitting in an armchair, staring through the sliders without really seeing what's beyond the glass.

Astra and I perch lightly on the edge of the sofa, giving her a couple of moments to gather herself. I'm sure that after living in uncertainty for the last year, only to have her worst nightmare come true, has been a pain that rocked Mia to her very core.

"Ms. Burkett, I know this must be a horribly difficult time for you," I start. "All we need is to ask a few questions, and we'll be on our way."

"Fine. Ask your questions," she mutters, her voice hoarse and raspy. "But hurry up about it. I have to plan my daughter's funeral."

I frown and look down at my hands, feeling a sharp lance of guilt piercing me. Questioning somebody on the worst day of her life is never easy.

"I know it's been a long time, but do you remember where Stacy was the night she disappeared?" I ask.

She shakes her head miserably. "I don't. She and I were both busy—me with work and my boyfriend at the time, and Stacy with school and her friends. We didn't talk a whole lot. We were like ships passin' in the night most of the time," she says, the sound of guilt thick in her voice.

"Did she have a boyfriend at the time?" Astra asks.

Mia shrugs. "Maybe she did. We didn't talk a whole lot.

She was always a pretty and popular girl," she says. "But she never mentioned anything about a boyfriend to me."

"Do you recall her ever mentioning having trouble with anybody?" I ask. "Anybody watching her or maybe following her, or anything like that?"

Mia shakes her head again. "Not that I remember, no."

Her voice cracks, and I see the tears rolling down her face. She quickly wipes them away and clears her throat, trying to regain her composure.

"I wish—I wish I could do it all over again, you know?" she says. "I wish I would've taken more time for Stacy. I wish we'd been closer."

The regret in her voice is as thick as the guilt. My heart goes out to her. I can't imagine what she must be feeling right now. Knowing she'll never get the chance to see her daughter again, to grow closer to her and to celebrate all of life's milestones, has to be one of the most painful things a person can go through.

I have a small understanding of that feeling. Having had my kid sister ripped away from me and knowing I'll never see her again or get the chance to celebrate life's milestones with her is a gut punch. But I didn't give birth to Kit, so I imagine it's a thousand times worse for Mia.

"I always held out hope Stacy would come back to me, you know? I always made myself believe that she went off somewhere to live a little bit of life. I pretended she was traveling the world, seeing all the countries she talked about when she was a kid—France, Spain, even Japan," Mia says, almost as if she's speaking to herself. "And I always believed that one day she'd walk through that front door again and tell me all about her adventures. Kept her room just like it was the day she left. She always used to get on me about tryin' to pick up her room a little. I just couldn't bring myself to do nothin' else with it."

She falls silent and looks down at the coffee mug in her hand. I get the feeling she'd like nothing more than to crawl inside of it and drink until she blacks out, hoping she'll wake up to find this has all been a horribly vivid nightmare. But I can tell she knows the truth of it: there is no amount of alcohol that will make this any less real. Or any easier. She's a strong woman, but I can see the cracks forming in her. I just hope she's able to keep herself pieced together long enough to begin healing.

"For months and months, I held onto a thread of hope. Over time, that thread got a little frayed, but it held. I think in some ways, havin' that thread cut is probably a good thing. Maybe a little bit of a relief, if it don't sound too bad sayin' that," she goes on. "I mean, I guess on some level I always knew that phone call would come, but to finally get it and have that hope taken away—it hurts, yeah. But havin' to let go of that false hope I was clutchin'....it's a little bit of a relief. Does that make me a monster?"

Astra shakes her head. "No. Not at all, Ms. Burkett. It makes you human," she says. "And that relief you feel is you giving yourself permission to let go of the past and move forward. I'm sure Stacy would want you to do that. To live your life."

A low chuckle passes her lips. "Not sure I know how to do that anymore."

"It'll come back to you. In time," I say, thinking of the process it took for me to find my way back to life after my parents were killed. "It's like a muscle inside of you. It's a little weak and atrophied right now, but the more you use and exercise it, the stronger it will get."

She gives us both a tight smile. "I'm sorry to go on and on like this. You had some questions to ask me?"

At this point—and after all this time—I'm not sure Ms.

Burkett's going to be able to answer our questions. Especially given the fact that she and Stacy weren't all that close. But there is one thing I think she might be able to tell us.

"Ms. Burkett, in the days and maybe weeks before her disappearance, was Stacy acting any differently? Did she have any sort of a personality change?" I ask.

She looks at me with a frown on her face and the light of surprise in her eyes. She nods slowly, looking at me as if I'm clairvoyant or something.

"Actually, yeah. She was different in those last few weeks before she went missin'. I remember her goin' on and on' about how wasteful we are. She was addicted to her own phone and computer but said she wished we could just go back to simpler times when we didn't have all this technology that was keepin' people apart and all," she tells us. "Said the world would be a better place if we got rid of all the phones and computers and stuff. I thought she joined some environmentalist group at school or somethin', to be honest. I never paid it much mind. She went through phases sometimes. Didn't think it meant anything."

I exchange a subtle glance with Astra, who seems to be on the same page as I am. Something is beginning to take shape. I can't exactly see what it is. It's a silhouette through frosted glass, our view obscured and opaque. But I feel the shape of it, and judging by the look in her eye, Astra feels it, too.

I turn back to Ms. Burkett with one more question for her. "Ms. Burkett, what happened to Stacy's father?"

"Oh, him," she snorts. "Stacy's sperm donor ran off after I got pregnant. Never heard from that dirtbag again."

It's another possible link in the chain. Stacy and Selene had a few things in common, but at this point, it could just be a coincidence. However, three would be a pattern. And if I were a betting woman, I'd say that the other twenty women who

went missing all came from fatherless homes and had under-
gone something of a personality switch in the weeks before
their disappearances.

"Ms. Burkett, would you mind if we looked at Stacy's
room?" Astra asks.

"Help yourselves," she replies. "Second door on the right."

We make our way to the bedroom and go inside. It's messy
—just the way Stacy left it—with piles of clothes on the floor, an
unmade bed, and even an empty water bottle on the night-
stand. I can't count the number of rooms I've been in that have
been sealed off from the world like this. They stand like a
moment, frozen in time. As if all that's needed is for somebody
to hit *play* to un-pause this room and the life that once inhab-
ited it.

It's love and hope that keep them sealed. And it's that same
love and hope that keep people like Ms. Burkett from moving
on. But even more than that, it's guilt that drives behavior like
this. Guilt over the fact that they weren't close to their children,
or that they'd missed warning signs, or simply that they are still
alive while their loved ones are not. Survivor's guilt is a nasty
beast that will tear you apart from the inside out if you let it.

In truth, by sealing off Stacy's room, Ms. Burkett is sealing
herself away. This room might as well be the entire house.
Nothing in this room has changed over the last year that Stacy's
been missing, just as nothing has changed with Ms. Burkett
over that same period. She's every bit as frozen in time as
Stacy's room. My only hope is that now she has her answer and
knows that Stacy is never coming home, that she'll be able to
break free and unstick herself.

I walk to the desk and start looking through the pile of
books—mostly textbooks from school. But when I hit a familiar
title, I freeze and feel a jolt of adrenaline rush through me. I

pick it up and show Astra the copy of *Living Clean, Living Free* —the same book we found in Selene's condo.

"What are the odds?" she asks.

It's too early yet to be anything but a coincidence, but I am starting to have the feeling that the more we look into the rest of these girls, the more coincidences will start to pile up. I feel that churning in the pit of my stomach I get when the momentum of a case starts to move. There's a long way to go yet, but we're starting to pick up steam.

TWENTY-SIX

Criminal Data Analysis Unit; Seattle Field Office

"ALL RIGHT, so I can confirm that all twenty-two of our missing girls came from broken homes," Mo says. "Most of them lost their fathers either through death or divorce at a young age. There are a couple who don't have their fathers listed on their birth certificates at all."

"That's a whole lot of coincidences," Astra replies.

I nod. "And it gives us some insight into our trafficker," I say. "He's a predator. Knows how to spot the girls with absent fathers and then appeals to them. I think he's able to gain their trust, get them alone somehow, then does his thing."

"What makes you think he can gain their trust, though?" Mo asks.

"Because in none of the twenty-two cases have we run across a report of a violent abduction," I reply. "This wasn't a case of his rolling up in a van, throwing the women in the back, and speeding away. They all simply vanished without a trace.

That can't be a coincidence. That is a pattern. To me, that says they went with him willingly."

Mo nods, but I can see she's still not entirely convinced. I don't have the proof to back my theory up, of course, but it feels right. My gut tells me I'm on the right path.

"What else do we know about the girls?" I ask. "Have we found the nexus yet?"

Mo shakes her head. "Other than the fact that they were all students, I don't see any common trends among them. I've gone through all their socials with a fine-toothed comb and I don't see common friends, places they hung out, or anything like that."

"Okay, so they were all students," I say. "That's a start. That's a big commonality."

"The perp could have been staff or faculty," Astra offers.

"Exactly," I say.

"Except for the fact that there's very little overlap among them," Mo says. "I mean, there are only so many schools around here, but they didn't all go to the same one. Stacy Burkett went to Evergreen Junior College, Selene Hedlund went to Marchmont—we've got some who went to UW, Washington State, and a few who went to different community colleges in the area."

"Huh," I say, letting my mind work.

"What about this book—*Living Clean, Living Free*," Astra brings up. "Two of the missing girls had it, which seems like an odd coincidence."

"From what I've seen in online chatter, that book is popular with off-the-grid prepper types," Rick offers. "They go on and on about traditional values and simpler living and decreasing reliance on technology. Probably half of them are flagrantly racist and sexist, of course. They literally want to go back to the 1800s, backwards social climate and all."

"Wait, and they have online communities?"

Rick merely shrugs. "I don't get it, either. You'd think social media and the Internet would be included in their whole, 'no television, no computers' thing. I'm pretty sure the nineteenth century didn't have Twitter."

"Yeah, because that was such a great time to be alive," Astra cracks. "Cholera, typhoid, a life expectancy of about thirty years. What's not to like?"

"What's the point of living if it's not to advance our society through better technology?" Rick adds. "Technology makes the world a better place for everybody. These guys are as freakish and bizarre as Flat Earthers."

"Forgive Rick," Astra turns to me. "He can't contemplate a world without Tinder."

"Are you still mad I didn't swipe right on you?" he shoots back. "I told you it would just be awkward because we work together."

Astra laughs and throws her pen at him. "Oh, my God, I hate you so much right now."

I laugh along with them, but cross my arms over my chest and pace the front of the room, absorbing all the information. There are still too many disparate pieces to form a cohesive narrative right now. The answer is there, so close I can practically smell it. But it remains just out of my reach. There's something I'm not seeing. Something I'm still missing, and it's frustrating me to no end. This case has had more twists and turns than I'm used to. Even though I feel the pace of the investigation speeding up and we're gaining that momentum I love so much, some pieces still won't line up for me.

The one thing that's standing out to me for some reason is the book. It seems an odd title for both Selene Hedlund and Stacy Burkett—two women from completely different backgrounds and socioeconomic stations—to have in their possession. I don't know what it is that's flashing wrong about it for me, but my brain keeps circling back to it.

"What do we know about this book—*Living Clean, Living Free?*" I ask.

Mo turns back to her computer. "Written by Arnold Merrick, who was a leading member of an organization called the Natural Living Federation at the time. It was published in 1986 and advocated for a technology-free, vegan lifestylein which humans live in harmony with nature," she reads off her screen. "The book has been highly influential and is still in wide circulation today. It's even become a preferred textbook on a lot of college campuses."

"So, it was science fiction," Astra says. "Got it."

"Without the science," Rick chimes in. "I'd call it more pure fantasy."

"I'd call it a handbook for self-flagellation," Mo says. "Who wants to live in a world where you can't get a big, juicy steak?"

"Not me," I agree. "But with all these new vegan restaurants popping up around town these days, it seems there are more and more people who do want to live in that world."

I pace back and forth as I stare at the floor, trying to get these square pegs to somehow line up and fit into the round holes. I know there's something there that will make them fit, but for the life of me, I can't see it right now. But then a thought occurs to me, and I stop pacing.

"Mo, can you see if there were any common instructors at those schools?" I ask. "Did the same professor teach at the schools the girls disappeared from?"

"Good thinking," Astra adds. "You'll also want to run the names of the staff, too. Janitors, admissions people —everybody."

"Go back six years," I say. "The disappearances started five years ago, but it was going to take a little time for our guy to groom the first girl. Time to get his methodology down."

"On it," she nods. "But that's a lot of names, so it's going to take me a minute."

I nod. "Copy that," I say. "But just get to it as fast as you can."

"Roger," she says.

I resume my pacing, letting my mind keep working the problem. Walking and talking things out has always helped me work through a problem. I've always believed there's something about being in motion that helps my brain function better.

"It seems we have two different tracks to this investigation," I state to nobody in particular. "We've got the girls and the trafficker. And we've got the man in the hoodie. They converge somewhere. We need to figure out where. We figure that out, we can solve this case."

"Here's another factor," Mo starts. "Why is Stacy Burkett the only one who was found? Where are the other twenty-one?"

I shake my head. "That's an excellent question," I reply. "But the fact that she was alive, a year after she was taken—that gives me some small measure of hope the rest might still be out there."

"Be careful with that hope," Astra tells me. "I don't want to see you set yourself up to fall. I mean, even if they are alive, we don't know what sort of condition they'll be in."

"I know. But I need to hang onto it until it's proven otherwise," I say. "I mean, why feed and care for Stacy Burkett for more than a year?"

"Why beat her so severely she dies of her internal injuries?" Astra counters.

"Touché." I nod, conceding her point.

It's just another one of those inconsistencies that aren't

adding up for me. One of those things that makes no sense. Trafficked girls are usually in pretty rough shape when they're recovered. They're used up and then thrown away like garbage, and the trafficker moves onto somebody else. But Stacy was cared for. Fed. Clothed. Those details are driving me up a wall.

"Hey, boss," Rick calls. "Prepare to tell me just how much you love me."

"If you have something good, it'll be a lot."

"I have something great," he says.

He looks at me with a wide smile and a goofy expression on his face, but doesn't say more. We stand there staring at each other for a long moment as I wait, but he remains silent.

"Well, what is it?" I ask.

"Oh. Yeah. Right. Sorry," he mutters. "I finally have the location for the store that sold the burner phone that called Tony's Auto."

"Excellent. That is the first bit of good news we've had in forever. Great work, Rick," I say. "Text the information to my phone. Astra, let's roll."

"Right behind you."

TWENTY-SEVEN

Mickey's Corner Market, Northgate District; Seattle, WA

THE NORTHGATE DISTRICT, like some of the others in the city, is a depressed and poor neighborhood where violent crime is simply a way of life. Gangs control the streets, drugs flow unchecked, and the violence is off the charts. According to the last study I read, you're three times more likely to be the victim of a violent crime here than almost anywhere else in the country. It's gotten so bad, the SPD has all but ceded the territory to the criminals, preferring to let them settle their own beefs than come in and put a stop to it.

We get out of the car and walk toward a couple of twenty-something men standing against the wall of the convenience store; I'm sure they're holding and dealing right there in the open. Such is the way in Northgate. I'm well aware of the way they're looking at us—like lions on the savannah deciding whether to take a run at the gazelle or not. I fix them with a cold glare as we walk by, and they both turn away, snickering and speaking in low murmurs to one another. Score one for the gazelle.

The electronic bell chimes as we step into the store, and I look around. Like most of the neighborhood that surrounds it, Mickey's is a bit run-down and threadbare. The linoleum that covers the floor is cracked and pitted. There are a couple of sections completely missing, revealing the concrete slab underneath. One of the cooler doors is cracked and held together by duct tape, the acoustic tile overhead is a dull, dingy gray, and the whole place could use a power cleaning and a fresh coat of paint.

Despite the disrepair, though, everything is tidy. Clean. There's not a speck of dust I can see anywhere, and everything on the shelves is neat and orderly. Whoever owns this place obviously takes great pride in orderliness. It's good to see that even though the area around the store is falling to pieces, the owner of the market is still holding onto his piece of the pie and is doing what he can to maintain his obviously high standards.

The front counter is about chest high, and as in the ME's office, is topped with an inch-thick piece of plexiglass that makes it a booth of its own. There's a steel door in the booth, but it sits empty at the moment.

"You two look as out of place as a fish walkin' on land."

We both turn and find ourselves facing a tall black man with a warm smile and an even warmer demeanor. He's got thick dark hair cropped close to his skull and is starting to turn silver, along with a neatly trimmed goatee with a silver patch. Although he's lean, he's getting that paunch around the middle that seems inevitable as we age. I'd put him in his mid-fifties, but he still looks like a man who can take care of himself. I suppose you'd have to be, to survive in a neighborhood like this one.

We badge him and the smile on his face grows even wider.

"Well, I didn't know the FBI was hirin' supermodels these days. Must be my lucky day. If I'm gonna get arrested for somethin', I'd prefer you two over some sweaty, three-hundred-pound city cop who smells like fried food and doughnuts. Just be careful when you're friskin' me. I'm a bit ticklish."

I can't stop the smile that touches my lips. The man has a disarming charm and a personality that just puts you at ease.

Astra smiles at him. "We're actually only here because we have a few questions."

He gives us a faux pout. "Well, that's too bad. I ain't had a good friskin' in a long while," he says, drawing laughter from both of us. "I'm Mickey Morris, by the way. Owner of this fine establishment."

He says it with a self-deprecating chuckle that brings a wan smile to my lips. He's a man who's doing the best he can in tough circumstances and seems to know it. But he just keeps plugging on. I can't help but admire that sort of strength.

"Blake," I say. "This is Astra."

He nods. "Pleased to meet you both," he says. "So, what can I help you with, Agents?"

I point to the disposable phones on the pegboard in his plexiglass booth. "We actually have information about a phone that was purchased from here and need to see if there is a receipt to go with it."

He frowns as he looks at the phones. "I hate sellin' 'em because I know what they're used for," he says. "But I sell a lot of 'em and I need to keep the lights on around here."

"Oh, absolutely. You're not in any trouble," I nod. "We just need to see if we can find out who purchased a phone on a particular day."

"They do somethin' bad with it?"

I shrug. "Unfortunately, we wouldn't be here if he hadn't."

He shakes his head sadly. "I remember when this was a

good neighborhood. I raised three kids here myself," he says. "But over the last twenty years or so, it's gone straight into the toilet. Pardon my language."

"Don't worry, Mickey," Astra says. "I say worse on a daily basis."

"Daily? More like hourly."

That gets a chuckle out of him. "Well, come on to the back," he says. "Let's take a look at the receipts."

We follow him into a small office in the back. Like the front, it's all perfectly organized and clean. On the wall hang photos of Mickey when he was in the military. There's a photo of him and what I assume to be his unit in what looks like Afghanistan, judging by the tall, craggy mountains in the distance behind them.

"How long were you in?" I ask, gesturing to the photos.

"Twenty-five years," he smiles. "Went in when I was eighteen, came home a little more than a decade ago. Seems like two very different lives."

"I bet."

He nods. "I tell you, though, I was never as scared over there as I am here sometimes," he says. "At least there, we knew what the danger was. We knew who wanted to kill us. Here? Hell, could be anybody."

I frown and nod. It's true. You just never know who's going to kill you here. The line between good and bad gets so blurred as to be indistinguishable. I clear my throat and pull myself out of my head, then check my phone for the notes Rick texted to me.

"We're looking for somebody who bought a phone on August twelfth," I say. "At six-forty in the evening."

Mickey scans his receipts log, and I'm grateful to the man for being so organized. After a couple of minutes, he nods.

"Yeah, here's the receipt for it," he shows us. "But the guy paid cash."

I grimace. I thought that might be the case, but hoped it would be otherwise.

"Did you recognize him, Mickey?" Astra asks. "Do you happen to know who he is?"

He shakes his head. "Not by name. But yeah, I've seen him in here plenty of times. He buys a lot of them phones too," he says. "He comes in often enough that I just assume he's from the neighborhood. Don't make much sense to drive in from somewhere else when these phones can be had anywhere."

It's a really good point. Burners can be bought almost anywhere these days. And if you're paying cash for it, that makes it virtually untraceable. So why would the man in the hoodie go out of his way to grab a phone from somewhere else? He'd probably get them where it was convenient for him.

"What about security cameras?" I ask.

He smiles. "Oh, yeah. Got plenty of 'em. My son works for a security firm," he says. "He hooked me up real good. Got six cameras mounted on the wall that you can see out there. But there's six more you can't see."

"That's good news for us," I say. "Is the footage archived?"

He nods. "In the cloud."

"That's even better news. Can you possibly pull up the footage from that date?" I ask. "I want to see who our mystery phone buyer is."

"You got it," he nods.

He taps away at his computer keyboard and a moment later, a split eight-screen comes up. Four camera shots on top, four below, each one showing a different angle of the store. The entire floor is covered. Nothing that happens goes unseen. Mickey taps a few more keys, and the screen resolves into one image—that from right behind the counter, shooting directly at the customers as they make their purchases.

"Here we go," he says.

He taps out a few more commands. The screen blinks, and then the timestamp in the corner shows the time and date I wanted. And standing there at the counter is our man in the hoodie. He's probably in his early-to-mid thirties, with short dark hair and brown eyes. He's thin and I'd put him somewhere around five-ten, five-eleven, or so. But what draws my eye is the distinctive scar that runs down the left side of his face.

"That is amazing," I say. "Can you print out that photo for us?"

"Absolutely," he replies.

I hear the whirr of a printer warming up, and a moment later, I'm holding a photo of our mysterious man in the hoodie. It's a full-color glossy that should be good enough to get something through facial rec on it.

"Mickey, I can't tell you how thankful we are for your help," I tell him.

"Glad I could be of service," he says.

Astra shakes his hand, then pulls him down and plants a kiss on his cheek. His smile is wide and genuine, his day made.

"You all come on back when you feel the need to frisk somebody now," he chuckles. "I'll be here waitin'."

"You have a great day," I tell him.

We head out of the store and climb back into the car. "We need to stop by County," I say. "I want to run the photo by Burton. We need to know if the man who called Tony's Auto is the man in the hoodie."

"Here's hoping Burton's lucid," she comments.

I nod. "Here's hoping."

The feeling in the pit of my stomach is unmistakable and undeniable. The momentum of the case is propelling us forward. We're closing in on getting the answers we need. I can feel it down in my bones.

TWENTY-EIGHT

Criminal Data Analysis Unit; Seattle Field Office

I PULL up the text messages on my phone and call up the new one from my aunt Annie. She rarely texts me, but given that I've been ignoring her calls for the last few hours, she's resorting to alternative means.

Need to talk to you. Call me ASAP.

The second I close out of my text messages, my phone buzzes with an incoming call. I roll my eyes. I connect the call and press the phone to my ear.

"Annie, I can't talk right now but the second I have some time, I'll—"

"Blake?"

It's not Annie's voice. I freeze in my tracks. I look at the caller ID and see the number is blocked. I know I don't recognize the voice, and yet there's some faint tingle of familiarity in it. I don't know what's ringing those bells, though.

"Yes, this is SSA Wilder," I say in my official voice. "Who am I speaking to, please?"

There's a loud sniff, as if the person on the other end of the line is crying. I cock my head and listen harder, straining my ears, but can't hear anything else.

"Hello?" I ask. "Who is this?"

The line goes dead in my hand. Whoever it was hung up without saying anything else.

"What the hell?" I mutter.

"Who was that?" Astra asks.

"No idea. It was a blocked number."

"Heavy breathing? Did they say perverted things?" she quips.

"No, nothing like that," I frown, shaking my head. "She just said my name. That's all."

"So why do you look as if you've seen a ghost?"

I shrug. "I don't know. I almost recognized the voice—or at least some part of my brain did. But I just can't place it."

"That's odd and creepy," she notes.

I nod. "Yeah. But whatever," I say. "I don't have time for it right now."

I give my head a shake and pull myself back to the present. I fire off a quick text to Annie, telling her I'm in the middle of a case and I'll call her as soon as I get a moment. She's not going to like it—she hates being put off more than anything—but I'm not going to stop the momentum we're building just to go and listen to her ranting about one thing or another.

If I had to guess, I'd say it'd most likely be about my cousin Maisey, who has begun asserting her independence more frequently and forcefully. And although Annie has come a long way in terms of being able to let go and let Maisey be her own person, there have been a few bumps in the road now and then —bumps I have no time for at the moment.

"Rick, can you put it up on the screens, please?"

"Your wish is my command, my liege," he replies.

"Do you think he's ever not weird?" Astra asks.

I shrug. "Maybe when he sleeps?"

"No, I'm pretty sure he even sleeps weird."

"What? Sleeping while hanging upside down like a bat is perfectly normal," he chirps.

The screens behind me pop to life with the mugshot of the man we've been looking for. I take a moment to study him. He's clean-shaven—face and head—with a strong jawline and piercing blue eyes. There's a hardness about him that only comes from growing up rough, fast, and having done some time.

"This is Alex Dansby, thirty-nine years old," I say. "He's a two-time loser, having done a nickel for aggravated assault and another nickel for attempted robbery of a bank—he was the wheelman."

"The wheelman who crashed into a city bus during the big getaway," Astra adds, drawing a laugh from everybody.

"Alex Dansby, as we confirmed with Sergeant Burton, who is currently residing at County, is the man in the hoodie. This is the man who gave Burton the debit cards and the instructions to bleed the accounts," I continue. "This is also the man who is the layer of insulation for our trafficker."

"Are we sure of that?" Mo asks.

"As sure as we can be," I nod. "What we are fairly certain of is that Dansby is not the mastermind—he's not the one trafficking the girls. He's the one doing the dirty work, such as running the bleeders and ditching the cars. I'm almost positive the person actually behind the scheme wouldn't risk himself that way."

"But why would Dansby take on that kind of weight for somebody?" Mo asks. "We can tie him to the missing girls via the debit cards. That means he's taking the weight for them—and with Stacy Burkett turning up dead, he's looking at twenty-two murder charges, bodies or not."

"It's a question I've asked myself a thousand times already. The only reason I can come up with is loyalty," I say. "For some reason, Dansby is so loyal to our trafficker that he's willing to take the bullet for him. In my experience, he's only going to have that sort of loyalty for a lifelong friend or a relative. Maybe a brother. His father. Somebody closer to him than his own skin. So, we need to do a deep dive on him. We need to figure out who engenders that sort of loyalty in him."

"On it," Rick says. "I'll get into every nook and cranny on the guy."

"Yeah, that doesn't sound disgusting and wrong," Astra says.

Rick chuckles. "Sounds like a typical Friday night for you."

"Children, let's focus," I say, laughing to myself. "Mo, have you had any luck cross-referencing the employment histories at the schools?"

"I'm so glad you asked," she says. "As a matter of fact, I have stumbled across an interesting nugget of information."

"Do tell," I say.

"As it turns out, your dreamy philosophy professor, Dr. Crawford, was an instructor at each of the institutions where some of these girls went missing," she says. "It took some doing, because he's never been part of the official full-time faculty anywhere but Marchmont—he was at those other schools as a part-time professor and guest lecturer. So, while he wasn't necessarily there at the exact times the girls disappeared, it's curious that he was at each of the schools where girls went missing. Only instructor I've found who was."

I nod, feeling my stomach starting to churn even more wildly. I can see the pieces lining up in some semblance of order. They're not quite falling into place just yet, but I think we're starting to get somewhere.

"That's great work, Mo. Really great work," I tell her. "But do me a favor and go deeper with that. I want to know if these girls had classes with him."

"For this theory to work out, if Crawford is our trafficker—which I assume is where you're going with this—what's the connection between him and Dansby?" Astra asks.

"That's a great question," I say. "Why don't we go ask him?"

"Should we do that?" Astra asks. "I mean, we risk tipping him off if we do, and if we spook him—and assuming the girls are still alive—we could force him to liquidate."

"Liquidate? That's really disturbing and dehumanizing," Rick chimes in. "Why can't you say something normal like 'murder everybody he's holding'? It's terrible, but sounds a lot better than liquidating people."

"You're such a wuss," Astra says.

"I prefer the term, 'gentler of constitution.'"

"Yeah, so you're a wuss," Mo cracks.

As they banter back and forth, I'm forced to think about Astra's point, and I come to the conclusion that she's right. I mean, we don't really have the evidence to confront him. The fact that he has been at each of the schools where the girls went missing is an anomaly, but it's far from damning. And she's also right in that if we spook him, he could kill the girls who are still alive—if there are any.

But the other side of that coin is that if we give him a clue that we're looking at him, it could force him to slip up. He seemed very calm and in control of himself when we last spoke with him. But I'm curious to see how he'd react to having a little pressure put on. How he would react if we started to squeeze him—if only a little bit. We could do that and then put some-body on him. We tail him everywhere and see where he goes. With any luck, he might just lead us to the girls.

It's a gamble, no question about it. But if we're ever going to blow this case open and find these girls—or find where they're buried—we're going to need to take some risks. It's the only way this is going to happen. But—perhaps we could help mitigate those risks.

"Astra, let's go," I say. "Let's go scoop Dansby up."

"On what charge?"

"If nothing else, we have him on the fraud charge," I say. "That's good enough to hold him for a little while. Hopefully long enough to squeeze him until he cracks. I want to know if there's any connection between him and Crawford. Because if there's not, we need to find out who he's taking his orders from."

"Or find out that he's the head of the snake."

I shrug. "Whichever. As long as we can figure out the whos and wheres," I say. "I just want to find these girls and bring their families a sense of peace, one way or the other."

"All right," she says, even though I can tell she's not convinced. "Let's do it."

TWENTY-NINE

Interrogation Suite Charlie-3; Seattle Field Office

"You HAD no right to pick me up like that," he snaps. "You had no cause to bust into my place of work and drag me out of there."

"Sure, we did," I reply. "You're on probation, and your name came up in our criminal investigation. A federal investigation, just so you know, so depending on what you tell us versus what we figure out on our own, you could be in very serious trouble."

"What she's saying is that because you're out on parole, your leash is especially short," Astra says. "So the choice is yours. You can either loosen it with us—or we can tighten it."

"But you should know that by now, as this isn't your first rodeo, cowboy," I add.

Dansby sits across the table glowering at us. "Lawyer," he sneers.

I shrug. "That's your right, of course. But I should tell you now that we already have you on bank fraud. That's federal weight," I tell him.

"We've also got you on the murder of Stacy Burkett," Astra adds.

I watch him closely, looking for a tell. But Dansby is well versed in keeping his features controlled. He gives me absolutely nothing. We obviously don't have him on the murder, but we were hoping to rattle him enough that he would give something away. It's a gambit we use all the time. Sometimes it works, sometimes it doesn't. This time, unfortunately, it's falling into the latter category.

"Who?" he asks smugly.

No choice but to play it out now. "The girl found out on Highway 12. Beaten within an inch of her life," I tell him. "But you already knew that. Died of her injuries, by the way."

"What did you use?" Astra presses. "Baseball bat? Steel pipe? Your fists?"

"I got no idea what you're talkin' about," he says.

"We can tie you directly to twenty-two girls who've gone missing," I tell him. "One of whom is dead. Think it'll take a jury long to connect all the dots?"

"This won't get to a jury," he says.

He's looking at us with a smug smirk on his lips that I don't like. He's acting as if he's got an ace up his sleeve. It reminds me a lot of the night Stephen Petrosyan got his bodyguard to fall on his sword for him. We had Petrosyan dead to rights, but I had to watch him waltz out the door, anyway. This is definitely feeling a lot like that.

"And what makes you think that?" Astra asks. "We've got you dead to rights, Alex."

"You've actually got nothing."

"We can prove you hired Leonard Burton to withdraw cash from the bank accounts of the twenty-two girls who went missing and funnel it to you. We can prove that you turned Selene Hedlund's Tesla—she's another girl who's missing—over to a chop shop in the Othello district," Astra says. "We can connect you directly to Stacy Burkett—that's the dead girl, just in case you forgot. How am I doing so far?"

He laughs slowly and shakes his head. "You people don't know anything, do you? This ain't what you think it is."

"No?" I raise an eyebrow. "Then educate us. Tell us what we're missing."

"I'd be glad to," he says. "In the presence of my lawyer."

"If you lawyer up, we can't help you."

"The only help I'll need from you is when you hold the door open for me as I walk out of here," he fires back.

"You do realize that's not going to happen, right?" Astra says. "We've got you cold—"

"You've got nothing. Nothing but a lack of understanding," he says. "You don't know nothin'. You may think you do, but you don't."

"Then educate us," I press.

"I will. Once my lawyer gets here," he says. "I'm takin' a temporary vow of silence now. I ain't gonna say another word 'til my lawyer gets here. Got it? Run along now and fetch my lawyer."

Astra and I exchange a frustrated glance but get to our feet, head out the door, and step into the pod. We stand in silence for a moment, glaring at him through the glass. Through the speakers on the tech's control board, we hear him humming to himself.

"Turn that off," I snap.

The tech does, plunging the room into silence, and I turn to Astra. "What are we missing here?" I ask. "He's way too smug to not have something up his sleeve. This is like dealing with Petrosyan all over again."

"I was thinking the same thing," she replies. "I have no idea what he's got. I mean, he doesn't have the money Petrosyan's got, so he's not going to be able to buy his way out of this. The money he bled out of those accounts isn't nearly enough for a lawyer of that caliber. But..."

"But he's acting as if he's got us by the shorts," I say. "It makes no sense whatsoever."

It's then that the door to the interrogation room opens and we watch as uniformed security lets a man enter the room. And when we see who walks in, I turn to Astra, my eyes wide and my mouth practically scraping the floor.

"What in the hell is going on?" I ask.

We watch as Palmer Tinsley, one of the slimiest—and most expensive—criminal defense attorneys in all of Seattle, quietly confers with Alex Dansby, who is apparently his new client. Astra and I open the door and step into the interview room again. Tinsley stands up, a wide grin on his face.

"Agents Wilder and Russo," he greets us. "How lovely to see you again."

He holds out a hand for me to shake, but I leave him hanging. I don't want to get contaminated. Tinsley plays it off by sticking his hand back in his pocket and clearing his throat. I'm reminded of the old joke about the difference between a catfish and a lawyer: one's a scum-sucking bottom feeder, and the other's a fish.

"What are you doing here, Tinsley?"

"Well, right now I'm conferring with my client," he says.

"Your client?" Astra asks. "Him?"

"Unless there is another wrongfully arrested man in this room I'm not seeing, then, yes, him," Tinsley says sarcastically. "Now, I'm going to need a little time to confer with my client, so do me a favor and turn off all those pesky recording devices on your way out. I'll give you a call when we're ready to talk."

"You should know," I start, "that we have your client directly linked to twenty-two missing women. One of whom recently turned up dead after being savagely beaten. We've got him dead to rights, counselor."

Tinsley chuckles. "I seem to recall hearing that somewhere before. Recently, too, if memory serves me correctly."

Astra grabs hold of my arm and drags me back to the door that leads into the pod before I can do something stupid. The rage burning in me is making my blood boil, though, so it's probably a good thing that Astra's got hold of me, all things considered. She shoves me into the pod and shuts the door behind me.

"Let's take a walk," she says, then turns to the tech. "Give us a page when the slimebag says he's ready."

"You got it."

Astra escorts me back to the shop, all but pushing me along the entire way. Still agitated, I cross my arms over my chest and start vigorously pacing the room as Astra drops into the chair at her workstation.

"Those don't look like the faces of conquering heroes," Rick observes.

"No, those look like the faces of a couple of women who just got their butts handed to them," Mo offers.

"You would be right about that," Astra mutters.

"So... I take it the case isn't being blown open," Mo says.

I shake my head. "Find out who retained Palmer Tinsley on Dansby's behalf," I say. "Rick, can you do that?"

"On it, boss."

"Not to throw more gasoline onto the fire or anything, but I did what you asked and looked at class schedules for all the missing girls," Mo says. "Some of them had the same professors, of course. But there's only one instructor they all shared in common."

"Silas Crawford," I say.

"Give that woman a cookie," Mo says.

"Hey, boss, here's another coincidence for you to chew on—Silas Crawford is the one who retained Palmer Tinsley," Rick calls over. "He's actually had Tinsley on retainer for years. Tinsley is the Crawford family's personal attorney. And just in case you were wondering, Crawford is loaded to the gills. Richer than God. His father invented some microprocessor and made a killing on it—still makes a killing on it."

"Sounds as though Crawford doesn't even need to work," Mo notes.

"But where would he then have access to emotionally damaged, impressionable young women of legal and consenting age?" I ask.

"You're saying he only works at the schools to recruit these girls?" Mo asks.

"Give that woman a cookie," I reply.

"Okay, let me see if I have our working theory straight," Astra says. "Dansby is out there doing the street-level garbage—ditching evidence, draining accounts, and all—in service to Crawford? And in return, he gets an expensive mouthpiece?"

"Seems that way," I say.

"But here's a question—why would Crawford be trafficking these girls?" Mo asks. "Obviously, he doesn't need the money. And from what you described, he doesn't have much trouble getting them to his office in the first place."

"Maybe it's something darker than we thought," I offer. "Maybe he's murdering these girls and Dansby is the one cleaning up after him. The debit cards, cars, and whatever other profit can be derived is his slice of the pie."

"But it still doesn't quite add up for me," Astra says. "Why risk keeping them for more than a year—as he did with Stacy

Burkett? If this is all about murder, why not just kill them and be done with it?"

"Because I think it's about more than just murder," I say. "As we can see with Burkett, it's about torture. Trauma. Crawford might be the type who needs to dominate these women. Control them. He seizes on their issues to draw them, in and when they're good and vulnerable, he strikes."

"I have a question that nobody's asking," Rick calls out. "You said that Stacy Burkett had just given birth, right?"

I nod. "That's what the ME told us."

"Then where's the baby?"

It's such a simple question, I can't believe it never occurred to me. And judging by the look on Astra's face, she's mortified that it hadn't crossed her mind, either. It's then we get a page from the tech in the pod. Tinsley's ready for us.

"Wait," Rick calls, stopping us in our tracks. "I just got a piece of intel you'll want. Silas Crawford is Alex Dansby's brother. Well—half-brother, apparently."

"That explains why Tinsley's in there," Astra says.

"That does," I nod. "And that's just one more curveball to this whole heaping pile of garbage. I honestly have no idea what's happening right now."

"That makes two of us, babe," Astra sighs. "But let's go see if that piece of garbage in the Armani suit can provide us with some clarity."

"That would be nice," I say. "It really would."

THIRTY

"So, is Silas Crawford paying you directly, Tinsley?" I ask. "Or are you on a permanent retainer?"

He chuckles softly. "I'm on retainer to the family," he says. "You certainly put that together very quickly."

"We're good at what we do," Astra says coldly.

"But not good enough to get to the truth of things, I fear," he says.

Dansby is sitting back in his chair, a smug smirk on his face, content to let his high-priced mouthpiece do the talking for him. I'm dying to come across the table and slap it right off him.

"Then why don't you lay it out for us?" I ask. "Tell us what your version of the truth is."

"How cynical, Agent Wilder. There aren't versions of the truth. There's only the truth and then what's left," Tinsley says.

"Let's not play games," Astra says. "I assume you're paid by the hour, so let's not pad your billing any more than you already do."

"Fine," Tinsley says. "I've consulted with my client as well as Dr. Crawford, and I can assure you that no crimes have been committed. Your suspicions and allegations are entirely incorrect."

"I'm waiting to hear your version of the truth," I say.

"Dr. Crawford is a man who believes in living simply. He longs for a return to a world where knowledge is valued simply for the sake of itself," Tinsley intones. "He desires to live in a world where we aren't glued to our screens twenty-four hours a day—"

"Get to it, Counselor, or I'm apt to arrest you for felony waste of my time," Astra snaps.

He chuckles. "Fine. To that end, Dr. Crawford has established a compound on a piece of land he owns south of here. Near Mt. St. Helens, to be precise."

"A compound?"

"A ranch, really. It's where people of like mind have been living for a little more than five years now," he explains. "A ranch of people living simply, and without all of the modern flourishes we have all come to take for granted."

"So, he established a cult," Astra replies.

"That's such an ugly and inaccurate word," Tinsley protests. "It's merely a haven, a simple world where people can live clean and live free. To live as they want and not as society dictates that they should."

"So....a cult," Astra repeats.

"You people wouldn't understand what my brother has created out there," Dansby finally says. "Your little minds couldn't possibly grasp it. You wouldn't know what it is to live free. To live your truth."

"Wow. Sounds like somebody drank a second glass of the Kool-Aid," I mutter.

He smirks. "Your feeble attempts to get under my skin

won't work, Agent," he says. "I have transcended and live well above your comprehension."

"Yeah, this sounds totally normal and not cult-like at all," Astra comments.

"What it sounds like is a group of consenting adults who have chosen to live a certain way—a way that you might not like, but a way that isn't in any way illegal," Tinsley replies. "There is no crime being committed."

"Except for the case of bank fraud," I say. "We have your client—"

"Oh, right. That," Tinsley cuts me off.

He pulls his phone out and scrolls through his files, then turns the screen to me. I give him a wry smile.

"I thought you folks wanted to cut technology out of your lives," I note. "Seems a little ironic to show me your proof on that snazzy new iPhone."

"I don't live there, Agent Wilder," he says dryly. "I do, however, defend their right to live as they see fit, free of government interference—as is their right. Now, just watch."

He hits the button, and the video starts to play. I recognize Selene Hedlund instantly and feel my heart drop into my stomach.

"My name is Selene Hedlund and I, being of sound mind and body, have made the conscious decision to uncouple from the modern world. I have made the conscious decision to live clean and live free," she says. "As I have made this decision, I am relinquishing my worldly possessions. I hereby give permission for those things that tie me to the so-called civilized world to be severed. Car, bank account, everything in my apartment—I am donating everything to Haven, and the proceeds of anything sold on my behalf will go to the same."

The video ends and I'm left speechless as I stare at the

blank screen. I manage to gather myself and glance at Astra, who looks as shaken as I feel right now.

"There are signed and notarized affidavits from all the residents of Haven on file, of course, that state the same thing," Tinsley says. "So again I repeat, no crimes are being committed here. It's simply a group of people, all of them of age and consenting, who choose to live in a way that—although you might not agree with it—is not criminal."

I clear my throat and turn my gaze to Dansby. "And what's your part in all of this?"

"I deal with logistics. I clean out houses and apartments, sell the belongings of our flock," he says. "I handle the worldly side of things."

"And I'm sure you take a healthy cut of the proceeds as well," Astra says.

"Last I checked, earning a wage for an honest day's work isn't a crime, Agent Russo," Tinsley replies.

"So, you're intimately familiar with the inner workings of your cult—sorry, I mean your group," I say. "You're involved with the decision-making? Have your fingers in all the pies to make sure you're doing Silas' bidding correctly?"

"I'm his right-hand man," Dansby says. "There's nothin' that goes on in Haven that I don't know about. Got to. Got to protect what we built from you people."

"So why all the subterfuge? Why are you hiring bleeders to drain the accounts?" I press. "Why do everything under the veil of secrecy?"

"Because we know what you people would do if you found us. We're an exclusive world. Only those truly of like mind are allowed to enter the gates of Haven. The only reason I'm revealing the existence of Haven to you now is that I have no choice. Silas doesn't want to see me prosecuted for something that's not a crime," he says. "He's good to our people that way. He doesn't turn on us the way you people turn on each other."

"Heartwarming. No, really, that's touching," I say. "But we still have the death of Stacy Burkett to contend with. She was a resident of Haven, no?"

"She was for a time," Dansby says.

"Uh-huh," Astra says. "So, how did she die? She was worked over pretty good. Who tuned her up, Alex?"

He shrugs. "She left Haven. Wanted to live amongst the animals again, I suppose," he says. "But nobody is forced to remain. And so we let her leave. What happened to her after she left Haven is a mystery to me. One of your people must have killed her. That's what you do."

"And what about the baby?" I ask. "We know she gave birth less than a month ago. Where is her child?"

He shrugs again. "I have no idea. She didn't have a child inside Haven, that much I can tell you. What she did outside our walls ain't my business."

Tinsley puts his hand on Dansby's arm and leans over, whispering to his client. Dansby's face immediately tightens, and he falls silent. Tinsley's smart enough to know what I just did, and he's slightly rattled. I can see it in his eyes—he's already trying to figure a way out of the can of worms his client just opened up all over himself. We got him on the record. Tinsley knows that if we find evidence of Stacy's baby, they're screwed.

"We're going to need to visit Haven," I say. "We're going to need to interview the residents and confirm all of this ourselves."

"You callin' me a liar?" Dansby growls.

Tinsley puts his hand on the man's arm again and shakes his head. Dansby settles back into his seat and glares at me with pure hate in his eyes.

"It's not that I don't trust the veracity of your statements, Mr. Dansby, it's just that—oh, wait, I do doubt your truthfulness," I say. "I have this funny thing about taking career criminals at face value."

Before Dansby can say anything, Tinsley sits forward. "Silas anticipated this and has welcomed you and your team—and your team only—to tour Haven," he says. "He invites you to see what they've built, to prove that these outrageous allegations you're making have no merit. He has nothing to hide."

"I appreciate that, but I'm also going to be bringing along a couple of crime scene techs," I say, then pin Dansby to his chair with my gaze. "We're going to be looking for DNA from Stacy Burkett's child. And believe me when I say that my techs are the best around. And if they so much as find a drop of that child's blood, I'm going to put the needle in you myself."

"There's no need for hyperbolic and ultimately empty threats, Agent Wilder," Tinsley fires back. "As I said, Silas has nothing to hide and welcomes your visit."

"That's good," I say. "Because we'll be heading out there. In the meantime, your client's not going anywhere. Not until we verify everything that's been said. "

Tinsley inclines his head. "Of course. I expected nothing less from you, Agent Wilder. You have never been anything but thorough."

I flash him a grin. "That's good, because I'm about to be more thorough than your proctologist."

"Charming," Tinsley says with a grimace. "As always."

THIRTY-ONE

Haven; Clark County, WA

JUST A FEW DOZEN miles north of Yacolt, in an unincorporated stretch of land—one hundred acres to be exact—is Haven. I had figured Tinsley's use of the word "compound" was an exaggeration, but it wasn't exactly wrong. The premises are surrounded by a ten-foot-high wooden wall that's been reinforced with steel on the back side. A long catwalk runs all the way around the wall, with ladders stationed every so often to give people access to the top of the wall. It's empty at the moment, but it's not hard for me to imagine armed men patrolling the catwalk. It provides a high, very defensible vantage point in the case of a firefight.

The gates themselves are just as tall as the fence and are also reinforced with steel. I can't tell whether that's to keep people out—or keep them in. They open as we drive up, and I cast a glance over at Astra.

"I kind of feel as if we're entering Jurassic Park," I comment.

"Really? I kind of had the feeling we were entering the Branch Davidian compound," Astra replies. "Or maybe Jonestown."

"That's comforting."

"Let's just hope it turns out better for us than it did in any of those places," she says.

Astra pulls the SUV into a dirt lot that sits in front of a brick-and-wood structure. The second SUV with our techs pulls in beside us, and we all climb out and huddle up. There's a certain sense of peace out here, I won't deny that. To be out of the city, away from the blaring horns and buzz of traffic and people—it's nice. The quiet out here is so absolute, it almost seems we've stepped into a vacuum.

Except, of course, for the massive walls locking us in.

"All right, keep your eyes peeled," I announce. "We're looking for evidence of anything illegal. Anything at all. Listen to the people. I mean really listen to them. I want to know if they sound stressed. If they're being told what to say under duress. And I want DNA swabs—as many as we can get. I want to know if that baby was born out here."

"Agents Wilder and Russo," comes a voice.

We turn to see Dr. Crawford walking toward us with a wide, welcoming smile on his face.

"Dr. Crawford," I say. "This is quite the place."

"It's my life's work," he says.

"That you forgot to mention the last time we talked."

He shrugs. "It didn't come up," he says. "And I hope you can understand my need to protect my home—and my people. The influence of the outside world is something we have all actively sought to shun. That's why we're here—to live in harmony with nature and with each other."

"That's beautiful," Astra says dryly.

Crawford frowns but quickly recovers. "I know our ways

seem strange to you. But we are living our own truth out here," he says. "I admit it's not for everybody, and that's all right. You are free to live as you see fit—as are we."

An awkward, tension-filled silence descends over us for a moment and we all stand there looking at each other. Crawford finally breaks the ice.

"Please, let me show you around. I understand you will want to speak with some of our residents," he says. "And as I've been informed, take DNA samples."

"That's correct," I nod. "Your brother is already on record. He told us Stacy Burkett didn't have her child in Haven. And that she was killed outside the walls."

He nods. "That's true. And such a tragedy. Stacy was a pure soul," he sighs. "I wish she'd never made the decision to recouple with the outside world. But she did. And that was her decision to make, as we all enjoy free will."

"Great," I say. "Let's have the nickel tour, huh?"

"It would be my pleasure."

Over the next hour, Crawford walks us around Haven like a proud father. It's a self-sustaining community that relies on solar and wind power, and crops they grow themselves. They've got a well that's fed by an underground spring, and all the buildings are made of the same uniform brick and wood. There are dormitories for the single residents—of which there are roughly fifty or sixty—with small cottages for families.

He leads us into the main dining hall. Three rows of long banquet tables sit in front of a dais that holds one long table perpendicular to the others. That's obviously where the leaders of this community sit. We take a seat at one of the long tables, Crawford sitting across from us. My four techs start spreading out through the community, taking swabs and samples. I told them to focus on the infirmary first, then hit Stacy's living area.

When I gave those orders, I saw Crawford tighten up, but

he managed to keep his cool. What he doesn't know is I told my techs—as well as Astra, who's speaking with the residents—to look for a baseball bat or a steel pipe. I need them to find something that could have been used to bludgeon Stacy Burkett to death and test it for blood.

Any rational person would have disposed of it. But Crawford is a classic narcissist. He doesn't think he can do any wrong and practically considers himself a god. I've learned that much over the last hour with him—and that gives me hope that he held onto that bat.

"Everybody pulls his or her weight and contributes to the welfare of our community," Crawford tells me. "What I've created here is a utopia for those who want to unplug from the world as it is today. People who want to live a simpler, better, cleaner life."

"I'll admit, it's impressive," I say. "A self-sustaining, green community with almost no carbon footprint. Impressive, Dr. Crawford. Honestly."

He gives me a beatific smile. "It started off as a thought experiment by Arnold Merrick. I just took the next step and then perfected it."

"I can tell you're very proud of Haven," I say. "But I would like to speak with some of your residents now. And I'd like to start with Selene Hedlund please."

A grin curls a corner of his mouth upward. "I thought you might."

"Did you, now?"

He nods. "I know you better than you might think."

"Oh, I think that goes both ways, Dr. Crawford."

"Maybe so," he replies. "At any rate, I'll have her sent in."

"Thank you."

"Of course," he says graciously.

I wait for a few minutes before Selene walks in. She has a

small smile playing across her lips as she sits down across from me. She's far from being the nearly out-of-control party girl everybody said she was. There's a certain peace about her. She looks like a woman perfectly in control of herself. More than that, a woman who's at peace with herself. There's a quiet confidence and tranquility about her that I can't deny. This is not a victim of trafficking. This is a woman who made a choice —one in which she found serenity.

"Selene," I start. "I'm Blake Wilder with the FBI. It's nice to meet you."

"It's nice to meet you as well, Agent Wilder."

"We've been expending a lot of energy and resources looking for you."

Her smile is soft, but her eyes twinkle mischievously. "And I've been here all along."

"Your mother is very worried about you, Selene."

"She doesn't need to be. I'm right where I belong now. I'm living my truth," she says. "And I'm happier than I've ever been. I feel at peace in Haven—something I never once felt in the outside world."

"Why didn't you tell your mother—"

"Because she would have tried to stop me. She would have tried to make me doubt myself," she says. "Silas believes the best way is to simply cut ties all at once. Leave your past where it belongs and never explain yourself to the outside world, because they won't understand. Worse, they'll try to talk you out of it. And he's right—as he is in most things."

Wow. "As he is in most things"? She sounds brainwashed, saying things like that, but when I look into her eyes, I can see that she truly believes it. She truly believes in Silas. He has managed to build a strong, resilient community. He's given these young people a confidence they perhaps didn't have before. It would be a remarkable and even admirable thing if he wasn't setting himself up as their savior, their father or god figure, or whatever he considers himself.

"What you need to understand is that my mother isn't worried about me. She's worried about her image—or what I might do to her image. I've never been anything more than a prop to her," she continues. "It took me awhile to understand that, but now that I have, everything makes so much more sense. I've come to understand that my mother is not interested in my happiness—she never has been. For her, it's all about her career. Her image. And I deserve better than that. I deserve more than that."

The horrible thing about all of this is that Selene is right. She deserves more than to simply be a prop for her mother's ambitions. I have little doubt that her feelings are valid. That her mother only ever worried about her image—and what Selene's transgressions would do to her image. It's never been about Selene as a person. It's only ever been about what Selene could do for her mother. And that's a tragedy.

"Just so I'm clear, you were not coerced to give up your life and come to Haven in any way, whatsoever?" I ask. "You made this decision of your own free will?"

She smiles. "I didn't give up my life, Agent Wilder. I found my life, I found myself," she says. "So yes, I am here of my own free will—as I believe my video and signed affidavit attest."

"And you were not under duress when you signed that?"

"No. Far from it," she replies. "For the first time in my life, I'm happy, Agent Wilder. Why can you not accept that as truth?"

I look at her closely, staring into her eyes. And what I see is that she isn't lying. She's not reciting a script that was forced upon her. She truly is here of her own free will. More than that, Selene genuinely seems happy. She seems at peace.

"I think you should call your mother," I tell her. "You should at least tell her what you've told me."

"She's part of my old life. She's as irrelevant to me as I was to her when I was growing up," she says. "And you can tell her I said that."

"Blake."

I look to the doorway and see Astra leaning in. She holds up a bat she's got bagged and nods to me. I turn back to Selene and feel a sharp stab of guilt, knowing we are about to blow up her entire world. We are going to destroy the peace and happiness she had been waiting her entire life to find. To say I'm conflicted would be a vast understatement. I find myself wondering if Haven can survive without Crawford.

"Okay, that's all I have for the moment, Selene," I tell her as I get to my feet. "Thank you for speaking with me."

She nods. "Of course. I hope we can put this whole silly affair to rest now."

I give her a weak smile, knowing this isn't over yet. Not by a long shot. I can't tell her that, though. I walk out of the dining hall and join Astra as we walk back to the SUVs. I look around, but don't see Crawford anywhere, and feel a shudder of concern as images of him and his men arming up flash through my mind. The last thing I want is for this to turn into another Waco or Ruby Ridge.

"Talk to me," I say.

"You were right, he kept the bat. It wasn't even hidden very well," she says. "Guzman checked it out and it tested positive for blood. He thinks there's enough still in the grain of the wood for DNA. What about Selene? Brainwashed? Drugged?"

I shake my head. "Fully coherent. Fully present. And fully on board with Crawford's message and Haven," I tell her. "She genuinely seems happy and at peace with herself. She doesn't want to leave."

"Same with everybody else I talked to—the men and the women," she says. "They were all students of Crawford at one point and decided that life at Haven would be better for them than life in the outside world."

"And now we're going to burn it all to the ground," I say.

"You don't think this place can survive without him?"

I shrug. "I don't know. Gut instinct tells me *no*. He's the glue that holds it all together."

"Well, I guess they're going to find out one way or another," she says.

She puts the bat in the back of the SUV as the techs start loading their gear into the back of theirs. I look over and see Crawford walking toward us. Selene and the rest of his flock walk behind him—he's smiling, but they all look pensive. I walk over to him.

"Dr. Crawford, I'm placing you under arrest for the murder of Stacy Burkett," I say.

He gives me a small smile. "This is why we have all chosen to seek refuge and live our lives out here—free of the interference of your world."

"Murder is murder, Dr. Crawford," I tell him. "Be it in our world or yours, you can't simply murder somebody."

"Well, I'd say you have an uphill battle to prove that. But good luck with that," he says, then turns to his flock, some of whom are crying as I put the handcuffs on him. "Worry not, everybody. This is how they treat those who are different from them. Who refuse to live by their norms and notions of society. But don't worry. I'll be back before you know it. I promise you. And when I am, we shall celebrate."

"Good luck with that," I mutter and push him toward the SUV.

THIRTY-TWO

Interrogation Suite Alpha-4; Seattle Field Office

"I MEANT it when I said I was impressed with Haven," I tell him. "It's a remarkable achievement."

"It is, isn't it?" Crawford asks.

"Do you think it'll be able to function without you?" Astra asks.

"Oh, I'm sure it could. No one man is bigger than Haven. Our ideals are bigger than any individual," he says. "We are a family, and we all work for the betterment of our world."

"That's good," Astra counters. "Because they're going to need to find somebody to fill your shoes for the next twenty years or so."

He chuckles softly. "And what is it you believe you have on me?" he asks. "You have clearly seen these young women are not being trafficked. You have heard them tell you they gave permission for their bank accounts to be accessed and their worldly possessions sold. So, where is the crime you are attempting to persecute me with?"

"'Persecute'. That's a pretty bold choice of words," I comment.

"And what would you call it?" he asks.

"I'd call it being held accountable for your actions," I tell him. "You killed Stacy Burkett, and now you're going to pay for it."

He laughs softly. "Why would I kill Stacy Burkett? Because she wanted to leave Haven and rejoin the ugliness of your world?" he asks. "Why would I want somebody who did not believe in what we're doing out there to remain among us? Haven is only for those who believe and will work to better themselves and our community."

"Where is Stacy Burkett's child?" I ask.

"I couldn't tell you," he replies.

"You do know we have the bat you used to beat Stacy to death, right?" Astra asks.

I see concern briefly flash through his eyes, but it disappears just as quickly. Crawford is a master at controlling his emotions and his expressions. But for just a split second, the mask slipped, and I got a peek at how concerned he is. The feeling is satisfying, albeit short-lived. The last thing I'm going to do is allow myself to feel any sort of way until we have Crawford in bracelets and heading down to a cell. Been there, done that with Petrosyan—and I have no desire to repeat the experience.

"I don't know what you're talking about," he says smoothly.

"Oh, you tried washing it down, but the problem is that blood seeped into the wood grain," I tell him. "We're currently pulling DNA from it, and when it matches Stacy Burkett's, you are going to be going away for a very long time."

"So, why did you kill her, Dr. Crawford?" Astra asks.

"I didn't."

"Was it simply because she wanted to leave?" Astra

presses. "Could you not tolerate the fact that she didn't want to be part of your little commune anymore?"

He laughs softly and shakes his head. "As amusing as all of this is, I'm afraid it's beginning to get tiresome," he says. "And I don't feel like continuing this circular argument with you anymore."

"Well, you could save us all a lot of time and confess to what you did," I offer.

His smile is wide. "I could do that. But instead, I think I'll ask for my lawyer," he says. "I would like to get back to my people. You left them in crisis, and I need to get back to help allay their fears and ensure they remain calm."

"Don't you mean you need to get back to soak up their worship of you?" Astra fires back. "I can almost picture you walking through the gates of Haven, wailing and moaning like a horribly misunderstood and persecuted man—"

"Isn't that what I am?"

"No," I say. "You're a murderer."

"An allegation that has not been proven," he counters. "And once again, I will ask for my lawyer, which is my right under the Miranda warning you gave me. Until Mr. Tinsley arrives, I will have nothing further to say."

"You have this one chance to help yourself, Dr. Crawford," I tell him. "Once we walk out that door and your lawyer walks in the other one, we'll be coming after you for the whole boat. You'll be staring down a murder charge, Silas. There won't be any helping you after that."

"I need no help," he insists. "I'm innocent of all charges."

"All right. Good luck to you, then," I say. "I'll have your lawyer sent in."

Astra and I get to our feet and walk into the pod, closing the door behind us and staring at him through the glass for a moment. He sits at the table, completely self-possessed and confident. He truly believes he did nothing wrong and that he won't suffer the consequences of his actions. Like any other true narcissist.

I turn and look through the glass at the observation room behind us. Tinsley is sitting with Dansby, neither of them speaking. Dansby looks pensive. Far tenser than his half-brother. There's a tightness in his eyes and in his body that tells me he's nervous. Scared. And added to all of that the fact that Dansby isn't exactly the brightest crayon in the box, he very well could be ripe for the picking.

"I have an idea," I mention to Astra.

"On a scale of one to ten—with ten being a really horrible idea—where does your idea land?" Astra asks.

"Probably a twelve. Maybe thirteen."

"Oh, I'm so in," she grins.

"Toni," I turn to the tech. "Do me a favor and send a text message to Tinsley. Inform him that Dr. Crawford is asking for him."

"You got it," she says and does as I ask.

"And once Tinsley leaves Alpha-2, turn on the audio/visual equipment," I say.

"Done," she says.

I turn to Astra. "Just follow my lead."

We watch through the glass as Tinsley picks up his phone and reads the message. He gets up without a word and leaves Dansby sitting there alone. When we see Tinsley enter the room with Dr. Crawford, I give Astra a nod and we walk out of the pod and into Dansby's interrogation room, quickly taking seats at the table across from him.

I look at him for a long moment in silence, amping up his fear. It's amusing to me how tough and macho he acts when he's got Tinsley to hide behind, but put him alone in the room with us and he looks like he's about to wet himself.

"You ain't supposed to be talkin' to me without my lawyer present," he mutters.

"Nothing in the rules says we can't sit in the room until your lawyer comes back," I counter.

"Yeah, whatever," Dansby snaps.

"Your brother," I say. "He's an impressive guy. Makes sense that Tinsley would rather defend him than you."

"What are you talkin' about?"

I shrug. "He sure bugged out of here real quick, didn't he?"

"Really quick," Astra adds. "Almost as if he was summoned by a more important person."

"Well, to be fair, Crawford is the one bankrolling this whole thing," I say.

Astra nods. "But Alex here provides a vital function to Haven."

"That's right. I do," he says.

"He doesn't do anything a trained monkey couldn't do," I say. "Crawford could replace him in a heartbeat. My guess is it's only because Alex here is family—sort of—that Crawford gave him a job. Probably felt sorry for him."

"Hey, shut up. Just shut your mouth."

"Yeah, I can see that," Astra nods. "In Crawford's place, I'd probably feel sorry for him, too. But I don't know that I'd trust him to help run my passion project."

"I said, shut your mouth," he snaps.

"I get the feeling with the way things are shaking out, Crawford's going to have to look out for number one," I tell her. "Probably going to cut the dead weight and make sure he can cut a good deal to get back to Haven as fast as he can."

Astra cuts a quick look at Dansby and returns her gaze right to me. "He'd be the dead weight in that scenario, right?"

"Why are you sayin' this garbage? You better shut your mouths," he growls. "Right now. I mean it."

I go on as though he's not even there, looking at Astra instead of him. "With the evidence we have, Crawford is looking at some serious time."

"He's going to cut a deal," Astra says. "I'm sure that's what he and Tinsley are talking about right now."

"But what's he got to offer up?" I ask. "The AUSA isn't going to cut him a deal out of the goodness of his heart. He's going to need to get something in return—something he can feel good about."

We both turn and look at Dansby pointedly. It takes him almost a full minute before the light bulb goes on over his head and he sputters.

"You're talkin' about me?" he spits. "You think my brother would give me up in return for a deal?"

I shrug and turn back to Astra. Technically, I'm not talking to him or questioning him without his lawyer present. "I don't know. Do you really think Crawford would use Alex as a human shield for himself if it meant protecting Haven?"

Dansby opens his mouth—I'm sure to vigorously deny it—but he hesitates, and the words seem to die on his lips. He sits back in his seat and looks down at his hands for a moment. It's then I know for sure we're on the right track. There's a crack in the foundation as he thinks about how much Haven means to his half-brother. Dansby seems to realize that there isn't anything—including serving him up on a silver platter—that would prevent Crawford from protecting his life's work.

"I can't go back to prison. It'd be my third strike," he mutters to himself. "But no. He wouldn't sell me out. He hired a top-shelf lawyer for me after all."

Astra keeps her gaze steeled right on me. "It's just a shame we can't get in there to talk to Tinsley yet with Crawford. They're probably cooking up a deal as we speak."

Dansby's eyes widen at her words, and I see that he's just

about there. He's just about at the tipping point. The specter of taking a third strike and going to prison for the rest of his life is hanging heavy over Dansby's head. I just need to give him one final push to get him there.

"If Crawford's smart—and he is very smart—he'd definitely be talking deal," I tell her. "All he cares about is Haven."

"I want a deal," Dansby blurts out. "I want a deal now."

"Sorry, Alex," I finally turn to him. "We can't help you. Your lawyer advised us—"

"He's not my lawyer anymore. He's fired," he says. "I want to talk. I'll tell you everything you want to know. Just get me a deal. I can't have a third strike. I can't go back. I can't spend the rest of my life in prison."

"So, am I correct in saying that you have fired your counsel, you are waiving your right to counsel, and you are willing to cooperate?" I ask.

He nods vigorously. "Yes. That's correct. All of it," he says. "Now, get me a deal."

"Toni, can you bring in the form he needs to sign to waive his rights?" I ask.

A moment later, the door to the pod opens and she comes in with a clipboard and hands it to me. I give her a smile.

"Thanks, Toni."

"Anytime."

The door to the pod closes again, leaving us alone with Dansby. I slide the form over to him and point out where he needs to sign to waive his right to counsel. He scrawls his name and pushes the clipboard back to me.

"Now, make me a deal," he demands.

The door opens and Tinsley steps in, his expression darkens quickly. "What do you two think you're doing in here?" he asks. "I should actually thank you since you've violated—"

"You're fired," Dansby snaps.

Tinsley looks at him. "Excuse me?"

"You're fired. Get out."

"Alex, I just spoke with your brother and—"

"I bet you did," Dansby snaps. "You're fired. You are no longer my lawyer. Now, get the hell out."

"Alex, think this through. I don't know what these two agents told you, but they're trying to manipulate you," he says. "They're trying to use you. They want to have you thrown in prison forever. This is your third strike, Alex. They'll throw away the key."

"Get the hell out of here!" Dansby yells. "Go try to cut a sweet deal for my brother without me. You are fired."

Tinsley stands in the doorway for a long moment just staring at Dansby. There's a look of real concern on his face. I start to wonder if I was actually right, and they really were going to serve Dansby up to cut a deal for Crawford. That'd be rich.

"I think he was pretty clear, Counselor," I shrug.

"Your services are no longer required," Astra adds.

I tap on the clipboard. "We even have his signature to prove it."

Tinsley shakes his head, that light of concern still in his eyes, but he backs out of the room, no doubt trying to downshift into Plan B. When we're alone with him again, Dansby turns to us, tapping his foot on the ground nervously.

"Now, get me a deal," he repeats.

"All right. Tell us what you have, and we'll take it to the AUSA," I say. "If you're fully forthcoming and honest, I'll personally make a recommendation for leniency."

Dansby starts talking, telling us everything—including how Stacy Burkett came to wind up on a slab in the ME's office. His story is long and detailed and takes some turns I didn't see coming. And when he's finished, both Astra and I are left wide-eyed and speechless. This whole thing is even darker and more twisted than we realized.

I sit back in my chair and let out a low whistle. Astra is staring at him slack-jawed, seemingly only able to shake her head. I understand the feeling.

"So? You think that's good enough to get a deal?" he asks with desperation in his voice. "A good deal?"

"Do you have proof of all of these allegations?" I ask, finally coming back to myself. "Without proof backing them up, these are just the words of a co-conspirator. The AUSA is going to need actual evidence if he's going to cut you a deal."

"Of course I've got proof. Do I look like an idiot?" he scoffs. "I love my brother, but he always acted like he was better than me because I'm the illegitimate one. I'm the bastard. And because of that, I always figured he'd throw me under the bus if push came to shove. My brother is self-serving, in case you hadn't noticed. He'd cut me loose in the blink of an eye to cover his own butt—and protect Haven. So, I kept records of things for a rainy day, and it's storming out right now."

"That's good, Alex," I nod. "That proof is very good. That makes me think the AUSA is going to cut you a deal you can live with."

Dansby nods to himself, a satisfied smile on his face. "Good. That's good."

THIRTY-THREE

Interrogation Suite Alpha-2; Seattle Field Office

"As we go on the record, take note that in the room are Supervisory Special Agent Blake Wilder, Special Agent Astra Russo, defendant Alex Dansby, and Assistant US Attorney Piper Harvin," I say as we get this show underway.

"AUSA Harvin for the people," she says. "We have a proffer for Mr. Dansby, which I am extending to him now. In exchange for his truthful testimony, we are giving Mr. Dansby immunity from all charges. However, if Mr. Dansby is to lie, mislead, or in any way contradict his sworn affidavit in any way whatsoever, this proffer will be null and void, and he will be prosecuted for all of his crimes without consideration. Are these terms agreeable to you, Mr. Dansby?"

He nods and doesn't look up.

"We need you to verbally acknowledge the proffer," Harvin says.

"Yes. Fine. The terms are fine," he says. "Can we get on with it?"

Ordinarily, I would have balked at immunity. Dansby did play a role in Stacy Burkett's death—her blood was found on the clothing he turned over as part of his plea agreement. To my mind, he should pay the price for it. But the information he's providing us is so explosive and so much more than we had originally thought, even his public defender was able to wrangle an immunity deal from the AUSA. So, even though I still think it stinks, I have no choice but to suck it up and deal with it, because it serves a far greater good.

"All right, Mr. Dansby," I start. "Tell us about the night Stacy Burkett was killed."

"She was gonna snitch. She was upset Silas had taken her child from her. He said it was for the good of Haven, but she didn't like that," he starts. "So, we get wind of her plan to escape and before she can get too far, we catch up with her. Silas worked her over with the bat real good. We both thought she was dead, and he told me to take care of the body. But it turns out, she wasn't dead, and got away. I chased her through the woods, and she ended up on Highway 12. Almost got hit by a car. But as I learned, she died of her wounds later."

"So, you were with Dr. Crawford when he beat her with a baseball bat," Harvin says.

"Yeah. That's right," he nods. "I watched him tune her up."

"Have you seen Dr. Crawford murder anybody else while at Haven?"

He shrugs. "A couple of people a few years back now," he says casually. "Once you're a part of Haven, you don't get to go unless Silas says you can go. And he never lets nobody go."

"The people we spoke with all seemed very happy to be there," I bring up.

He nods. "Of course. Because they are. Some people love the way of life at Haven," he goes on. "But before you agents got there, Silas had the people who aren't real thrilled with bein' at Haven—the nonbelievers—locked up in the underground bunker. Can't see or hear 'em in there, no matter how loud they scream."

For the next forty-five minutes or so, Harvin guides him through a series of questions as she builds her case. He's provided the corroborating evidence of his claims, which should make her case bulletproof.

"What about the children?" I ask. "Walk us through that, please."

Dansby nods. "Silas—he don't really like kids, to be honest. And he also needs to keep Haven flush, if you know what I mean. He don't get all the money in his trust 'til his dad kicks off," he explains. "So, for the last five years, ever since he founded Haven, he's been sellin' some of the kids born there."

"Selling them how?" I ask.

"He's got an arrangement with an adoption agency—Willet House. The director there, Artie Holbrook, is an old friend of his," he tells us. "Anyway, Artie and Silas worked out a deal. Silas gets fifty grand for every kid he brings in, then Artie turns around and sells them to couples desperate for a kid for twice that. Artie mostly sells the newborns to desperate parents. But sometimes, he'll sell the younger kids—five, six years old—to people for other purposes, if you know what I mean."

"Please say it plainly," Harvin says.

"The younger kids are sold to pedophiles," Danby admits, with a grimace.

"And how does Stacy Burkett's murder tie into this?"

"She found out about the scheme,'" Dansby says. "She was gonna snitch and had this grand plan of gettin' her kid back and livin' happily ever after with it. She was gonna jeopardize Haven by tellin' everybody about it. Silas couldn't have that. So he killed her. She knew too much and couldn't be a loose cannon out there ruinin' everything."

"Are there guns at Haven, Mr. Dansby?" Harvin asks. "Any kind of weapons or ammunition stockpiles?"

I look at her curiously, because that wasn't part of our script. It leaves me wondering where she got that intel. I turn back to Dansby, who's nodding.

"Yeah. Lots of guns. MRs, AKs, M16s, loads of handguns. Yeah, we got weapons out there," he says. "We wanted to be able to defend ourselves if the worst came to pass—society breakin' down, chaos, destruction. We still got a Second Amendment and a right to own guns. A right to defend ourselves."

"That's funny," I say. "You reject society and shun the laws that govern this land. And yet, you'll still cling to that Second Amendment like a drowning man hangs onto a piece of driftwood."

"Whatever," he grunts.

"One more question from me—did you hire Sergeant Leonard Burton to deplete the bank accounts of Haven residents by using their ATM cards?"

"Yeah. Sure did," he says. "That was my idea. A good one, too, since it benefitted all of Haven."

"Yeah, you're a real philanthropist," Astra mutters.

"AUSA Harvin, I've heard all I need to. I'll be stepping out of the room," I say. "But you can carry on with Mr. Dansby. When you're done, just let the tech in the pod know to call and have Mr. Dansby taken back to lockup."

"Thanks, SSA Wilder," she says. "You and Special Agent Russo did fantastic work."

I give her a nod, then Astra and I step out of the room and into the pod where Rosie has been joined by Congresswoman Hedlund. I feel myself automatically tense and grit my teeth With everything going on, I hadn't had a chance to contact her yet. And judging by the look on her face, she's not about to let me forget it. But she turns away and watches the interview for a moment. As we stand there in silence, it hits me—the question about the guns came from Hedlund. It had to have. But why did she need to know, is my question. Washington State has pretty permissive gun laws—if those weapons were purchased legally, there should be no problem.

"Did you see Selene?" Hedlund asks me suddenly.

I nod. "I did. I spoke with her for a little while."

"And? What did she say?"

"That she was happy at Haven," I reply. "Said she'd never felt as at peace and happy as she did there."

"She's obviously been brainwashed," Hedlund snaps. "Either that or they're keeping her drugged to the gills."

I shake my head. "No, ma'am. She was sober as a judge," I say. "I've seen enough people drunk or on drugs to know when somebody's high. Your daughter was very much in her right mind. I know you don't want to hear that, but it doesn't make it any less true."

"What else did she say?" Hedlund demands.

"That she wanted you both to be happy. But she told me she was tired of being your prop," I continue. "She said she deserved to be happy, that she's finally found herself. And she told me to tell you..." I trail off, trying to figure out how to put it delicately.

"What? What did she say?"

I take a deep sigh and try to muster as neutral a voice as I can. "She told me to tell you that you are as irrelevant to her life as she was to yours when she was growing up. I'm sorry."

Hedlund's expression darkens further. Her lip begins to tremble, but she hardens her face, masking the emotions I know must be roiling around inside of her. But she bites them back. I turn to Rosie and give her a nod.

"If you've got things under control here, I've got a baby seller to snatch up," I say.

"Go get him. And be careful, Blake," she says. "Make sure you and Astra have each other's backs."

"Yes, ma'am," I reply. "Consider our backs had."

THIRTY-FOUR

Willet House, Ravenna District; Seattle, WA

THE ONE AREA where Dansby's evidence was weak was when it came to Crawford's arrangement with Artie Holbrook, the director of Willet House. There wasn't enough there for Harvin to feel comfortable including a trafficking charge along with the laundry list of offenses she's assembling to indict Crawford. She said they had enough without it to put him away for basically the rest of his life, but it wouldn't satisfy me to not include a trafficking charge. Stacy Burkett deserved at least that much.

Astra parks the car, and we climb out and I look around. The Ravenna district is a nice upper-middle-class neighborhood just north of the University district. Willet House is in a glen of trees just behind a neighborhood of single-family homes. It's a tall, three-story building that isn't much aesthetically, looking a lot like an old, squared-off, u-shaped motel, but it's nicely maintained and well-kept.

"Ready for this?" I ask.

"Of course, sweetheart," she replies. "Been looking forward to this all day."

I laugh softly. "Good, then let's go meet Mr. Holbrook."

We're both dressed in tasteful pantsuits—Astra is wearing blue with a white blouse under her jacket and I'm in black with a green blouse. Very tasteful. Very professional. Very conservative. We're trying to project the image of a power couple. I put on a pair of glasses with a camera built into the frame, and we've both got earbuds, with mics tucked into the inside pockets of our jackets.

"Testing, testing," I say. "Are we broadcasting?"

"Loud and clear. We have eyes and ears on," Mo replies. "And for the record, let me just say you two make a very cute couple."

"Yeah, we kind of do, don't we?" Astra asks.

"Very," Rick says. "I'll be thinking about—"

"Stop making it weird, Rick," Astra snaps.

Mo and Rick are in a van halfway down the block running the audio and visual equipment for our sting. After one final check and a smoothing out of our clothes, Astra takes my hand and we walk across the parking lot, mounting the steps and heading into the lobby of Willet House. It's tasteful in design, with a lot of soft, earthy tones, and what seems to me to be an excessive number of plants. It's like a jungle in here.

We walk to the desk that stands across from the front doors, and are greeted by a middle-aged woman with blonde hair that spills down to her shoulders, green eyes, and a warm, welcoming smile.

"Good afternoon," she smiles. "And welcome to Willet House."

"Thank you," I reply. "Blake Jenkins and Astra Wagner. We have an appointment with Mr. Holbrook."

The woman pecks at the keys on her keyboard and reads

from her screen. She turns back to us, her smile not having slipped a fraction of an inch.

"And so you do," she says and gestures to the hallway on our left. "Just head down that hallway, turn left at the junction, and it will be the door at the end of the hall."

"Thank you," I say.

"You're very welcome. And good luck to you."

Hand in hand, Astra and I follow her instructions and make our way to Holbrook's office, stopping when we reach the door.

"Be careful," Astra says quietly. "Don't do the cop knock."

"What? I don't do a cop knock."

"You totally do," she says.

"Yeah, you kind of do, boss," Rick says in my ear.

"Gotta agree with everybody else," Mo chimes in.

"You all can kiss my butt," I say.

"Watch," Astra says. "You do it this way."

She raises a hand and gently raps on the door with the back of her knuckles. She turns to me and smiles.

"See? That's a normal-person knock," she says.

A moment later, the door opens to reveal a man who stands all of about five-five or so. He's lean and fit, with a stylishly groomed shock of thick, wavy dark hair. He's wearing a very nice—and obviously expensive—three-piece suit and a pair of Bally's on his feet that probably set him back five or six hundred bucks. He's obviously a man doing well for himself. But then, trafficking children is a lucrative business.

Holbrook ushers us inside and closes the door. He directs us to the chairs in front of his desk and takes the seat behind it. His quick smile and friendly demeanor are comforting.

"So, Ms. Jenkins and Ms. Wagner, what can I do for you today?" he starts.

I look at Astra then turn back to him, hoping I'm conveying the right level of desperation and desire for a child.

"Mr. Dansby told me he'd called you on our behalf," I say. "That he vouched for us?"

"He did," Holbrook nods. "Said you two were ideal candidates for a special program we run here at Willet House."

Astra nods. "We would very much like to participate in your special program," she says. "And, as I hope Mr. Dansby said, we are willing and able to pay for your services."

I can practically see the dollar signs floating above his head. The unmitigated greed of the man turns my stomach. That he would manipulate people through their desperation to have families, all in the name of making a few bucks, is sickening. It's what's wrong with the world—a thought that leads me straight back to the Thirteen. I quickly banish the thought, though, and try to stay in character. This op demands that I do. If we're going to take down this sleazy ring, I need to keep myself focused and sharp.

"Yes, he mentioned that you are quite....motivated," Holbrook replies smoothly.

"That's an understatement, Mr. Holbrook," I tell him. "It's hard for a couple like us to secure an adoptive child through normal channels. We've been turned down three times now. I just can't let my heart keep being broken like that."

"It's why we've sought out—alternative means," Astra finishes.

He stares at us both for a long minute. Perhaps he's trying to determine our truthfulness. Maybe he thinks he's good at reading people and seeing into the depths of their souls. And the fact that he nods and gives us another smile tells me he's not very good at it.

"Well then, I do believe I can assist you," he finally says. "And tell me, what is it you're looking for exactly?"

Astra and I exchange a passably excited look. "We want a little boy. Six months old or less. Hair and eye color don't matter to us. Just so long as he's healthy."

Holbrook nods. "I do believe I have what you're looking for," he says. "He's five months old and matches your preferred physical description."

"Oh, that's wonderful," Astra grins. "More than wonderful. Wouldn't you agree, darling?"

I give her a smile. "It sounds more than wonderful. Almost —miraculous."

"Well, as I hope Mr. Dansby mentioned, there is a fifty-thousand-dollar fee to get the ball rolling," he says. "And the balance is due when you pick up your little bundle of joy."

"Yes, he did explain that," I say.

Astra reaches into her jacket pocket, pulls out an envelope, slides it across the desk to Holbrook. He stares at it for a moment as if it were a snake, coiled and ready to strike. But his greed wins out and he picks it up. Pulling the flap open, he looks inside, nodding with the light of joy in his eyes.

"Excellent," he says. "This will get the ball rolling, as I said—"

"Oh, there's one thing I should mention that seems kind of important," I say.

"And what is that, my dear?"

Astra and I get to our feet and badge him. Holbrook's face immediately turns whiter than milk and his eyes widen with shock.

"You're under arrest," I say, unable to keep the note of glee out of my voice.

THIRTY-FIVE

Situation Room; Seattle Field Office

WHEN ROSIE's text came through, instructing me to get to the situation room ASAP, my first thought was that we'd had a terrorist attack somewhere in Seattle. But when I walked in and found Rosie standing with Hedlund and a few men in suits, a flutter of worry passed through me, ruining what had been a good morning. We busted up a trafficking ring and put a narcissistic groomer behind bars all in one case. I should be walking on sunshine right now and feeling pretty good about myself.

But then Rosie had to go and send me the message. The situation room is typically reserved for monitoring actions that are taking place. Filed ops. Raids. Takedowns. Things of that nature. But so far as I'm aware, nothing was scheduled to be on the books today. But the large screens that line the far wall of the room show a SWAT team in motion.

"Rosie, what's happening?" I ask as I step up beside her.

She gives me a frustrated look then turns and stares at

Hedlund. The Congresswoman looks back at me with a malignant gleam of joy in her eyes.

"I have a joint FBI-ATF team raiding Haven," she says simply.

"You're what?" I gasp.

"Mr. Dansby said they were stockpiling illegal weapons," Hedlund says. "It's up to us to disarm them."

"You can't do that, Congresswoman. There are women and children in Haven," I argue. "You send in an ops team and something goes wrong, a lot of people die."

"As long as they do what they're told, when they're told to do it, there shouldn't even be a need for shooting," Hedlund says.

"I'm sure the same thing was said at Ruby Ridge and Waco. Why don't we go talk to them about how it—oh wait, we can't. They're all dead because of actions just like this one."

"I have faith in your SWAT team," she says.

"All well and good—and they're deserving of everybody's faith and trust," I counter. "The people in Haven are emotionally volatile and on edge, because we have Crawford in custody. You send in the army and I can guarantee you that people are going to die. Call this off, Congresswoman."

"I can't," she spits. "I won't."

"Your own daughter is in there, Kathryn," I spit. "How are you going to feel if she gets caught in the crossfire?"

"First of all, you don't know this will break down into gunfire," she fires back.

"Historically speaking, people who willingly live the way the people in Haven do don't react well when you try to disarm them."

"Secondly," she goes on as if I hadn't just spoken. "My daughter has made her choice. As far as I'm concerned, she is dead to me. I no longer have a daughter. I have already started taking steps to expunge her from my life."

I stand there, gaping at her. "You are an absolute monster."

"Call me what you will, but this is still happening."

I glance up at the monitors and the screen shifts to another POV that shows the teams approaching the gates of Haven. I turn away, knowing already that this is going to be a bloodbath. A lot of people are going to die out there, and for what?

I turn to Rosie who just shrugs. "The AG signed off on it. There's nothing we could do," she says. "There's still nothing we can do about this."

"Why did you call me in here?" I ask.

"I didn't," she replies.

"I did," Hedlund says. "I wanted you to see what bold, swift, and decisive action looked like for a change."

"Are you this desperate for a headline?" I sneer. "You'd actually kill your own daughter to generate a little sympathy for yourself? To increase your odds of re-election? You're more of a monster than I ever thought possible."

I turn and head for the door just as the sound of gunfire erupts. As I step out of the situation room, I hear the anguished wailing of somebody who's been shot.

"And let the bloodbath begin. I'm sure it'll look terrific in tomorrow's poll numbers," I mutter to myself as I walk away.

THIRTY-SIX

Wilder Residence; The Emerald Pines Luxury Apartments,
Downtown Seattle

I PULL into the underground garage and into my assigned space, then sit there for a long few minutes, trying to summon the energy to get out of my car. All I want is a glass of wine and a hot shower to wash off the stink of the day. I can't get the sound of the gunfire that had erupted at Haven out of my mind. That Hedlund had orchestrated that attack for nothing more than exacting revenge on a daughter who'd rejected her, and a bounce in her poll numbers, makes me sick. I can still taste bile in the back of my throat.

With a heavy sigh, I get out of my car and turn to head for the elevators, only to find myself face to face with a man who seems to have materialized out of thin air. Instinctively, I drop my bag, and knowing I don't have time to pull my sidearm, lash out with a fist. He easily deflects it and dances back a step.

"Agent Wilder," he says. "Calm down. It's me."

The blind fear that jolted me ebbs when I realize who's

standing before me. "Fish?" I ask, my voice quavering. "Jesus, you scared the hell out of me."

"Apologies, Agent Wilder. I didn't mean to startle you."

"Yeah well, lurking around in a dark garage and popping in out of nowhere tends to do that to a person."

He bows his head. "Apologies."

"What are you doing here?" I ask. "If you have information, I could have stopped by the Pearl—"

He shakes his head. "No, I needed to see you immediately —and in secret."

The tone of his voice puts another charge of fear-fueled adrenaline through me. Gone is the playful, flirtatious Fish. And in its place is one who sounds—scared. Fish doesn't scare easily, so the fact that he seems rattled can't be a good thing.

"All right," I say. "What's going on?"

"Concerning the matter you asked me to look into, I am sorry, but even with my considerable resources, I have not been able to discover his true identity," he says, sounding surprised himself. "He is truly a ghost. There is nothing to be found about Mark Walton anywhere. The backstopped information is all there is."

"How can that be possible?" I ask. "Everybody has a digital trail. It's almost impossible to be completely off the grid."

"'Almost' is the operative word there, Agent Wilder," he replies softly. "I have checked with overseas contacts, domestic contacts—there is absolutely no trace of him."

"Wow," I say. "That's—disturbing."

"To put it mildly, yes."

I run a hand through my hair, trying to wrap my mind around that piece of intel. The fact that Mark is truly a ghost— that neither Brody nor Fish has been able to find a single scrap of information about him—is worrisome on so many levels. But

I get the feeling that Fish has even more to tell me that I'm not going to like.

"What else is there, Fish? What aren't you telling me?"

"You have made some very powerful enemies, Agent Wilder," he says. "Perhaps even more powerful than you know."

I shake my head. "No, I think I'm pretty aware of who's gunning for me these days. It's a pretty lengthy list."

The gate to the garage rumbles up and a black Audi drives in. Fish melts into the shadows so effectively, I can barely see him. He waits until the car has passed by without incident before he emerges again.

"Why are you so jumpy, Fish?"

"Because I fear I may have drawn the eye of those who hunt you," he says. "My inquiries may not have gone unnoticed."

My stomach churns wildly and I feel I'm going to be sick. It's then I realize that Fish has become part of my pack. Part of my tribe. It's the strangest thing, given that we exist on opposite sides of the legal spectrum, but I have to admit that I have a genuine affection for him. And the thought that to him—because of a favor he was doing for me, no less—sends an intense lightning bolt of fear shooting through me.

Even in the darkness, I can see his smile. "Don't worry for me, Agent Wilder. I'm protected. I will be fine," he says. "I will probably go underground for a little while. But I will always be reachable to you. Always."

"Thank you, Fish," I say. "And I'm sorry I brought this down on you."

He laughs softly. "Knowing you certainly keeps life interesting. I will say that."

"Well, here's to many, many more years of it being interesting."

"Well said."

"But tell me, what is it that has you so rattled?" I ask.

He sighs. "There is an assassin on US soil right now. The person is a legend, somebody even monsters fear—"

"You're not saying 'he' or 'she,'" I interrupt.

"That is because nobody knows who the assassin is, whether male or female, or which nationality," he explains. I can hear the nervous tension in his voice. "There is only one thing that is known about this person. And that is he or she is called Đavole."

"Zavol-ay?" I pronounce.

"Closer to a D and J at the same time," Fish explains. "Đavole—that is Serbian for 'devil'. Nobody knows where the name came from, but this fearsome beast's reputation certainly lives up to it."

"Okay, why is this Đavole here?" I ask.

"If my information is correct—and it usually is—then Đavole is here for you," he says. "He or she has been hired by somebody to kill you."

His words freeze the blood in my veins, and all I can do is stare at Fish. I take a couple of beats to process it and gather myself.

"They're trying to stop me from investigating. They don't want me to find the secrets they're hiding," I say.

"Đavole would be an effective way to do just that," he nods.

"Do we have any idea where this assassin is?" I ask.

He shakes his head. "Not specifically, but there was chatter that Đavole is still on the east coast at present. Perhaps tying up some loose ends for his or her employer before coming west," he tells me. "But that is speculation. There is no way of knowing for sure. Not until Đavole shows up at your door to kill you, anyway."

"Thank you, Fish. For everything you've done for me," I tell him.

"Of course. And thank you for all you've done for me as well."

I give him an awkward smile. "Why does this feel as if we're saying goodbye forever?"

Fish smiles. "Let us hope it is not," he says. "Please be careful, Agent Wilder. Watch your surroundings. And be careful of who enters your life."

I laugh softly. "A few years too late for that one," I say. "But point taken. And thank you, Fish. You watch your back and stay safe. When this is all over, I'll look forward to seeing you in those shiny suits you love to wear."

His smile is sad. I get the feeling he thinks he's looking at a dead woman. It's not a comforting feeling, to say the least. Fish surprises me by pulling me into a tight embrace. After a couple of moments, he steps back.

"Be careful, Agent Wilder."

"You too, Fish."

I watch him walk away and melt into the shadows. And then he's gone, like a spirit in the night. I pick up my bag and head to the elevator, keeping a cautious eye out. I scan the parking lot, looking for something—or somebody—that doesn't belong. Looking for movement in the shadows. But I make it to the bank of elevators and am on my way up without incident.

Keeping my shooting hand free, I cautiously peek out of the elevator, first one way and then the other, before stepping off on my floor. I walk down to my door and quickly open it, step inside, and close it behind me, throwing all the locks I had installed. I drop my keys in the dish and my bag on the floor, then pull my gun and move from room to room, clearing my entire apartment before I let myself relax—a little bit.

I'm on edge. All my defenses are up. Which I like to think

is somewhat understandable, given the fact that Fish just told me some notorious assassin who everybody fears is coming for me. Part of me feels I would probably have a better chance of stopping a freight train with a blade of grass than this mysterious killer.

I pour myself a glass of wine, then move around my place, turning out all the lights as I go. When the house is darkened, I sit down in one of the chairs in the living room area with my wine in one hand and my weapon in my lap, and consider. I'm not paranoid enough that I think Fish's visit has somehow conjured up *Davole* tonight. It could be days or weeks—or, yes, hours—before the assassin comes for me. But I'm going to have to be a lot more careful, much more prepared, from now on. I'll have to come up with a strategy to protect myself and those around me. For tonight, though, I'm on guard, just in case. Nobody gets the drop on me.

Fish has me so worked up that sleep, I fear, is going to be a long way off. Maybe for the foreseeable future.

THIRTY-SEVEN

Criminal Data Analysis Unit; Seattle Field Office

"... *two ATF agents were killed in the firefight with homegrown, domestic terrorists in southern Washington last night. I will never waver in my fight against those who'd harm our great country. Yes, it's a tragedy that twenty-seven domestic terrorists lost their lives. They were Americans, once upon a time. But they chose a different path. They chose the way of violence and treachery to our nation. So, don't mourn them too much. Instead, celebrate the teams of FBI and ATF agents who took up that fight, some of them paying the ultimate price, to defend this country and everybody in it from those who seek to do us harm...*"

The screens go dark as Rick cuts off the news feed. Silence descends over the shop as we take in the toll of the tragedy Representative Hedlund engineered. The tragedy she is now trying to capitalize on.

"Did you notice that she didn't mention her daughter once?" Mo points out.

"I'm guessing that ordering the gunfight that killed your own daughter doesn't play well in the polls," Astra says.

"On the other hand, showing that she's so committed to this fight against terrorism that she'll even order the death of her own daughter should have been good for a point or two bounce in the polls," I offer.

There is a pall that's been cast over the shop. Everybody's feeling it. The energy that usually suffuses the place is absent, and everybody just seems to be suffering from an emotional hangover. The ending of our case—and how it ultimately turned out—is taking a toll on all of us.

What bothers me the most about how this all shook out is that the people in Haven did nothing wrong. Their only crime was in living differently. In wanting something other than society today has become. They wanted to live a simple, peaceful life, isolated and free from the world around them. And although it's not one I would choose for myself, I can't deny that I see the appeal.

Haven was much more than Silas Crawford. It was an idea and a belief, and those are greater than any one man. I would have liked to have seen if those beliefs and ideals could have withstood the absence of the man who found Haven. I like to think they could have. I would like to think the people could have collectively banded together and built Haven into something even greater than Crawford had ever intended. That they could have taken that next logical step and truly perfected it.

This case took something out of me. Out of my team. I think on some level, we all identified with somebody in this whole mess. We all recognized the idea behind Haven, and I think we all crave the sort of peace and happiness they found. Or perhaps I'm just projecting again. Either way, we're all feeling a bit down in the wake of yesterday's wholesale slaughter of people who just wanted to live their lives.

"The real tragedy here is that Hedlund isn't ever going to face charges over this whole mess," Mo says. "As far as I'm concerned, there are twenty-nine deaths on that woman's conscience—including her own daughter's."

"People like Hedlund don't get charged. They get promoted," Astra mutters. "They get rewarded. Pats on the back and awards. Hell, they get highways and buildings named after them."

"It's depressing as hell to think about, but every word of what Astra just said is right. People like Hedlund are never held accountable. They never face repercussions for their actions. They just keep on going, destroying lives, and ruining everything they touch as they continue climbing that ladder. These people always, always fail upward."

My phone buzzes, and I pull it out of my pocket and call up my texts. It's from Rosie, and when I read it, I feel an ice-cold hand wrap itself around my heart and squeeze.

My office. Now. Torres is here and on a warpath. Be ready.

Christ. Can't I just have one day?

"Because today apparently couldn't suck anymore, enter Deputy Chief Torres," I mutter.

"What does that loser want?" Astra snaps.

My phone buzzes again, but this time it's Annie. Her text is telling me she needs to talk to me right now. I shoot her a quick message back, telling her I'm in the middle of something and that I'd call her as soon as I can. I send the message, then look up at Astra again.

"Crap, I keep forgetting to call Annie. I'm sure she's going to try to find a way to blame all of those deaths on me," I tell Astra. "I can see the headline tomorrow—FBI Agent murders twenty-nine."

"Good thing you have an alibi—you were in the situation

room with the woman who planned the slaughter herself," Astra says.

"That won't stop her from trying, anyway. But I should go see what that putz wants," I say. "While I'm gone, let's start getting back into the Angel of Mercy case. Now that the Hedlund case is over, we should get back into the swing of things. And I want to nail Nurse Crane in the worst way possible. Do something unambiguously good."

"And something that definitely won't end up with a firefight and lots of people being killed," Astra says.

"That, too."

I head out of the shop and take the elevator up to the main floor, then make my way through the warren of corridors until I find myself standing outside Rosie's office. Her assistant, Stephen, the prissiest and snobbiest person on the entire planet, is glaring at me. He's preventing me from going in right now. I am in no mood for this rank pettiness, though. He is literally the gatekeeper right now.

"So, any chance of your letting me get in there today?" I ask. "I mean, she did text me to come. Even said it's an emergency."

He sighs. "Fine. Go in."

"Thanks. That wasn't so hard, now, was it? Even a simpleton would get that."

Before he can say anything, I disappear inside Rosie's office and close the door behind me. Torres is standing off to the side staring at me. Rosie is sitting behind her desk, her expression dark, her face tight and pinched. But Torres is looking at me as though he's the cat that ate the canary. He's got a smug smile on his face that makes me want to smack him.

"What can I do for you, Deputy Chief?" I ask.

"You really think you're so above the law that consequences don't apply to you, don't you?" he begins.

"My name isn't Kathryn Hedlund, so, no. I don't think that. Not at all, in fact," I reply.

"Blake," Rosie warns.

"Fine. I personally don't believe I'm above the law. In fact, I go to great lengths to preserve and enforce the law," I say. "But you obviously believe otherwise, so let's unpack that. What is your gripe today, Deputy Chief?"

He smirks at me and shakes his head. He makes a show of smoothing out the lapels of his jacket, then straightening the badge-shaped SPD pin. He looks at me as he pulls at his cuffs and squares his shoulders.

I roll my eyes. "Are you done primping, princess?"

"Take it down a couple of notches, Blake."

I turn to Rosie. "Did you know the Deputy Chief here is running a pool around the SPD?" I ask. "Apparently, people are betting on how long it will take him to indict me for Gina Aoki's murder—a murder he knows damn well I had nothing to do with."

Torres looks at Rosie and shrugs. "I have no knowledge of that. Nor would I condone it."

"Uh-huh," Rosie says. "Blake's here now, as requested. So, do you mind telling us what this is all about? We both have important work to be doing."

Torres swivels his eyes over to me again, that cocksure smirk on his face. "Where were you last night, Agent Wilder?"

"I was at home."

"Alone?"

"Yes, I was home alone last night."

Torres' smirk gets even greasier. "So, there's nobody who can verify the fact that you were home last night?"

"That's usually what being home alone means," I snap. "Mind telling me what this little song and dance is all about?"

"Who's Mark Walton to you?"

I freeze in place and feel my heart stop dead in my chest. What in the hell is he playing at here? But then the fear melts away, replaced by burning anger. Torres is now crossing a line and violating my personal space. My personal life. To what end, though? What sort of leverage does he think Mark gives him? What does he know about Mark? Does he somehow know Mark was a plant in my life? An imposter? And if so, how?

"I don't believe that's any of your business," I start. "My personal life is my own and—"

"So, your relationship with him is—personal?"

"What are you driving at, Deputy Chief?" Rosie cuts in. "I'm getting tired of these games. Get to the point or get out."

Torres' face darkens. He was obviously enjoying himself. Just like the bully he is, he wants to drag the drama on for a little while longer and doesn't appreciate Rosie's raining on his parade. My phone buzzes with an incoming text. It's Annie again—911 this time. I shoot her a quick reply telling her I'm in a meeting and will touch base later, and to stop blowing up my phone. She doesn't reply again, so I think I'm in the clear. For now.

"I ask again, who is Mark Walton to you, Agent Wilder?"

"He was somebody I was seeing for awhile," I shrug. "Again, my personal life is not your business."

"It is when the people in your life turn up dead, Agent Wilder."

I cock my head at him, sure I'm not following. "What did you say?"

"Mark Walton is the second person connected to you who's turned up dead. First, Gina Aoki, and now him," Torres says. "That's some string of bad luck, isn't it?"

I'm hearing his words, but they make absolutely no sense to me. I look at Torres, confused, trying to understand what he's saying. But no matter how many times I replay the words in my head, they don't make sense. I turn to Rosie. She's looking back at me with wide eyes and an expression of confusion I'm sure matches my own. I turn back to Torres again and see that cocksure little smile on his face and feel the anger within me snuffed out by confusion and fear.

"What are you talking about?" I frown. "Mark isn't dead—"

"Oh, but I'm afraid he is," Torres interrupts. "His body was found in the duck pond at Wilbury Park. He'd been beaten and then shot at close range. Two in the back of the head, in fact. Say, isn't that the exact way your parents were killed? A double-tap to the back of the head? Odd coincidence, that."

"Deputy Chief Torres, do you have proof to back up your claims?" Rosie asks.

"We found a hair on him that looks a lot like hers."

"They were seeing each other, so that's not very surprising, now, is it?

I slump down into the chair and bury my face in my hands, trying to get my mind around all this. Given the fact that Mark was a spy, somebody who was planted in my life to watch me, I shouldn't be feeling anything about his death. Maybe relief. Maybe joy. But not this. I feel I've been punched in the gut. I'm finding it hard to breathe and my heart is beating a staccato rhythm inside of me.

It makes no sense, given who—and what—he was, but I'm actually feeling grief. Sadness. Even though he betrayed me, I still opened myself up to him. I gave him pieces of myself and my heart I'd never given to anybody before. Before I found out what he was, I allowed myself to care for him very deeply. Care for him in ways I'd never cared for anybody before. And now he's dead. I can't help but feel that sharp stab of grief and loss. It's surprising to me, but I had never been able to entirely shut that off.

"That's two people around you dead, Wilder," he says.

"And I've never believed in coincidences. Where there's smoke, there is usually fire."

I turn and look at him, though my vision is blurry with the tears welling in my eyes. I fight them off and fight to maintain my composure. I will not give him the satisfaction of letting him see my emotions. I grit my teeth and narrow my eyes at him.

"It's easy to see the fire through the smoke if you're the one intentionally setting it," I hiss.

"You have no alibi for either murder," he counters. "And your hair was found on Walton. Do you really think a jury won't be able to connect the dots?"

"And what would be my motivation for killing him?" I ask.

Torres shrugs. "Don't rightly know. Jealousy? You catch him with another woman?" he asks. "Maybe he tried to break up with you."

"You're so full of crap. You know I'm not good for either of these murders," I growl. "You know it every bit as well as I do."

"I don't know anything, other than that you have a lot of anger and hostility in you. You tend to fly off the handle a lot," he says. "So, maybe you two had a fight and it just got out of hand. Is that what happened?"

I shake my head and refuse to look at him. As I stare into nothing, Astra's words from the other day echo through my mind. He is going to wage a PR war against me. He is trying to smear me. He knows damn well I had nothing to do with either murder, but he thinks if he layers on enough innuendo and accusation, facts or not, he is going to cause me problems in the Bureau. If he keeps this up, all but calling me a serial killer, somebody up the command structure is going to see me as a liability to the Bureau's image and kick me loose.

"This the time you want to get out ahead of all this, Wilder," Torres pushes. "Now's the time to confess and let us help you."

I shake my head. "My God, how did somebody so bad at cop work become the Deputy Chief?" I ask. "I'd be willing to bet you went through ChapStick like crazy. I bet your lips got really dry and cracked after all the ass you had to kiss to get to where you are."

His expression darkens for a moment before he's able to reel it back in and put that arrogant smirk back on his face again.

"Your time is up, Wilder."

"If you keep this up, I'm going to rain hell down on you, Deputy Chief. If you persist in this, the gloves are definitely coming off," I say, my voice low and dripping with rage.

"Easy. Both of you," Rosie orders. "Deputy Chief, I sure don't appreciate your coming in here and ambushing my agent with what are, so far, baseless accusations."

"I have proof," he says.

"And what is it?" Rosie asks.

"You'll see it when it's time."

"You have nothing, because I didn't kill anybody!" I raise my voice. "But if you're going to proceed with this trumped-up charge, then you had best prepare yourself for the fight of your life. And when I'm done with you, you'll be lucky if you can still score a job as night-shift security down at the mall."

"Deputy Chief, I have, as a courtesy, let you come in to talk to Blake several times now," Rosie says. "And each time, you have come in and thrown baseless accusations all over the place like glitter, hoping enough of it will stick to her that it will cause problems for her in the Bureau. I will not be a party to this attempted character assassination any longer. Leave the field office now. You are no longer welcome in my building."

Torres smirks, his eyes glued to mine. "Last chance to get out in front of all this," he says. "Last chance to come clean."

"Get out of my office and get out of my building, Deputy Chief," Roses growls as she gets to her feet.

"Consider this your official notice that you are a suspect in two homicides, Agent Wilder," he says with a slow smile. "Don't leave town, because I'll be in touch. We're going to want to have you in for questioning. Soon."

Torres chuckles and finally walks out of his own accord. I bury my face in my hands and sob—and I don't know why. Rosie gives me a minute before she takes my hands in hers and forces me to look up at her. She gives me a tight smile and a look of calm reassurance.

"We're going to fight him with everything we have," she tells me. "We know he's got nothing on you. And if he persists, we will absolutely bury him, Blake. Trust me, everything is going to be all right. You are going to be all right. I promise you."

My smile is weak and shaky. And though I want to believe her, I just don't right now. I feel as if my entire world is crashing down around me in a fiery heap. Not only is there nothing I can do about it, I feel anything I do is only throwing more gasoline onto it. And underneath all of that is the maddening and inexplicable grief I feel over Mark's death.

My world is falling to pieces and there's nothing I can do to stop it.

EPILOGUE

I PULL to a stop in Annie's driveway, cut the engine, and sit there for a few minutes, the reality of the last couple of hours starting to sink deeply into my bones. The grief I felt about Mark's death is still there, but it's now being tempered by the white-hot rage I feel about Torres' trying to throw me under the bus. Trying to frame me for a murder—two murders—he knows I didn't do. That's a situation I'm going to need to handle, there's no question.

As I think about Torres' description of how Mark's body was found, I get angrier. And that is soon followed by a wave of fear so thick, I'm practically choking on it. The thought that pops into my mind is accompanied by Fish's voice—trust no one and watch my back. The next thought that pops into my mind is that this is the *Davole*. The assassin is already here and is just letting me know by killing somebody he thought was close to me.

Or perhaps he was under orders to kill Mark? If the Thirteen thought he was compromised or had his cover blown, he might become expendable to them. They might engage the *Davole* to cut their losses for them. But even in that scenario, I don't see a happy ending for me. If I blew Mark's cover, and they know I'm getting close to some answers about the deaths of my folks, they'd be highly motivated to keep me quiet. Forever.

There are so many questions, and more are piling up each and every day. But I want to feel that there are answers on the horizon. It seems things are gaining momentum—but I know I'm not in control right now. I'm reacting to events rather than taking control and leading the way. That needs to change. And it needs to change soon.

I sigh as I get out of the car, trying like hell to get rid of the heaviness in my heart. Mark doesn't deserve it. He lied to me. Used me. He treated me like an idiot. It's not the first time I ever got played in my life, but it is the worst case of it. When I was younger, I'd usually been able to figure out in time that I was being played. And when I did figure it out, I'd put a stop to it immediately—usually in the form of some public humiliation or another. But Mark? Never saw it coming. He had me fooled every which way he could.

I do what I can to push all of that to the back of my mind as I trudge up the steps to the back porch. Annie has been blowing me up all day, which, in addition to annoying me to no end, is kind of freaking me out. Annie isn't one to text over and over and over again. She's really not one to text at all. So, to see all the missed calls and texts I've gotten from her—just today— tells me something is up. Something big.

Before I even get to the door, though, it opens and reveals my aunt, looking somewhat harried and somewhat stressed. She steps outside and closes the door behind her, leaning back against it. She obviously doesn't want me to go inside for whatever reason. She's acting so strangely and un-Annie-like that my curiosity is piqued.

"So, I'm here," I announce. "The house is still standing and isn't on fire. There's no chainsaw-wielding mass murderer running around. What's up, Annie? Why have you been blowing me up today? What's the emergency?"

She clears her throat and tries to stand up a little bit straighter. She looks me in the eye, and reflected back in hers, I see both fear and hope, which only deepens my curiosity.

"Blake, there is somebody here that I want you to see," she starts.

"Oh, God, you're not trying to set me up again, are you?"

"No, nothing like that. Not this time," she says.

"But before I take you inside, I need you to really get control of yourself. I need you to be strong, Blake. I need you to get as tight a grip on yourself as you can. Can you do that for me, Blake?"

"Annie, what are you talking about?" I ask. "You're making no sense at all."

"Please. I need you to give me your word that you will keep hold of yourself."

I open my mouth to reply, but close it again. None of this is making sense, and after the day I've had, I really don't want to play these games anymore. I turn to leave, but Annie takes hold of my hands. Hers are warm and soft. Her expression is earnest. Honestly, she's being so weirdly insistent, she's starting to freak me out.

"Okay, fine. I promise to keep my cool," I say. "I don't know who you're about to introduce me to, but know this—if you're trying to set me up on a blind date again, I will burn your house down. I'll burn it to the ground."

Nothing. Not even a courtesy laugh from her. Whatever is going on and whoever is in the house are serious business. She turns and I follow her inside. We enter through the kitchen and I'm immediately inundated by a thousand different aromas, each one better than the last. They're obviously making dinner for her mystery guest.

We make it to the archway that leads out to the living room, where her mystery guest is stashed, and Annie turns, planting her hand on my chest to stop me. At this point, I have no idea who's out there or what in the hell is going on. I've run through a list in my mind, trying to figure out who could be out there— who could be eliciting this sort of a response from her. And why Annie is so insistent that I maintain my emotions.

"Remember. You promised to—"

"Yeah, yeah, yeah," I wave her off. "I'm fine. I'll keep my head about me. I promise you."

She still looks a bit uncertain, but she gives me a nod and turns, leading me through the archway and into the living room. Annie stands in front of her guest, hands clasped at her waist, an expression of stark naked fear on her face. She looks up at me, the question in her eyes—are you ready? I give her a firm nod and Annie steps aside, revealing her guest.

I fall straight to my knees, my eyes locked onto the woman in the chair. It's been more than twenty years, but I know her anyway. I know her just as well as I know myself.

I open my mouth to speak, but nothing comes out. But she looks at me with those dazzling green eyes and a smile that's so beautiful and so pure, it steals the breath from my lungs.

I shake my head in disbelief and give my arm a vicious twist. The resulting pain tells me this is no dream. This is reality. I stare into her eyes, watching my vision waver and shimmer as the tears start to well.

"Kit," I whisper. "How? How are you here? Where have you been? I don't understand."

"And we have all the time in the world to catch up, Blake. I have so much to tell you."

Kit smiles and takes my hand in hers. I revel in the warmth of her hand. In the feel of her skin. In the way her eyes sparkle as she looks at me. Waves of disbelief wash over me so fast and thick, I can hardly breathe. I can't believe it. My baby sister is back.

After almost twenty years, Kit, my baby sister, is alive. She's home.

NOTE FROM ELLE GRAY

I hope you enjoyed *The Lost Girls*, book 6 in the *Blake Wilder FBI Mystery Thriller series*.

My intention is to give you a thrilling adventure and an entertaining escape with each and every book.

However, I need your help to continue writing and bring you more books!

Being a new indie writer is tough.

I don't have a large budget, huge following, or any of the cutting edge marketing techniques.

So, all I kindly ask is that if you enjoyed this book, please take a moment of your time and leave me a review and maybe recommend the book to a fellow book lover or two.

This way I can continue to write all day and night and bring you more books in the *Blake Wilder* series.

By the way, if you find any typos or want to reach out to me, feel free to email me at egray@ellegraybooks.com

Your writer friend,
Elle Gray

ALSO BY ELLE GRAY

Printed in Great Britain
by Amazon

62769891R00161